THE WHITE PEOPLE ARE COMING

to settle this land. There is no stopping them. Soon it will be impossible for anyone to live upon game; it will all be driven away or killed off. Far better for everyone to make up his mind to plant crops and raise cattle or sheep and make his living in that way. In no time the Apache will be wealthier than the Mexican. I offer complete amnesty to all who have committed crimes in the past, and I swear to enforce the laws fairly and equally for whites and Indians alike. If everyone came in without necessitating a resort to bloodshed, I should be very glad. But, if any should refuse, I will expect the good men to assist me in bringing in the bad ones. This is the way the white people do things; if there are bad men in the area, all law-abiding citizens turn out to assist the officers of the law in arresting those who will not behave themselves.

By Hank Edwards

THE JUDGE

WAR CLOUDS

GUN GLORY

TEXAS FEUD

STEEL JUSTICE

LAWLESS LAND

BAD BLOOD

RIVER RAID

BORDER WAR

DEATH WARRANT

IRON ROAD

LADY OUTLAW

THIRTEEN NOTCHES

RIDE FOR RIMFIRE

GRAY WARRIOR

APACHE SUNDOWN

Published by HarperPaperbacks

APACHE SUNDOWN

HANK EDWARDS

HarperPaperbacks
A Division of HarperCollins*Publishers*

This is a work of fiction. The characters, incidents, and dialogues are products of the author's imagination and are not to be construed as real. Any resemblance to actual events or persons, living or dead, is entirely coincidental.

HarperPaperbacks   *A Division of* HarperCollins*Publishers*
10 East 53rd Street, New York, N.Y. 10022

Copyright © 1996 by Jason Manning
All rights reserved. No part of this book may be used or reproduced in any manner whatsoever without written permission of the publisher, except in the case of brief quotations embodied in critical articles and reviews. For information address HarperCollins*Publishers*, 10 East 53rd Street New York, N.Y. 10022.

Cover illustration by Tony Gabrielle

First HarperPaperbacks printing: August 1996

Printed in the United States of America

HarperPaperbacks and colophon are trademarks of HarperCollins*Publishers*

❖ 10 9 8 7 6 5 4 3 2 1

PREFACE

By 1886 there were only thirty-four of them left—men, women, and children. These were the last of the free Apaches, the *bronchos*, the Wild Ones. This small band of Chiricahuas were the last Indians to wage war against the United States. It took five thousand U.S. troops and three thousand Mexican soldiers five months to run them into the ground. Their leader was called Goyahkla, "One Who Yawns." Americans knew him better by the name Mexicans had bestowed upon this cunning warrior— Geronimo.

On and off for twenty-five years the Chiricahuas had fought against the Mexican and American interlopers of *Apacheria*. They were the finest guerrilla fighters the world has ever known. Their leaders included Mangas Colorado, Cochise and Victorio, Nana, and Ulzana. For a quarter of a century they fought far superior numbers to a standstill.

The average United States infantryman or cavalry trooper was no match for an Apache warrior, who could go for days without food or water, who could run all day from sun up to sundown without respite, who could blend into his environment so well that it was said you did not see the *broncho* Apache until he was in the process of killing you. The Mexicans called them *Los Barbaros*, The Barbarians, because the Apache showed no mercy. Neither was he shown any by his enemies. Far better, the old veterans told the greenhorns on their first campaign, to save the last bullet for yourself than to fall into the hands of the Apaches.

They were neither "noble savages" nor, as General John Pope said of them, "a miserable, brutal race, cruel, deceitful and wholly irreclaimable." Rather, they were just human beings who lived in a harsh land surrounded by harsh foes, and they fought to the last breath to defend their territory against invasion and to protect their way of life.

Believing there was merit in the old adage that one fought fire with fire, the United States Army eventually began to employ Apache scouts. Some of these were lured into service with the *Pinda Lickoyi*—the "White Eyes"—with gold and whiskey. Others served because they believed that continued resistance by the renegades, the troublemakers, the *teiltcohes*, would destroy the Apaches completely.

This is the story of one such scout, one of the "wolves in blue," the Chihenne Chiricahua named Kayitah, but better known to history as Soldado.

1861

Against the wishes of his parents, ten-year-old Kayitah, Chihenne Apache, son of Kaywaykla, ventured out into the storm. The afternoon was as dark as night. Great, towering, black-bellied thunderclouds had gathered to blot out the blazing summer sun. The wind had risen, throwing up a choking haze of red dust, but soon the lashing rain came to settle the dust. Jagged bolts of lightning angrily struck the earth and made it shudder beneath Kayitah's bare feet, while the thunder rolled, like a thousand giant drums, so loud it seemed to rattle the teeth in the Apache boy's mouth.

Kayitah knew that the *Ittinde*, the lightning bolts, were the arrows of the Thunder People, supernatural beings who had once upon a time hunted for the Apaches, supplying them with all the game they could use. The chipped flints that littered this desert land were all that remained of these lightning arrows. In time the Apaches had made a cardinal mistake; they had taken the largesse of the Thunder People for granted, and the Thunder People had responded by ceasing to help the Apaches.

Every now and then they hurled their lightning arrows to the ground, just to remind the Apaches that they still existed. Not to cause harm, but merely to humble.

Each time lightning struck close by, Kayitah made a spitting sound, a show of respect. One had to be careful, for the Thunder People sometimes struck down human beings with their arrows, in order to demonstrate their power and superiority. Apaches used charms to protect themselves, amulets called *tzidaltai*, often fashioned from the wood of a lightning-riven tree, or wore sage in their hair. They made certain never to wear anything red, as it was common knowledge that red attracted the attention of the Thunder People, who were strongly prejudiced against that color.

Kayitah was afraid, but he kept his fear in check. He wanted desperately to see the great Chokonen war leader, Cochise, who had responded to the summons of Mangas Colorado, chief of the Chihenne. Standing outside his family's jacal, Kayitah wiped the rain from his eyes and looked about him. The village appeared to be deserted. No one else dared venture out into the storm for fear that they personally would be punished by the Thunder People for the past ingratitude of the Apaches. Even the camp dogs cowered in whatever shelter they could find.

"Kayitah!"

This was his mother, calling to him from within the jacal.

"Kayitah, come back inside, you foolish boy."

He did not obey, and he knew neither his mother nor his father would come out after him. Apache parents believed their children had to learn the lessons of life through experience. They would give advice, issue warnings. But if a child as hardheaded as Kayitah ignored them, then he would have to learn the hard way. It was in the hands of Ussen, the Apache god.

Realizing he would gain nothing by standing here in front of his jacal, Kayitah ventured boldly forth into the darkness, battered by silver sheets of rain. He wore only a breechcloth, and the rain struck his flesh like cold needles.

But what was a little discomfort compared to the opportunity to lay eyes upon the heroic Cochise? Kayitah knew which jacal Cochise occupied, and he bent his steps in that direction.

As he neared his destination a bolt of lightning struck so near that the loud *crack!* took his breath away, and the pungent odor of the *Ittinde* filled his nostrils. If a person inhaled the lightning "powder" he could fall ill, and perhaps even die. Kayitah realized it was too late for him. Momentarily blinded, he heard laughter, deep and rumbling, and thought it must be the Thunder People, amused at his fatal foolishness.

But then, when he could see again, he realized that the laughter came, not from the heavens, but rather from the man who stood but a few feet in front of him.

Kayitah knew right away it was Cochise, having seen the Chokonen chief at a distance that morning when he had entered the *che-wa-ki*, the village of the Chihenne, accompanied by Janos and the dark and brooding Victorio. Cochise stood tall for an Apache, six feet in height. Though nearly fifty summers old, his body was trim and muscled, the physique of someone half his age. Wet black hair clung to his thick neck and stout shoulders. From each ear dangled three large brass rings. He wore a breechcloth, deerskin leggings, and *n'deh b'keh*, desert moccasins. Kayitah had heard that Cochise never smiled. But Cochise was smiling now.

"*Ish-ke-ne*," said Cochise, using the Apache word for boy. "What are you doing out in this storm. Are you not afraid?"

"No," said Kayitah.

In the electric blue flash of lightning the eyes of Cochise seemed to glitter like polished obsidian.

"Maybe I am," said Kayitah, equivocating. "A little."

Cochise nodded. "Yet here you are. Tell me why."

"To see you."

Cochise sat on his heels so that his eyes were level with those of the Chihenne youth.

"How are you called, *ish-ke-ne?*"

Kayitah told him.

"Who is your father?"

"I am the son of Kaywaykla."

"He must be very proud to have a son whose heart is so strong. Already you are brave enough to ride with Cochise. Perhaps in a few years you will also be big enough."

"In a few years there will be no yellowlegs left to fight," muttered Kayitah. "Cochise will have killed them all."

As he smiled, a twinge of bitterness touched the corners of Cochise's mouth. "No. There are too many *Pinda Lickoyi*."

"But is it not true that every day there are fewer and fewer White Eyes in *Apacheria?* Is it not so that you have come to tell Mangas Colorado that the Chokonen will join the Chihenne to drive the rest of the *indah* out of our land forever?"

Cochise put a hand on the boy's shoulder. "Perhaps it will be so." He stood up. "Come with me, Kayitah. I go now to speak with your great *nantan*, Mangas. I want you to hear what is said."

"Me? But I am just a boy. I am not allowed to sit at a council fire."

"Your future will be decided today, Kayitah, so it is only fitting that you be present." Cochise turned away and made a curt gesture. "Come. If you are to ride someday with Cochise you must learn to obey orders."

Heart pounding in his chest, Kayitah followed the Chokonen war leader through the driving rain to the jacal of the chief of the Chihenne, Mangas Colorado.

Mangas Colorado, chief of the Chihenne, was seventy years old. But he was still a vigorous and powerful man. Standing six feet four inches tall and weighing two hundred and fifty pounds, he was a giant among his people. None surpassed him in courage or wisdom. His people adored him. His enemies feared him, for he was a military genius, and no one could best him in one-to-one combat, even now.

His people were called the Warm Springs Apaches, but they were still Chiricahua, and the name they gave themselves—*Chihenne*—meant "Red Paint People" because it was their custom in certain rituals to daub their faces with the clay found in the vicinity of the spring near their sacred home, at the head of the Canyon Alamosa.

The Chihenne and the Chokonen were cousins, an affiliation strengthened by the marriage of Cochise, the Chokonen leader, to the daughter of Mangas. But Cochise had not come to Canada Alamosa merely to pay a social call on his famous father-in-law. Indeed, he was answering a summons. Mangas sought to ally the Chihenne and the Chokonen, and perhaps even the Mescalero and Coyotero Apaches, against the whites.

The hatred Mangas Colorado harbored for the *Pinda Lickoyi* was a fierce and unrelenting cancer in his soul. It had started twenty-five years before, when a blackhearted scalp hunter named John Johnson and his gang of Missouri riffraff lured a group of Chihenne Apaches into an ambush. Johnson had passed himself off as a trader and a friend of the Indians, and when the Apaches sat down to barter the scalp hunters fell upon them, killing more than twenty. The Mexican state of Chihuahua was offering a bounty for Apache scalps—a hundred pesos for the topknot of a man, fifty pesos for a woman's, twenty-five for a child's—and John Johnson intended to have his share of that blood money.

Mangas witnessed the massacre, and barely managed to escape with his life.

Then, in 1851, gold was discovered at Pinos Altos, and the flood of white prospectors was a cause for grave concern among the Apaches. Symbol of the sun, gold was sacred to Ussen, the Apache god, and no one was permitted to take it out of the ground. Mangas tried to talk the whites into looking for gold somewhere else. He knew of a place in Mexico where it was plentiful, far from Apache land, and he offered to lead the prospectors there. Mistrusting Mangas, the whites seized him, tied him to a tree, and applied an ox whip to his back, beating him to within an inch of his life. Mangas still bore the scars, inside as well as out. Those scars marked the transformation of a peace-loving man into a ruthless antagonist of the *Pinda Lickoyi*.

Kayitah was filled with mortal dread when Cochise brought him into the jacal of Mangas Colorado. Mangas was alone, a brooding copper-skinned giant sitting cross-legged beside a dying fire. His hair was streaked with gray. A brown blanket was draped over his massive shoulders.

"Why have you brought the boy along, Cochise?" asked the Chihenne leader, his voice deep and rumbling like the thunder which shook the world.

"It is about him that we will speak, *jefe*."

Mangas looked at Kayitah. The stern lines of his craggy face softened. Then he nodded. Cochise motioned for Kayitah to sit just inside the deerskin flap that covered the entrance to the jacal.

"It is time," said Mangas, as Cochise settled across the fire from him. "Time for us to drive the *Pinda Lickoyi* from our land forever. If we succeed, perhaps young Kayitah will be able to live in peace."

Kayitah was aghast. He did not want peace. That was the last thing he wanted. He dreamed of growing up to become a great warrior, to kill many of the *indah*.

"Anh." Cochise nodded, *yes*. "The medicine men all say that these lightning storms are an auspicious sign. Now that the White Eyes are busy killing each other, they are as weak as they have ever been, or are ever likely to be again."

Again Mangas nodded gravely. He did not fully understand the reasons for the civil war now raging between the White Eyes, but he was glad of it. Sometimes the various bands of the Apaches had warred upon one another, and conflict with their distant cousins, the Navajos, was commonplace. The White Eyes were a violent and treacherous race who would kill with little or no provocation, and Mangas could only hope many thousands would die while the feud lasted.

The White Eyes' war was good for the Apaches. Hundreds of the *Pinda Lickoyi* had left their ranches, mines, and settlements and headed east—Mangas presumed to participate in the bloodletting. Many of the yellowleg soldiers had also departed *Apacheria*. A few months earlier the Butterfield Stage Line had ceased operations. Some weeks later all the soldiers had marched out of Fort Breckenridge on the San Pedro River, north of Tucson. Then, two weeks after that, the last remaining army outpost in Arizona, Fort Buchanan, had been abandoned and burned to the ground.

"Now only the mining camp at Pinos Altos and the village called Tucson remain," continued Cochise. "Less than three hundred White Eyes. We must destroy them all."

"Tucson will not be easy," said Mangas. He knew the men who populated that town were hardcase cutthroats, all armed to the teeth. "Even now there are soldiers coming to defend it."

The bronze features of Cochise darkened with concern. This was news to him. "How do you know this, *jefe?*"

"Goyahkla has told me."

Cochise knew Goyahkla well. The young man was not Chihenne or Chokonen, but rather Bedonkohe. But he fought like a Chokonen Chiricahua. He had led many successful raids against the *Nakai-Ye*—the Mexicans—and the *Pinda Lickoyi*, and both Cochise and Mangas trusted him implicitly.

"How many soldiers does Goyahkla say are coming?" asked Cochise.

"He says a hundred. They bring several hundred head of cattle with them, no doubt to feed the people of Tucson."

For weeks Tucson had been a town besieged. Continually harassed by Apache raiders emboldened by the departure of the outpost garrisons, the inhabitants of the settlement scarcely dared emerge from their houses into the light of day. Cochise realized that Mangas was right. The soldiers were on their way to rescue Tucson.

"The yellowlegs must be stopped," decided the Chokonen leader. He knew this was easier said than done. Attacking a hundred soldiers was not the same thing as raiding a small mining camp or hitting an isolated ranch.

"In three days time they will pass through Skeleton Canyon," said Mangas. "There I will strike."

"It is a very good place for an ambush, *jefe*. But it is also nearby. If we should fail. . . "

"We must not fail. We cannot. There will be no soldiers left alive to attack our women and children. A hundred men will ride with me. Will you, Cochise?"

"*Anh*. You know I would be honored, *jefe*. I will send

Janos back to my *che-wa-ki* to bring the others. In three days he should be back with eighty men. If we succeed it will be a great day for our people."

Mangas made no response. He could only hope that the destruction of the army detachment would convince the *Pinda Lickoyi* once and for all to abandon their dreams of taking *Apacheria* for themselves. If the ambush worked, he would then move against Tucson, kill all the White Eyes who lived there, and burn the town to the ground. Then the whites would think twice about settling on Apache land. Tucson would be a lesson they would not soon forget. Perhaps Kayitah and his generation could live in peace, after all. Peace was the reason Mangas Colorado was going to wage war.

3

The heavy iron shackles were painfully tight on Clancy St. John's thick wrists, but they were the least of the scout's worries. The sun was blazing in the summer sky. The soldiers were relieved that the storms had passed, but Clancy wasn't. The column was making much better time now that the ground was dry. Which meant they would reach Skeleton Canyon sooner. And that was what worried Clancy—that and the cloud of dun-colored dust kicked up by a hundred horses and over two hundred head of bawling beef.

Besides, he knew Indians didn't move around much in bad weather. They were like animals in that regard, and as long as the lightning storms were afoot he could rest assured that the Apaches were tucked away inside their jacales.

Clancy St. John was thirty years old, and he had spent the last ten years of an adventurous life in this godforsaken desert. A first generation Irishman from County Cork, he'd left the slums of Hell's Kitchen in New York to try his luck as a prospector out west, a way of life which had quickly soured. An excellent shot with rifle or pistol, Clancy then made a living hunting game for miners who were too busy seeking the mother lode to worry much about putting fresh meat on their tables. His knowledge of the land, and of the Indians who dwelled on it, had eventually steered him into service as an army scout. Right now, though, he wished he had never had anything to do with the United States Army.

He was a big man, three inches over six feet in his stocking feet, two hundred twenty pounds of brawn, as strong as an ox, with quick hard fists and a keen nose for trouble. He could smell trouble now. Plain as the ears on a mule.

"Sergeant Haney."

The noncom riding alongside Clancy glanced at the scout and sighed.

"Damn it, Clancy, you know I can't take those irons off. I'd like to, God knows, but orders is orders."

Clancy flashed a wicked grin. "Then how about a nip from that pocket flask of yours?"

Alarmed, Haney looked behind him. "Keep your damn voice down, Clancy, for Christ's sake! You know we ain't suppose to have no whiskey on patrol."

"But I know you, Sergeant."

"Not now," muttered the sergeant darkly. He tugged at the stiff collar of his sweat-stained shell jacket of blue cloth, with its yellow collar stripes and the chevrons on both arms. Then he pushed the black Hardee hat back on his head and wiped the sweat from a furrowed brow. "Damn, Clancy. It's so hot we'd have to visit hell just to cool off."

"I'm in no hurry," said Clancy, and silently chastised himself, for the thousandth time this week, for being such a fool. If only he had stayed home where he belonged and told the army to take a flying leap. Home with his pretty Mexican wife. But no, sympathy for the plight of the beleaguered inhabitants of Tucson, many of whom he knew by name, had prompted him to agree to scout for the army one more time.

Twisting in the saddle, Clancy glanced at the herd

bringing up the rear of the column, shaking his head as he dolefully watched the plume of thick dust rise into the sun-bleached sky.

"Reckon any Apache within a hundred miles knows we're here," said Sergeant Haney.

"You're not as dumb as you look, Sergeant."

"And you're an idiot, Clancy."

Haney smiled wearily. He and Clancy were drinking buddies from way back. Friends, although Clancy declared he never made any of those. On occasion they had fought side by side, in the desert against hostiles as well as in barroom fisticuffs. It was a comfort to have Clancy St. John along on this particular excursion—even if the Irishman was disarmed and wearing irons on his wrists. All because the fool didn't know when to keep his big trap shut. You just didn't talk to officers like that.

"Don't have to tell me—I know. The only thing that makes it any easier to swallow is the sure and certain knowledge that there are bigger idiots populating this old world. Take Captain Bascom, for instance . . . "

Haney looked to the head of the column, eyes narrowed against the dust. Forty troopers rode in front of them, by twos, and in front of them, up there where Old Glory and the regiment's colors fluttered wearily, rode Captain Ezra Bascom who, yesterday, had ordered his scout clapped in irons for rank insubordination. Haney's sympathies lay with Clancy. The scout had been right to point out that camping beside Dead Horse Spring had been asking for trouble. You got all the water you could carry and then moved up into the rocks before you pitched camp, instead of settling down for the night out in the open on the flats with no cover, right beside the only water source within fifty square miles, where any Tom, Dick, or "Cherry Cow" Apache might come along and stumble onto you.

But Bascom had refused to listen. That was the problem with those West Point boys. They always thought they knew better. It was Clancy's job to give advice, and he'd been concerned about the welfare of the men, and rightfully so. Because when Clancy took a scouting job, he felt it was his beholden duty to get every man through alive. That didn't always happen, but Clancy kept trying. But when the captain had insisted on camping right there beside the spring, Clancy had lost his Irish temper, which happened often, and given Bascom a good tongue lashing, spiced with a heady dose of profanity. The captain was an idiot, decided Sergeant Haney, but calling him every name in the book, and casting aspersions upon his ancestry to boot, made Clancy St. John just as big an idiot, in Haney's opinion.

"Well," drawled Clancy, "if you won't take these shackles off, and you won't give me a drink, then ride up there and tell that gold-braided jackass I want to have a word with him."

"Hell, Clancy, why can't you just leave well enough alone?"

"Sergeant, I don't fancy roasting upside down over a slow fire with a pack of Apache *bronchos* sticking their knives into my private parts," rasped Clancy. "See that high ground ahead? We're coming up on Skeleton Canyon. Got that name for a good reason. So be a good boy and go fetch the captain."

Haney grimaced, kicked his mount into a canter, and rode up to the head of the column.

A few minutes later the column halted and the sergeant came back with Captain Ezra Bascom.

"You have something important to tell me, Mr. St. John?" asked Bascom stiffly.

"You need to stop this column and let me ride up ahead and check out that canyon passage."

Bascom looked like he had just swallowed horse piss. "And you need to stop telling me what to do."

He was a young, slender man who, but for the coat of dust and the sweat stains, was impeccably clad in a blue double-breasted frock coat with three gold bars on the high collar and a gold braid "Austrian knot" on each sleeve. His horse furniture was a McClellan saddle, just like all the other cavalrymen in the detachment, and the pad beneath was blue with a broad yellow stripe around the border. He wore yellow calfskin gauntlets and a plume in his hat. All in all, mused Clancy wryly, he looked right pretty, the picture of the perfect horse soldier.

"I have dispatched outriders, Mr. St. John," he continued. "In front and on the flanks."

Clancy sighed. "Not good enough, Captain."

"You have a pretty low opinion of the United States cavalryman, don't you?"

"Except for Sergeant Haney and a few others, none of your men have been west of the Pecos. This is new country to them. It will take some getting used to—if they live long enough."

"This unit has acquitted itself well against the Comanches on the Texas frontier, sir—at least until those damned secessionists took over."

"This isn't Texas. And Comanches aren't Apaches."

"You are under arrest, St. John. You are no longer my scout. Please remember that."

"And you're a flamin' fool."

Sergeant Haney winced. It pained him to watch his quick-tempered friend dig himself into a deeper hole.

Bascom stiffened. His face turned beet red as he fought to control his own temper. Clancy St. John had been a thorn in his side from the first day out of the fort. But it would not do to vent his anger and resentment in front of the men. A commanding officer was supposed to be in control of the situation—and of himself—at all times. The morale of the troops depended on that.

"Aren't you the one," asked Bascom coldly, "who has been petitioning the army for years to employ Apache scouts?"

"I have."

"That in itself proves your judgment cannot be trusted. Everyone knows Apaches would make unreliable scouts. They are a savage, treacherous, and ignorant people."

"Honesty is the single most important virtue among the Apaches, Captain. If an Apache gives you his word, you can rely on him to keep it."

Bascom made a skeptical sound. "I have no more time to waste on you, St. John. The people of Tucson are counting on us to break through to them."

"Which you might not do if you don't scout the flanks of that canyon, Captain."

"Sergeant Haney, you are to gag Mr. St. John if he makes any more noise. Do you understand?"

"Yes, sir," sighed Haney.

Bascom galloped back to the head of the column, which began to move again. Riding stirrup to stirrup with Clancy, Haney shook his head.

"You just never know when to quit, do you, Clancy?"

A half hour later the column entered Skeleton Canyon. Steep slopes choked with brush and rocks loomed on either side of them. The clatter of ironshod hooves and the bawling of cattle echoed loudly in Clancy's ears. Choking dust filled the hot still air, stinging his eyes as he scanned the rimrock. He saw nothing out of the ordinary. But then that meant next to nothing where Apache *bronchos* were concerned.

"Maybe you were all wrong, Clancy," said Haney, when they were a mile deep into the canyon.

Just then a rifle spoke.

One of the troopers just in front of Clancy and Haney cried out and toppled from his horse.

The canyon slopes erupted with gunfire. Clancy heard the loud cracking noise of a bullet passing too close for comfort. There were more empty McClellan saddles. Clancy dismounted in a hurry and scurried in a crouch for the nearest cover, a jumble of rocks at the base of the southern slope. A bullet shimmied off a boulder and threw rock dust into his eyes. He hit the ground, looked back for Haney. The sergeant had also dismounted. Reins in one hand and pistol in the other, he was shooting up at the slopes while trying to hold onto his plunging horse and yelling hoarsely at the troopers to dismount. Most of the cavalrymen were still in their saddles, trying to return fire with their Army Colt revolver or Sharps carbine from the hurricane deck of a snorting, pivoting mount—an exercise in futility. Maybe, thought Clancy, you fought on horseback against the Comanches. But it wouldn't work here. The troopers made excellent targets, and one by one they were being picked off by the Apaches.

"Haney!" roared the scout. "Get your lazy butt over here!"

The sergeant's horse screamed and collapsed, hit by a bullet. Haney let go the reins, tugged the carbine out of its saddle boot, and sprinted for the rocks where Clancy was hunkered down. He was nearly home when an Apache bullet spun him around and dropped him.

"Hell," muttered Clancy.

He left his cover and ran to the sergeant. Bullets whined around his ears and kicked up dust at his feet. Grabbing Haney by the front of his blood-splattered shell jacket, Clancy dragged the sergeant into the rocks.

"How bad?" gasped Haney through clenched teeth.

Clancy tore open the shell jacket to check the sergeant's wound.

"You'll live, Sarge." The bullet had struck Haney in the shoulder.

"Will I?" Haney flashed a grin that was tight with pain.

Clancy knew what he meant. Would any of them get out of Skeleton Canyon alive?

"Need the key to these irons," he said.

"Pocket," wheezed Haney.

Clancy checked, but the key was gone, and he muttered a blistering curse. "Shoot 'em off, Sergeant." He laid the stout iron chain joining the shackles across the face of a rock. Haney put the barrel of his Army Colt right up to the chain and triggered the pistol. The chain separated, the bullet ricocheted away. Haney had managed to hold onto his Sharps, so Clancy appropriated the carbine for his own use. His rifle, a Henry repeater, was still on the sergeant's saddle, Bascom having ordered him disarmed at the moment of his arrest. The Henry now lay under a half ton of dead horse.

"You might need this, too," said Haney, tugging Clancy's pistol from his belt. It was a Texas-made Dance Brothers copy of the .36 caliber Colt Navy revolver.

Clancy transferred the short gun to his own belt. He checked the Sharps. A Model 1859, it was .56 caliber and used special linen cartridges.

"What do we do now, Clancy?" asked Haney. "Must be a hundred of 'em up there in those rocks. They've got us pinned down good."

The Irishman grinned. A tremendous calm came over him in times of crisis, and this time was no exception.

"What do we do? Why, we do what they least expect of us, Sergeant."

"I'm almost afraid to ask."

"Just lie still."

And with that Clancy was gone.

The gunfire was a constant din. Men and horses were falling on all sides of Clancy. Bullets filled the air with angry sound. It was a nightmare. A living hell. Clancy had been through this kind of hell several times before. He didn't get rattled, but kept his wits about him, and was aware of everything going on with astonishing clarity.

The cavalrymen were shooting back now, but there wasn't really anything to shoot at. None of them saw an Apache. All they could see was a muzzle flash here and a puff of smoke there. The Apaches knew how to use the jumbled rocks on the slopes for cover. And they knew to move to a different position after each shot, so that when a trooper fired at a puff of smoke he was wasting his ammunition.

By now most of the troopers who were still alive had come to the conclusion that staying in the saddle was just plain suicidal. So they dismounted and sought cover in the rocks, as Clancy and Sergeant Haney had done at the outset. But Captain Ezra Bascom had other ideas. Clancy saw him galloping down the canyon yelling hoarsely at his men.

"Stay with your mounts, men! Stay with the horses! Damn it to hell, that's an order!"

The troopers weren't listening, and that infuriated Bascom. He was brandishing his Model 1833 dragoon saber over his head, and Clancy wondered if he was going to use it on his own men. He looked mad enough to do just that.

Bascom made a perfect target, and Clancy could scarcely believe the Apaches had not yet cut him down. But then, mused the scout, wasn't that always the way in battle? The good men died and the jackass officer seemed immortal.

Clancy leaped out into the open as Bascom thundered by. He latched onto the bridle of the captain's horse. The horse snorted, balked, and reared. Bascom tumbled backwards out of his McClellan. Clancy let the horse go and helped the stunned officer over into the rocks.

"Damn you!" rasped Bascom as it finally registered in his befuddled mind what Clancy had done.

"Captain, if you get your ass shot off, that's okay with me. But I'm afraid some of these boys might be stupid enough to obey your orders, which means they'd get their asses shot off, too, and that is something I'd purely hate to see."

"We need our horses . . . "

"Dead men can't ride, Captain. Don't worry about the bloody horses. They won't go far."

Bascom looked around. A hint of fear glimmered in his eyes. Clancy figured he wasn't so much worried about the men under his command, but rather about his fledgling career as a field officer. Wouldn't look good on Bascom's record, mused Clancy, if his first command was wiped out in an Apache ambush. Clancy decided now wasn't the time for I-told-you-so's.

"The cattle . . ." said Bascom, realizing the herd that had been bringing up the rear of the column was nowhere to be seen.

"Stampeded."

"How many Apaches up in those rocks, Mr. St. John?"

Clancy's cold green eyes scanned the slopes. "Maybe a hundred."

"Good God!" croaked Bascom. "Then we are outnumbered."

Clancy nodded, bleakly scanning the dead and dying troopers who littered the canyon floor. "We are now, for certain."

Bascom swallowed his pride. "What do you suggest?"

"Attack, of course."

"Attack?"

"Yeah. We charge straight up this side and clear 'em out. Once we've gotten to the top, we can turn around and pick off the ones on the other slope."

"That's suicide."

"So is staying down here. We're on our own, Captain. Won't be any rescue. Long as we stay put they'll stay up there and pick us off one by one. Sure, we'll lose a lot of men in an attack, Captain, but you might just win the fight. The Apaches won't be expecting it."

Bascom tried to swallow, but his throat was too dry. He nodded. "Okay. We'll attack."

"Better death than dishonor, right, Captain?"

Bascom didn't bother with a response. Standing up, he brandished his saber and yelled at his men to follow and began to clamber up the steep slope. All along the canyon men in blue began to climb and shoot, shoot and climb. Born with a panther-like grace and ability, Clancy was well in front of the rest. Cavalrymen were falling left and right, many shot in the back by the Apaches on the other side of the canyon. But the *bronchos* on this side were surprised, as Clancy had expected them to be. Most of them began to fall back, and in doing so showed themselves for the first time. Clancy didn't shoot until he had a sure target, but when he did shoot he always hit his mark, accounting for three Apaches with three shots.

A few of the Apaches chose to remain hunkered down in the rocks until the soldiers drew near, then jumped them. One of the *bronchos* tried that on Clancy, but the scout hammered him to the ground with the Sharps, shattering the carbine's stock in the process. Drawing the Dance Brothers revolver, Clancy put a bullet in the Apache's brainpan before the Indian could get back on his feet. Delayed in this manner, Clancy lost the lead to the young trooper who gallantly bore the colors. But an Apache bullet pierced the man's throat, and the Stars and Stripes fluttered to the ground. Clancy didn't give a hoot about the honor of the flag, but he didn't want to reach the top all by his lonesome, either, so he took up Old Glory and shouted at the remaining cavalrymen to follow him. A ragged cheer answered his call, and the troopers climbed with renewed vigor.

When he reached the rimrock, Clancy was somewhat amazed to find that he was still alive. The Apaches were on the run now, darting through the brush. Clancy wedged the flagstaff between a couple of rocks and proceeded to fire at the *bronchos* on the other side of the canyon. He could see them a lot better from this vantage point than he had been able to from the canyon floor. About two dozen troopers joined him at the top and followed his lead, laying down a withering fire on the north slope. The Apaches didn't stand their ground for long. Clancy knew they wouldn't. Unless he had a clear advantage, an Indian generally preferred to live to fight another day. He and the troopers accounted for about ten of the *bronchos* before the survivors quit the slope and melted into the brush beyond the rimrock. Bascom ordered the men to stop firing. Those who had canteens of water shared them with those who did not. The wounded were attended to by the unscathed.

As Bascom approached, Clancy noticed the officer's blood-soaked sleeve and ashen complexion. He held his left arm stiffly against his side. At least the man had guts, thought Clancy, even if he was short on good sense.

"Appears you were right, Mr. St. John," conceded Bascom.

"You'd better sit down, Captain, before you fall down."

"I'm fine. Just a scratch. What will the hostiles do now? I mean, do you think they will come back?"

"I doubt it. But they might go after the cattle. I think the detail you assigned to the herd is still with those beeves."

Bascom glanced bleakly at the blue-clad bodies on the slope below, and on the serpentine trail winding through the bottom of the canyon. "Brave men," he muttered. "Brave men all. We must try to help that detail, Mr. St. John."

"Best way is to draw the Apaches away from the herd."

Bascom nodded. He realized that he didn't have enough men to go riding into another full-fledged fight—and those he had were shot to pieces. "What do you have in mind?"

"The Chihenne village is only a few miles from here, Captain. We gather what horses we can and ride like hell right for it. The Apaches will have left one or two men to watch us, see what we do next. If they think we're going to attack their *che-wa-ki*, they'll come running. We'll make a feint at the village and break off, circle around, and rejoin the herd. By then it will be dark, and if we push hard all night, we should be nearly to Tucson by daybreak. The Apaches won't come at us in the dark."

Bascom stared at the scout. "Mr. St. John, I . . . "

"Forget it." Clancy wasn't interested in apologies. "The dead are dead."

Clancy made his way down the rocky slope to the bottom of the canyon. He found Sergeant Haney, right where he'd left him. The bullet had entered the right temple, killing Haney instantly. Clancy heaved a deep sigh and closed Haney's staring eyes.

"And I thought only the good died young, Sergeant."

He turned and proceeded to look for his horse.

5

Looking back on it—as he often did, for the nightmares would trouble his sleep until the day he died—Clancy St. John figured his mistake was in leaving what remained of the cavalry detachment before it reached the village of the Chihenne Chiricahua.

Of the nearly one hundred soldiers who rode into Skeleton Canyon that day, only twenty-five were able to follow Captain Bascom south towards the *che-wa-ki* of Mangas Colorado. Bascom's command was scattered all over the desert now, with a dozen men presumably still with the herd of beeves destined for a starving Tucson, twenty-eight lying dead in the canyon, and thirty-one wounded in the scrape with the *bronchos*. Four were missing, and presumed dead.

Bascom hadn't liked the idea, but Clancy had convinced him to leave the wounded in the canyon. With the exception of the commanding officer, of course. They had to move fast, and injured men would only slow them down. If they succeeded in drawing the Apaches toward the village by making them think that the yellowlegs were about to descend upon their defenseless women and children, the wounded would be safe enough. Once they reached Tucson with the herd, assuming they could recover the cattle, they would return to the canyon with enough wagons to move those unable to stay in a saddle. And with the help of armed civilians, they could make this rescue operation so imposing that the Apaches would not dare attack it. The wounded were left with enough water and ammunition to last them several days, and all but a dozen were able to shoot if they had to. By Clancy's calculations, they could get the herd to Tucson tomorrow and be back in Skeleton Canyon by early the day after.

The plan, as Clancy explained it to Bascom, was merely to make a feint at the Chihenne village in order to draw the *bronchos* away from the herd, which the scout was almost certain the Apaches were now after. Under no circumstances were the troopers to get tied up in a fight at the *che-wa-ki*. Clancy knew the ambushers had been Chiricahua, the bunch led by Mangas Colorado, with some Chokonen *bronchos* mixed in. He'd taken a look at every dead Apache he could find in the rocks while the soldier boys gathered up enough mounts to make the ride, and he had recognized a handful of them. Figuring that at least a hundred Apaches had participated in the ambush, Clancy was sure that only a few warriors had remained behind in the Chihenne village. So there was nothing to be gained militarily by actually launching an attack. Besides, he didn't think there was much fight left in Bascom's men.

He forgot to consider one thing. Revenge.

Leaving the column a couple miles shy of the *che-wa-ki*, Clancy circled back in hopes of confirming that the Apaches were by now aware of Bascom's move on their village. The sight of a cloud of dust far to the northeast across the heat-shimmering plain brought a smile to his gaunt and dusty face. That had to be Mangas and his bunch. The scout just prayed they had been drawn away from the herd and that twelve-man detail in time.

Just as he turned his horse to head south again,

intending to rejoin Bascom, Clancy heard, very faintly but unmistakably, the sound of gunfire.

That shooting—and there was suddenly a lot of it—came from the direction of the Chihenne village.

Clancy kicked his horse into a stretched-out gallop. A chill traveled up his spine. Either the soldiers had run into another band of renegade Apaches or. . .

He didn't even want to think about the other possibility.

It took almost killing his horse, but he got there in a hurry.

From the high ground, he could see the village from one end to the other—about sixty jacales clustered around the big flat red sandstone boulders where the springs were located. He stared in gut-churning horror at the scene below.

Bascom's soldier boys were on a bloody rampage.

They were riding through the village, shooting at anything that moved—man, woman, child, or dog. Some of the jacales were burning. Thick black pillars of smoke climbed into the colorless sky. Through the din of rifle and pistol fire, the screams of the dying reached Clancy's ears and then crawled down deep inside of him and clawed without mercy at his soul.

He had been right about one thing—Mangas had taken nearly every able-bodied man with him for the ambush. The few that remained had proven no match for the troopers.

An Apache woman was running up the slope towards him, a cavalryman in hot pursuit. The woman was grimly silent. She knew she stood no chance of escaping with her life. Yet she did not cry out in fear or despair. The horse soldier, on the other hand, was yelling like a banshee.

Clancy spurred his horse down-slope. He couldn't reach her in time. The soldier rode her down, checked his horse sharply, turned it, and fired his pistol point-blank into the Chihenne woman sprawled on the ground. The bullet struck her between the shoulder blades as she was trying to rise, and the impact slammed her into the ground.

In the next instant Clancy's horse collided with the

cavalryman's mount. Clancy managed to stay in the saddle, but the soldier's pony staggered and its rider lost his seat and went flying. Stunned, he rolled over and sat up and gaped at the mounted man looming over him. Clancy's Dance revolver gaped right back at him. The soldier looked at the expression of cold fury on Clancy's face and was suddenly so afraid he wet himself.

"You bastard," rasped Clancy.

"No, please! Don't shoot!" The man rolled over and curled up into a fetal ball, covering his head with his arms, as though that would protect him from the bullet Clancy wanted to put in him so bad he could taste it.

But Clancy couldn't bring himself to pull the trigger. He wasn't too sure why that was, but he just couldn't. With a cry of pure rage, he whirled his pony around and rode hell for leather into the *che-wa-ki*.

Reaching the jacales, he came out of the saddle and hurled himself at a young lieutenant who was about to smite an Apache boy with his dragoon saber. Clancy and the lieutenant crashed through the mud-stick wall of a jacal. The scout's big fist pummeled the officer senseless. Only then did Clancy realize that a pair of Chihenne women cowered in the jacal, one old, one young. Their dark eyes glittered with hatred. Clancy briefly considered leaving the unconscious lieutenant where he lay, knowing that the women would slit the man's throat as soon as he left. Yet, again, he found himself unable to give in to his darker whims, and dragged the lieutenant away.

The young boy who had been the lieutenant's intended victim stood there staring at Clancy.

"What is your name, *ish-ke-ne?*" asked the Irishman. He was fluent in the Apache tongue.

"Kayitah, son of Kaywaykla," was the boy's response.

"Where is your *dagotai?*"

"My father rides with Mangas Colorado and Cochise," said Kayitah proudly.

Clancy was impressed by the boy's courage. "And your mother?"

"My mother is dead," said Kayitah flatly.

The muscles in Clancy's jaws worked as he bit down hard on an angry curse. He knew Kayitah was hurting terribly, but Apaches were taught at a tender age to keep their feelings to themselves—particularly in the presence of the *indah*, the enemy.

A cavalryman appeared, galloping out of the smoke from the fires. Spotting Kayitah, he checked his mount so sharply that the horse seemed to sit down on its haunches. The soldier whipped out his Army Colt revolver. But Clancy was quicker on the draw. As he stepped between Kayitah and the trooper he drew the Dance and aimed it at the trooper, who was stunned by this unexpected turn of events.

"What the hell?" rasped the soldier in disbelief. "Stand aside, mister."

"No."

"What's the matter with you?" Fear put an edge on the man's words, for he recognized the expression on Clancy's face as the look of a man who wanted to kill. "We got to wipe 'em all out. Even the young ones. Nits make lice."

"You're proof of that."

The soldier's temper flared, but only briefly. "Goddamn Injun lover," he muttered and, savagely kicking his horse into motion, rode away.

The gunfire had become sporadic. Clancy could see precious little of what was going on around him, as the smoke from the burning jacales hung thick and heavy on the hot still air. Those Apaches who had not been killed straightaway had made their escape under cover of the smoke, and the soldiers had ceased finding targets.

Clancy turned to Kayitah and held out a hand. "Come with me, boy."

Kayitah's indecisiveness was short-lived. He realized that this White Eyes had for some reason saved his life. He had to assume that his father and the other warriors had lost the battle they had gone out, with such high hopes, to fight this very morning. Perhaps his father, like his mother, resided now in the *Chibin-di-Kungua*, the House of Spirits. If so, he was all alone. As far as he knew, there was no one left alive in the village. His family, his tribe—all gone. His world had fallen to pieces. There was only one person who did not want to kill him, who actually seemed to care about him. This man, who did not wear the blue clothes of the hated yellowlegs, and whom Kayitah did not fear.

He took Clancy's hand.

The scout's well-trained horse stood nearby. Clancy had invested a lot of time and effort into training it not to run off. He hoisted Kayitah into the saddle and swung up behind the Apache boy. At that moment Captain Bascom emerged from the stinging, choking smoke.

"St. John! Where are you going?"

"Home."

Bascom looked about him at the carnage his vengeful troops had wrought. He seemed to be in a daze.

"I didn't mean for this to happen," he said. "But when the men spotted the village they ... they went berserk." He shook his head. "There was no stopping them."

"They were under your command," said Clancy coldly.

Bascom nodded. He realized there would be no valid excuses for him. Closing his eyes, he swayed like a sapling in a strong breeze. Gruesome images flickered in his mind's eye—an Apache infant's skull being crushed beneath a trooper's boot heel, a young woman being raped in the doorway of a jacal, an old man whose body was riddled with bullets as he sat upon his blanket and accepted his fate with implacable courage.

He opened his eyes. "You can't leave," he told the scout. "We must recover the herd. We must reach Tucson. The people there are counting. . . "

"To hell with them," said Clancy. "And to hell with you, Captain. To the devil, in fact, with my whole bloody race."

Bascom stared at him, speechless.

Clancy thought, *In a little while Mangas and his bronchos will be here.* He could only hope Bascom and his butchering sons of bitches lingered long enough to find themselves face-to-face with Mangas Colorado. Then they would pay for their crimes. Then they would feel the sting of Apache revenge. Vengeance begat vengeance, after all.

He rode away with Kayitah, and never once looked back.

6

"Goddamn Injun lover."

Clancy turned, gripping the bottle of rotgut by its neck and smashing it into the head of the soldier who had muttered the epithet. The soldier's eyes rolled and he collapsed, hitting his chin on the edge of the counter.

On the other side of the counter, Wiley James, Fort Union's licensed sutler, winced. He did not care about the soldier's skull, but the bottle had been nearly full, and whiskey—even bad whiskey—was a prime commodity out here, and his major source of income.

The garrison commander, Colonel Warren, let him sell strong spirits in the fort because he wanted to keep his troops away from the nearby tent town, knowing he could better control them within the confines of the fort, and knowing, too, that a cavalryman without access to liquor could be a surly troublemaker at best, and a deserter at worst. This had prompted Warren to strike a bargain with Wiley James—an eminently sensible bargain, in the sutler's opinion. James could sell his whiskey, but he would be held accountable for any drunkenness or disorder which might result from that commerce. In other words, it was up to James to make sure his patrons didn't drink too much who-hit-john. Too much could make a man run amok.

The unconscious soldier's two drinking buddies looked at their whiskey-splattered uniforms, then at each other, and finally at Clancy St. John, who stood there with a faint and infuriating smile curling his lips. James knew what that smile meant. Clancy was in a highly inflammable mood, and perfectly willing to take on these other two soldiers, and even the entire garrison, if it came to that. And the soldier's two friends were ready to take him on. In unison they took a menacing step forward, broken glass crunching under their boot heels. Clancy dropped the bottleneck. It made a wicked weapon, but he was a firm believer in fair fights. He clenched his big hands into granite-hard fists.

James reached under the counter and brought out a sawed-off shotgun and leveled it at the pair of soldier boys.

"That's far enough."

"You won't shoot," said one of the soldiers, but his voice lacked conviction. Wiley James was a burly ruffian and it was said he had killed three men down on the Bloody Border in his younger days, one of them a notorious *pistolero*.

"Yes, I will," said James cheerfully. "I will blow both your kneecaps off and then sell you a pair of wooden legs. Now get out, and take your partner with you."

Clancy contemptuously turned his back on the soldiers and leaned against the counter and sipped his whiskey like he didn't have a care in the world. The ugly looks the soldiers fired his way were wasted.

Wiley James waited until the soldiers were gone, having carried away their unconscious friend, before stowing the scattergun back under the counter.

"Hellfire, Clancy," he rasped. "You and me go back a long ways. We're friends. Or rather, I'm as close to a friend as an ornery old coot like you will ever have. But I just don't understand you. Reckon I never have, come to think on it. Why'd you show up here? You must've known there'd be trouble like this, after what you done."

"What *I've* done?" Clancy snorted and knocked back the rest of his whiskey.

"You know what I'm talking about. Leaving Bascom and his bunch to fend for themselves, and riding off with that Apache kid the way you did."

"My presence was requested here, Wiley. Colonel Warren summoned me to testify at Bascom's court-martial. And I wasn't going to miss that for the world."

A corporal appeared in the doorway of the sutler's store. "St. John? The colonel wants to see you."

"God help you, Clancy," said James.

"And the devil take you, Wiley."

Clancy threw enough money on the counter to pay for the busted bottle of bravemaker, then forsook the cool dimness of the store to follow the two-striper across the sun-blistered hardpack of the fort's parade.

Colonel Joseph Warren was seated behind a battered kneehole desk in his office. The headquarters building was an adobe structure with a cedar roof, two rooms on either side of a wide dusty hallway with split-log benches against fly-specked walls and open doors at both ends to catch any errant breeze that had gotten lost and strayed into New Mexico Territory. Thick adobe walls and open windows made Warren's office one of the coolest places south of the Absaroka this time of year, and Clancy folded himself unbidden into a rickety chair across the desk from the fort's commanding officer, where he proceeded to build a smoke.

Clancy didn't use cigarettes when he was scouting—the smell of tobacco could give a man away when he was trying to remain hidden from Apaches—but he made up for it when he wasn't working. It occurred to Clancy that he wouldn't ever have to do without his "quirlings" again, since hell would freeze over before he agreed to scout for the army.

Joe Warren was a tall, spare man with a long sharp-featured face framed by flourishing sideburns. A career soldier, he had earned his commission on the battlefields of the

Mexican War by virtue of heroic acts far beyond the call of duty. Once upon a time Clancy had liked him, considering Warren a capable, commonsensical officer with the added advantage of not being a product of West Point. But right now Clancy didn't like anybody who wore a uniform.

"I've just received the finding of the court," said Warren. "Thought you would like to be made aware of the board's decision."

Clancy scratched a strike-anywhere to life with his thumbnail, fired the tip of his cigarette.

"Captain Bascom has been found guilty on all charges," said Warren. He watched Clancy for the Irishman's response. "I suppose that makes you happy."

"Not really."

"But you did come all this way to testify against him."

"I came to tell the truth about what happened."

Irritated, Warren got up and paced from one side of the office to the other, hands clasped behind his back. Hearing a distant gunshot, he paused at one of the windows and peered out. Seeing nothing of consequence, he shrugged it off and resumed his restless pacing.

"It was a bad business all around," he said. "What happened at Warm Springs has all the Apaches up in arms. Not just the Chiricahuas, but the Coyoteros and Mescaleros, too."

"So Mangas finally gets what he's been after. All the bands fighting side by side."

"I must say, Clancy, that I hold you at least partially to blame. Not for the massacre, or the ambush that preceded it. I am confident you did all you could to prevent both. But I do fault you for leaving those soldiers to fend for themselves, knowing the Apaches were riding hard for their *rancheria*. When you signed on as a scout you agreed . . ."

Clancy held up a hand. "Captain Bascom relieved me of my duties."

"Yes, yes, I know, but my God, man! You left those boys out there at the mercy of Mangas Colorado. We're lucky any of them got back alive."

"After what they did, they deserved to die."

Warren scowled at him. "Know what I think? I think you feel guilty, because riding on Warm Springs was your idea, wasn't it? Bascom wouldn't have thought of it."

"Go to hell, Colonel."

"I understand you took an Apache boy."

Clancy nodded. "Turns out his father was killed at Skeleton Canyon. His mother was cut open from sternum to crotch by one of your poor boys, Colonel. He opened her up and her guts fell out onto the ground."

"And what are your plans for this boy?"

"I plan to make sure he grows up. Something not many Apache boys or girls can count on these days."

"He may well turn on you when he is grown."

"I could hardly blame him, after what my kind has done to his people."

"In that regard our opinions differ. The Apaches make war on our women and children. They are the ones who refuse to abide by the treaty terms and leave their reserves to raid isolated farms and mining camps."

"Don't worry, Colonel. This is a war you can't lose. There just aren't enough Apaches to stop you. 'Course, it'll take you a good long while."

The two-striper knocked on the office door and was told to enter.

"Captain Bascom is dead, sir."

"Dead?" Warren was stunned. "Dead, you say?"

"Yes, sir. Blew his brains out as soon as he got back to his quarters."

"Christ."

Feeling cold clear through, Clancy got up. "Will that be all, Colonel?"

"Yes, damn you. Go home. You may rest assured the army will not require your services in the future."

"That's the first piece of good news I've had all day."

Clancy rode hard for three days to get home. He lived in a

small adobe house sheltered by a bosk of oaks on the banks of a nameless creek a few miles shy of the border. There was a small Mexican village a half day's ride to the south, but the nearest white man lived a hundred miles away. That suited Clancy just fine. He admired the Mexican people, the peons. They were brave, resilient, humble, devoted to family and God, simple in their ways, friendly to strangers, and stoic in their suffering.

Five years earlier, Clancy had made the acquaintance of a pretty, slender young girl named Maria Delgado in that village. Right away he discovered he could not get her off his mind. Eventually he broke down and married her, and he'd never had cause to regret that decision. In fact, he thanked God every day for Maria, and the blessing of happiness she had brought him. Maria had been happy, too—except for one thing. She'd not been able to give her husband the son she knew he wanted so badly. That was why, mused Clancy, she had been so taken with Kayitah.

Months had passed since the massacre at Warm Springs, and Kayitah was adapting to his new life far more swiftly than Clancy had expected. He was a bright lad. His *chin-da-see-le*—his homesickness—was offset by the knowledge that he was surrounded by people who cared about him. Clancy gave most of the credit for this to Maria, whose sweetness and goodness could not help but have a beneficial effect on a child, Apache or otherwise.

Clancy realized full well that in the future there would be problems. No matter what they did, Kayitah was still a Chihenne Apache. Already there were signs. The people in the village disapproved of Clancy and Maria attempting to raise a Chiricahua boy as their own. Only grief would come of such an ill-advised effort, regardless of good intentions. Clancy didn't blame them for their prejudices. The Apaches and the Mexicans had been warring for many years before the first White Eyes set foot on this land. As far as the villagers were concerned, Clancy and Maria were trying to tame a rattlesnake, and everyone knew this simply could not be done. Sooner or later the rattlesnake—or the Apache—would, by its very nature, bring harm to them.

But Clancy had always believed that worrying about the future was a fruitless enterprise. Tomorrow would take care of itself. If tomorrow even came. It was enough to live for today.

As he rode up to the adobe, Maria emerged. Clancy was quickly out of his saddle and in her arms.

"It's all over," he said. "I'm finished with the army."

"I am glad," she whispered, relieved beyond expression. Her husband's dangerous occupation had caused her much anxiety, many sleepless nights. She had always tried to keep her fears to herself, for she was not the kind of wife who would ever try to keep her man from doing what he thought he ought to do. But of course Clancy had known exactly how she felt.

"Reckon Luis and I can start looking for mavericks," he said.

Often he had told her that one day he would give up scouting and turn his attention to building a herd out of the wild cattle that abounded in this country. Luis was Maria's uncle. He had no family of his own, and for several years now he had lived here with them. Clancy was happy with the arrangement, for he did not like leaving Maria alone. Luis was a true *hombre del campo*. He knew everything there was to know about cattle and horses and this land, and he was a damned fine shot as well.

"Where is . . . ?" Clancy saw Kayitah running across the hardpack from the shed and the *ramada*, where he had been watching Luis shoe one of the horses in the shade of the cedar poles whose bark hung down like Spanish moss. Luis stepped out into the hard sunlight and waved. Clancy waved back, turned to his horse, and, when Kayitah reached him, had in hand the wooden rifle he had carved while sitting around at Fort Union waiting to testify at the court-martial of Ezra Bascom.

Sitting on his heels, Clancy presented the wooden rifle to the Apache youth, whose eyes lit up with delight.

"A little soldier shouldn't be without a gun," he said.

"*Gracias*," said Kayitah. A quick learner, he had picked up quite a bit of Spanish from Maria and Luis in a short time.

It was Luis who had taken to calling Kayitah "little soldier." Or Soldado, for short.

Clancy looked up at Maria. Her smile filled him with a warm contentment. *I'm home for good*, Clancy promised himself. *I have everything here that a man could possibly want. And with any luck the world and all its woes will leave us be.*

7

Standing on a windswept outcropping of rock high in the Dragoon Mountains, Cochise gazed out upon the desert plain and silently mourned the death of Mangas Colorado. He also mourned the fate of his people. He was certain now that the Apaches were doomed.

The war between the whites, which Cochise had hoped would work to the advantage of his own people, was over. Once again the *Pinda Lickoyi* were flooding back into Apacheria.

Worse still, the great leader of the Chihenne was gone. After the massacre of his village at Warm Springs, Mangas Colorado had fallen into a deep and long-lasting depression. In retrospect, Cochise concluded that the tragedy had taken much of the fight out of his father-in-law. How else to explain what had happened at Pinos Altos? Or perhaps Mangas had succumbed to that self-destructive streak in his character, weary of life and of the suffering which seemed so much the staff of life.

In 1863 a party of gold seekers led by a mountain man named James Reddeford Walker had arrived in Pinos Altos and set up camp. They told Mangas that they would sup-

ply his people—what was left of them after the massacre—
with food and blankets in exchange for a guarantee of
peace. This occurred in the middle of a particularly harsh
winter, and Mangas Colorado's people were hungry.

With only three warriors, Mangas had visited the
camp of the White Eyes to parley. The gold seekers flew a
white flag, but when the Apaches were securely in their
trap, they brandished weapons. The warriors were released
after being told that if the Apaches left the prospectors
alone for ten moons Mangas would be released as well.
Until then he would be held hostage.

Whether Walker and his men intended to keep their
word was a moot point, for soon after, the yellowleg soldiers heard that Mangas had been captured and arrived at
the gold camp to take charge of the famous Apache *nantan*.
That very night Mangas Colorado was shot to death.

The official explanation was that he had tried to
escape. But Cochise heard a different story—that his
father-in-law had been gunned down in cold blood. Even
worse, Mangas Colorado's head had been cut off and his
corpse discarded in a gully. The skull of the great Apache
leader was sent to a phrenologist back East who reported
that the cranial capacity was greater even than Daniel
Webster's.

The fate of Mangas Colorado horrified the Chihenne,
who believed that a person lived forever in the House of
Spirits in the physical state he or she had been in at the
moment of death. If Mangas had been decapitated while
still alive, his spirit would wander forever without its head.

To an Apache, revenge was a sacred duty, and for
years now Cochise and his Chiricahua had cut a bloody
swath of death and destruction across the Southwest. The
Dragoons, located in the southeastern corner of the
Arizona Territory, was their stronghold. Surrounded on all
sides by alkali flats, no enemy could approach undetected.
The mountains themselves were a maze of granite spires,
cliffs, and chasms, natural defenses so formidable that the
army dared not attack the *bronchos* there. The Dragoons

had plenty of year-round springs, and lots of game in the thickets of piton, mesquite, and alligator juniper.

Other Apache bands came to the Dragoons. Chief among these were the Mescaleros, who had been rounded up and herded onto a reservation at the Bosque Redondo. Here they joined what was left of the once-proud Navajo nation, living on land with soil so poor it could sustain few crops, whose streams were too alkaline to drink safely, and whose trees were so sparse that the women had to walk ten miles just to harvest an armful of firewood. For two years the Mescaleros had suffered in the Bosque Redondo. Then, one night, every Apache who could travel, who wasn't incapacitated by starvation or disease, simply vanished. Many of them made their way to the Dragoons and joined Cochise and his Chiricahua "wild ones."

Watching dust devils twist across the desert from his rocky aerie, Cochise pondered the inexorable march of time. Seven years had passed since the murder of Mangas Colorado, five years since the end of the war the whites had waged among themselves. Cochise had lost count of all the White Eyes he and his *bronchos* had killed in that time. Three or four hundred, at least. Yet the *Pinda Lickoyi* kept coming, more and more of them every year. So many years of war had depleted the Apache ranks. Even with the Mescaleros, Cochise could muster barely a hundred and fifty warriors. By comparison, over two thousand yellowlegs now garrisoned no less than fourteen posts in Apacheria. And there seemed to be no end to the steady influx of white civilians. Cochise knew this was a war he could not win. But he was determined to fight to the death. There could be no surrender.

Recently, word had reached him that the U.S. Army was preparing to launch a major campaign against him, spurred by hysterical petitions to Congress from the white inhabitants of the Arizona and New Mexico Territories. The civilians demanded protection from the Apache scourge. Before long the soldiers would come, led by Lieutenant Howard Cushing, renowned Indian fighter, a brave and energetic officer.

"*Jefe.*"

Cochise turned. Juh was climbing the rocks to join him. Though a heavyset man, Juh was as agile as a mountain goat.

"We are ready," said the Nednhi chieftain.

Cochise nodded. The Nednhi were the southernmost of the Chiricahua bands. Their homeland lay in Mexico, in the Sierra Madre. Cochise had spent the better part of two years helping Juh and his people resist the encroachments of ancient Apache enemies, the Yaquis and the Tarahumaras, who had been driven north from their traditional lands into the territory of the Nednhi. Now Juh and his warriors had crossed the border to fight for a time with Cochise.

Though he stuttered so badly that he had to give commands in sign language, Juh was a great warrior and a dynamic leader of men, and Cochise was glad to have his help. Juh was also a close friend of Geronimo. The two had grown up together, and Juh had married Geronimo's sister, the beautiful Ishton.

Juh had begged Cochise to let him deal with Cushing, because the lieutenant had led an attack against a band of peaceful Mescaleros two years ago, leaving only two women alive. Some of the dead had been Juh's friends, and he had sworn vengeance.

"Remember," counseled Cochise, "to burn the grass. Their horses will suffer. Then, when you strike, they will not be able to move quickly."

Juh nodded. He had vowed to kill Cushing and all of his men, even if it meant chasing the yellowlegs to the ends of the earth.

For three arduous days Lieutenant Cushing and his soldiers crossed scorched earth. The Apaches were burning the spring grass, and the horses of the detachment were beginning to suffer. But Cushing pressed resolutely onward, in the direction of the Dragoon Mountains.

Having sworn he would find and defeat Cochise, he was not going to be deterred.

Several miles north of the Babocomari River he discovered the tracks of a solitary Apache heading north. It was the first sign of the enemy they had found, though the smoke from distant grass fires was proof enough that the Indians lurked near at hand. Elated, Cushing dispatched three men to follow the trail at the double-quick, while he came along with the rest of the column as quickly as he was able.

Cushing had handpicked the men who rode with him, and every one of them was a veteran of at least one campaign against the Apaches. It soon became apparent to the three-man patrol that something was amiss. The trail was entirely too easy to follow. When the tracks of the lone Apache led them into a narrow canyon, the trio of horse soldiers hesitated, suspecting a trap. But it was too late. A dozen Nednhi *bronchos* emerged from an arroyo behind them and blocked their escape, while others materialized from deep within the canyon. Certain that they were doomed, the cavalrymen took cover and resolved to sell their lives dearly. But the Apaches did not attack. They hoped to lure Cushing and the main column into their trap, so they settled down to exchange fire with the patrol.

Cushing played right into their hands. Charging to the rescue of his patrol, he led the column straight into an Apache crossfire. The lieutenant was among the first to be cut down in a hail of bullets. The surviving soldiers scattered, fleeing for their lives. Juh ordered his Nednhi warriors to ride them down, every last one.

A pair of soldiers fled south, pursued by a dozen *bronchos*. They rode hard for hours. Finally one of their mounts stepped into a hole and broke its leg. Riding double now, the two men soon found themselves afoot, for the starving horse could not carry both of them more than a few miles before collapsing. The Apaches hot on their heels, the soldiers plunged into the brush and managed to elude their pursuers until night fell.

All through the night the soldiers staggered on. When morning came, they saw no sign of the Apaches. Relieved, they gave some thought to finding out exactly where they were and to locating some food and water. Early that afternoon a plume of chimney smoke led them to a small adobe house where they found a woman and an old man, both Mexican. One of the cavalrymen recognized the woman as the wife of the ex-scout, Clancy St. John.

Their arrival seemed to trouble the old man, Luis. But Maria took the soldiers into her home and gave them something to eat and drink. She explained that her husband and son were away, having driven a hundred head of cattle to a nearby fort, but they were due back today or tomorrow.

While the soldiers informed Maria of the ambush, Luis stood outside in a ribbon of shade, frowning as he watched and listened. He did not see or hear anything out of the ordinary. Still, he was worried. His instincts, sharply honed by a lifetime in *Apacheria,* warned him that there was danger. Finally he decided to take Maria away. The soldiers could stay or go their own way, it mattered not to him. Maria's safety was his first priority. He went to the shed to fetch two horses.

It was there that the *broncho* killed him. Luis had no chance. He died instantly, silently, unable even to shout a warning.

The Apaches had tracked the pair of yellowlegs all day. Now they moved in on the adobe house from all sides, committed to doing their part to fulfill Juh's promise that none of Cushing's command would survive.

8

For Clancy St. John the trip to Fort Stanton was both profitable and disturbing.

Since forsaking his career as a scout for the United States Army, Clancy had made a decent living providing army posts and mining camps in the southwestern portion of the New Mexico Territory with beef on the hoof. A business relationship with the boys in blue had been slow in coming, thanks to the lingering effects of official resentment towards him for abandoning Bascom's command at Warm Springs.

Finding his village sacked by the yellowlegs, and more than fifty of his people butchered, Mangas Colorado had hounded Bascom and his men to the outskirts of Tucson and then turned back to Skeleton Canyon to virtually wipe out the contingent of wounded soldiers left there. Of the more than one hundred troops who rode with Bascom, only two dozen survived, the greatest disaster in the annals of army campaigns in the Southwest. Worst of all, from the army's point of view, Clancy had remained stubbornly unrepentant.

Of course, the massacre at Warm Springs had inspired

the Apaches to renewed vigor in their fight against the white interlopers, and the past ten years had been the bloodiest the desert had ever seen. Clancy was glad to be out of it. He wanted nothing more to do with Indian fighting. The war had swirled all around his home in that remote corner of the Territory, but never too close.

In time the army's desperate need for beef to feed its burgeoning forces in *Apacheria* forced them to deal with Clancy. He had sold a hundred head to the commissary at Fort Stanton for sixteen dollars a head, his biggest transaction yet. Now he had more money than he knew what to do with—more than he had ever possessed at any one time in his life.

And yet, though the cattle he sold were much needed, his welcome at the outpost had not been a warm one. Even after all this time, bad feelings remained. But it wasn't just old grudges that had caused the soldiers to give him a cold shoulder. The presence of Soldado had bothered many of the troops posted there. An Apache was an Apache, and the only good one was a dead one. That was the way their minds worked, almost to a man.

Soldado—for years now Clancy had called him by that name—had handled the hostility of the soldiers with implacable grace. Even though he knew the Chihenne youth better than anyone, except perhaps Maria, Clancy couldn't tell what the lad was thinking. Soldado was a silent, inscrutable young man. His Apache upbringing had taught him to bear both physical and mental anguish with absolute stoicism.

Apache boys were very early schooled to endure pain. Sometimes dry sage was put on their skin and set afire; they were expected to let the sage burn to ashes without so much as flinching. They were encouraged to fight one another, and the fight wasn't called until blood had been drawn. They would be divided into teams and engage in child warfare using slingshots or arrows with wooden points. To the Apache, pain was an ever-present fact of life, and one demonstrated character by enduring it without complaint. This was a lesson Soldado had learned well before his tenth year.

He was twenty years old now, and he had grown tall and slender and agile. Though he wore the garb of a white man, he could not be mistaken for anything other than he was. Black hair grew long and straight to his shoulders. And he refused to wear boots, preferring instead the Apache *n'deh b'keh*, the desert moccasin.

Seldom did he speak, unless spoken to. Thanks to Maria and Luis he spoke fluent Spanish, but his English was rudimentary. Clancy himself usually communicated with his wife and her uncle in their native tongue, so English was rarely heard in the St. John household. Clancy could not remember ever having heard Soldado laugh. Nor had he ever seen the youth lose his temper. Sometimes he smiled, usually at Maria, because he had grown to love her. It was hard not to love Maria. But Soldado was a very solemn young man who kept his own counsel and only occasionally betrayed his true feelings.

So Clancy had no idea how Soldado felt about the way the soldiers had treated him at Fort Stanton. Clancy had always endeavored to keep Soldado away from soldiers, bearing in mind that the Apache youth had seen his mother murdered by a cavalryman. But he had needed help moving that hundred head of cattle. Soldado was a hard worker, and he rode a horse like a man born to the saddle. Clancy and Luis had taught him about horses and cattle and everything about this land that he had not already known. No man Clancy knew could ride better, track better, or shoot better than Soldado, and the Irishman was as proud of him as a man could be of his own flesh-and-blood son.

In ten years time Clancy had come to think of Soldado as his own, and loved him as though he were. But Clancy still wasn't sure how Soldado felt about him. Soldado never revealed his true feelings in this regard. He was apparent enough in his affection for Maria. Sometimes, when Soldado looked at him, Clancy thought he detected a kind of warmth in the Apache's dark eyes, but the Irishman realized this was probably just his imagination, fueled by wishful thinking. *He knows I rode with the soldiers who killed his parents and destroyed his home. Perhaps that is something he will never be able to forgive.*

A three-day ride separated Fort Stanton from Clancy's home. A *tinaja*, or spring-fed rock pool, marked the halfway point, and late in the second day of their return trip they thankfully drew near this water source. They moved with caution, as one always had to in those circumstances; bandits, hostile Indians, javelinas, and the occasional mountain lion also knew of this water. Their caution paid dividends this time. There were nine Apache *bronchos* at the *tinaja*.

The Apaches were lounging around in the scant shade of a few scrawny trees, all but two men, who were letting the horses drink from the water hole. The others were sharing a bottle of whiskey. They were well on their way to being certifiably drunk. A hundred yards away, concealed among the rocks on the rim of a hogback ridge north of the rock pool, Clancy watched one *broncho* get up, stagger, and then trip over the sprawled legs of one of his companions. The others laughed; they were making a lot more noise than sober Apaches ever would have dreamed of making. Clancy wondered where they had gotten the popskull liquor.

Then he saw Maria.

She was lying curled up at the base of one of the trees. He recognized the dress she was wearing.

"Oh Christ, no," he breathed.

He looked in horror at Soldado, who was watching him impassively.

"It's Maria," he said, his voice shaky and hoarse. "I've got to try to save her."

He knew now where that whiskey had come from—it was his own. And he also knew that Luis had to be dead. Luis would never have let the Indians take Maria while he lived.

Clancy realized that he had been a fool to think he could keep himself and his family divorced from the war between the Apaches and the *Pinda Lickoyi*. This was bound to have happened sooner or later.

Soldado said nothing. He watched Clancy like a hawk. This, thought the Irishman, was the moment of truth, the moment he had been dreading all these years, the moment that would put Soldado's loyalty to the supreme test. Those *bronchos* were his own people. Chiricahuas. Would Soldado raise his hand against them, even for Maria's sake? Clancy felt sorry for him. He couldn't ask Soldado to fight alongside him. So he turned and ran down the back side of the hogback to his horse and leaped into the saddle without touching boot to stirrup, drawing the Henry repeater from its boot. He never looked back to Soldado. It was his intention to ride straight into the Apache camp, guns blazing. He had one thing going for him. The Apaches were drunk. Would that be enough of an advantage, at nine-to-one odds? He hoped so. For Maria's sake, not his own. Because he was Maria's only chance.

He kicked the horse into a gallop.

9

Clancy galloped into the Apache camp with the setting sun at his back. The reins were clenched in his teeth, and he had the Dance revolver in one hand and the Henry repeating rifle in the other. He got right in among them before starting to shoot. It was difficult enough trying to hit anything from the saddle of a hard-running horse without making a long shot out of it. Before the fact that they were under attack could register in their whiskey-fogged brains, Clancy was right on them. Firing the pistol and the long gun almost simultaneously, he dropped two *bronchos* in their tracks. A third lunged at the head of his horse, brandishing his knife, planning to cut the animal's throat. Clancy clubbed him savagely with the barrel of the repeater, and the Apache lost his grip on the bridle and fell beneath the horse's hooves. Twisting in the saddle, Clancy triggered the Dance and put a bullet in the head of the fallen *broncho*.

In a matter of seconds he had passed straight through the camp. Now, as he checked and turned his horse, bullets began to burn the air in their search for him. The two Apaches with the horses were doing the shooting. Apparently they were not as inebriated as their companions. Clancy traded lead with them, hitting one of the Apaches squarely in the chest. The *broncho* threw up his arms and toppled backwards, splashing into the water of the shallow rock pool. The surface of the pool was stained red by the light of the setting sun and the blood of the dead man.

Shouting at the top of his lungs, Clancy spurred his horse and rode back towards the group. The Indians were ready for him now. The element of surprise no longer worked in his favor. The second horse holder rose to his full height with rifle to shoulder and fired. Wisely, he aimed for the bigger target—Clancy's horse. The animal screamed and went down, thrashing. Clancy kicked clear of the stirrups and landed on the run, plowing into an Apache. Both men went down in a kicking heap. The Indian was first on his feet, but Clancy rolled over on his back and triggered the Dance. Two bullets slammed into the *broncho*, and he was dead standing up.

As Clancy rose, a searing pain shot through him—he'd been hit. Nothing serious. A bullet had laid a deep furrow across his arm. A guttural scream spun him around. An Apache was running full tilt straight at him, bringing up a pistol as he closed in. Before Clancy could react, a rifle spoke and the Apache was hurled to the ground. Clancy turned to see Soldado riding into the fray.

Only five Apaches remained alive. Four of them had reached their ponies. The fifth was too slow, stumbling drunkenly towards the rock pool. Soldado's rifle spoke again. Here, it seemed, was one man who had no difficulty hitting his mark from the saddle. The drunken *broncho* dropped to his knees and then pitched abruptly forward onto his face. The other four swung aboard their horses and scattered. There was no more fight left in them.

Clancy turned and made for the trees where Maria lay. She was on her hands and knees now, trying to get to her feet, but having trouble doing so. She was hurt! Clancy called out to her and broke into a run. Mounted, Soldado swept past him, reaching the trees before him, aiming his rifle, pulling the trigger . . .

Clancy stared in uncomprehending horror as Soldado put a bullet into her at point-blank range.

An incoherent snarl of rage on his lips, the Irishman lurched forward. Then, as Maria was thrown against the tree by the bullet's impact, he realized it wasn't Maria at all, but a drunken Apache wearing Maria's dress. Astride his prancing horse, Soldado fired again. The Apache's face dissolved in a pink mist and he flopped forward, dead.

Staring at the Apache, Clancy realized that he could not save Maria. She was already dead.

Dismounting, Soldado walked over to him, leading the horse. The Chihenne said nothing, but a glimmer of silent grief briefly penetrated his inscrutable mask.

"I hoped they killed her quick," said Clancy, and his voice broke, because he knew that wasn't likely.

Soldado left him alone in his grief. Clancy's horse, mortally wounded, was still moving. The Apache put a bullet in the animal's brain to release it from its agony. Then he collected one of the ponies left by the departed *bronchos* and transferred Clancy's Texas-rigged saddle from the dead horse to the living one. This done, he brought the horse to Clancy, who hadn't moved from the spot where he stood.

"We go," said Soldado, offering the reins to Clancy.

Clancy nodded. There was grim but necessary work to be done.

When the soldiers came, Clancy calculated it had been two days since he and Soldado had buried Maria and Luis and the two cavalrymen, but he couldn't be sure because he'd lost track of time. Time meant nothing to him anymore, since he no longer had a future, at least none that he wished to contemplate.

He couldn't remember much about those days since discovering Maria's body, however many of them there had been. Occasionally Soldado brought him some food and water—he hadn't touched the food. He spent most of the time in the doorway of the adobe, falling asleep once from sheer exhaustion, otherwise staring out at nothing. Nightmares had awakened him that one time, nightmares so hideous that he didn't want to close his eyes again, ever, for fear they might revisit him.

Through it all Soldado had watched over him, day and night, never sleeping himself. The Apache youth rarely strayed from the corner of the adobe where he had posted himself, and where during most of the day there was a strip of shade. He sat on his heels, back braced against the wall, a rifle near at hand. Time meant nothing to him either. He had forgotten time, in the Apache way. He could wait forever.

When he heard the soldiers' horses Soldado didn't move. He knew right away, even before they emerged from the scrub, that these were yellowlegs, not Apaches. An Apache's pony was usually unshod, unless it had been stolen recently from a white, and with an Apache there would have been no rattle of bit chains, no creak of saddle leather, and none of the other telltale noises that, to Soldado's ears, made the passage of a cavalryman through the brush as loud as that an elephant might make blundering its way through a china shop.

There were five of them—again, Soldado knew this before they came into view. A lieutenant, a corporal, and three troopers. They had come a long way in a big hurry and their nerves were shot, and when they saw Soldado and recognized him for what he was, the hate blazed in their eyes. Soldado was unmoved.

The lieutenant took note of the fresh graves, then took Clancy's measure, and put two and two together. Keeping a wary eye on Soldado, he dismounted to stand before the adobe's doorway.

"Sir, might you be Clancy St. John?"

Without looking around Clancy nodded.

"General Crook sent me."

"Who?"

"General Crook. President Grant has relieved Stoneman and placed Crook in charge of operations against the Apaches." Again the lieutenant looked suspiciously at Soldado.

"Thanks for coming all this way to give me that piece of news," said Clancy.

The lieutenant was momentarily nonplussed. "Sir, I—I came to inform you that General Crook would like to see you as soon as is convenient for you. At Fort Apache, sir."

"Why?"

"He desires an interview with anyone who has knowledge about the Apache problem. Your name came up."

"The Apache problem?"

"Yes, sir." The lieutenant was wondering if maybe this Clancy St. John was a little loco.

Clancy got up. "Yes, Lieutenant. There is a problem." He walked stiffly over to Soldado. "Looks like I'll be scouting for the army again, after all," he told the Apache, speaking in Spanish. "Where the *bronchos* are concerned, I am now their worst enemy."

Soldado looked at the graves, at the soldiers, then back at Clancy.

"I go," he said.

Clancy breathed a sigh of relief.

10

General George Crook was forty-two years old, a hero of the Civil War, and a veteran of numerous Indian campaigns in the Northwest. His appointment as the new commander in the Southwest, charged with solving the "Apache problem" once and forever, had not been popular in the army. President Grant had passed over a number of senior officers to give Crook the job. Even William Tecumseh Sherman, Commanding General of the Army, had opposed Crook's promotion, claiming the officer was too unorthodox. Crook didn't give a damn about all that, or about who liked what. The President had given him a job and he was going to do it to the best of his ability.

Crook had a number of well-publicized eccentricities. He preferred civilian garb over his regulation uniform. He rode a mule rather than a horse. He was brutally outspoken, and his proclivity for letting his feelings be known regarding other officers had not endeared him to his superiors, whom, when the occasion warranted, Crook had variously described as incompetent, cowardly, or just plain stupid. The fact that he was usually right didn't help.

But he was a fighter, a wily strategist. He knew

Indians, and the enlisted men who served under him learned to idolize him, because in his dealings with his troops he was invariably honest, fair, and steadfast.

A stocky six-footer, Crook acknowledged the arrival of Clancy St. John in his Fort Apache office with a distracted wave of a hand, indicating the chair across from the desk where he was poring over a pile of charts. Clancy ignored the offer, and a moment later Crook fastened his steely blue-gray gaze on the Irishman and smiled faintly.

"Your hackles are up, Mr. St. John. Go on and tell me why that is."

"My son is having to wait outside because your dimwitted aide says an Apache is not allowed in the head-quarters building."

"Oh yes, I've heard you're raising an Apache lad. What is his name?'

"His Apache name is Kayitah. But he's known now as Soldado."

Crook nodded, rose wearily from his chair, and strode to the door. "Sergeant Milhouse! Let Soldado through."

"But General . . . "

"But what, mister?"

Even Milhouse's voice cringed. "Nothing, sir."

"I didn't damn well think so." Crook slammed the door and lumbered back to his chair, slacked into it as Soldado entered the room. The general gave him a curt nod. "Glad to make your acquaintance, son. Now, St. John, will you sit your butt down? I like to palaver eye-to-eye."

Clancy sat down. Soldado remained standing near the door.

"Mr. St. John, I've fought Indians for thirteen years now. But it is abundantly clear to me that the Apaches are a unique bit of work."

"You're right on the mark, General."

"I have no prejudice against them. I realize they are trying to hold onto their homeland. I know atrocities have been committed by both sides in this conflict. But I have a job to do, and, by God, I'm going to do it."

I think, mused Clancy, *that the Apaches have finally met their match.*

"When I first arrived, the territorial governor strongly suggested I employ Mexican scouts to help me track down and chastise the renegades. He told me such men could travel light and fight hard and, in his words, turn the Apache wrong side out in no time. So I employed fifty Mexican scouts, being an open-minded son of a bitch. Well, I can tell you that Mexican scouts are not the answer. They care about only one thing. Butchering Apaches and taking their scalps to collect that bounty the Republic of Mexico has recently instituted, damn them."

"Not the first time," said Clancy.

Crook grimaced. "A disgusting business. At any rate, I dismissed those Mexican scouts. Now I am giving serious thought to using Apache scouts."

Clancy sat up straight in his chair. "Well I'll be. It's about time."

"Yes, I've been told you recommended that the army use Apache scouts more than ten years ago. Now, as I understand it, there is long-standing enmity between some of the Apache bands. Of course, by our own stupidity we have driven some of the bands together. But I believe we could find some reliable scouts among the Coyoteros and the White Mountain band. What do you think?"

"Coyoteros, for sure. I also think you're going to catch pure hell, General. Not just from the army, either. The people in these parts will not be happy about this. They lump all Apaches together and figure the only good one is eating dust six feet under. They'll squawk."

"Let them," snarled Crook. "I'm not running for a damned elective office, so I don't care what the civilians say. If they manage to get me replaced, that'll suit me right down to the ground. I'm tired of Indian fighting anyway, Mr. St. John. Sick to death of it, frankly. That's just between you and me, of course."

Clancy thought, *I hope he isn't replaced any time soon.* Crook was just about the first high-ranking officer he'd met who talked sense. Clancy had a hunch that if George Crook were given a free hand he could eventually bring peace to the Arizona and New Mexico Territories. Best of all, he was not imbued with that irrational hatred of Apaches that seemed to afflict most other officers—that conviction that the Apache was little better than an animal, an unredeemable savage that needed exterminating. The Apaches, surmised Clancy, would get as fair a shake from Crook as they could expect to get from any White Eyes.

"My job is to persuade Cochise and Victorio to agree to a peace settlement," said Crook. "If they refuse, I will drive them out of the Dragoon Mountains. Should a campaign against them be necessary, I will want a capable man who understands the Apache and his ways for my chief of scouts. Would you be interested, Mr. St. John?"

"I'll do it. But you should know, there may be some resentment in this army towards me, because of . . . "

Crook made an impatient gesture. "I know all about that, and it is of no consequence whatsoever. You will answer solely to me. How does that suit you?"

"Fine."

"Good. Then your first task will be to raise a company of Apache scouts. I leave that entirely in your hands. You pick the men you want, bearing in mind that you will be responsible for their actions. Understood?"

"Yes."

"I have written a letter which you may want to use in recruiting these men, if you think it would help." Crook rummaged through the maps, found the letter, and passed it to Clancy.

Clancy read:

The white people are coming to settle this land. There is no stopping them. Soon it will be impossible for anyone to live upon game; it will all be driven away or killed off. Far better for everyone to make up his mind to plant crops and raise cattle or sheep

and make his living in that way. In no time the
Apache will be wealthier than the Mexican.

I offer complete amnesty to all who have committed crimes in the past, and I swear to enforce the
laws fairly and equally for whites and Indians alike.
If everyone came in without necessitating a resort to
bloodshed, I should be very glad. But, if any should
refuse, I will expect the good men to assist me in
bringing in the bad ones. This is the way the white
people do things; if there are bad men in the area, all
law-abiding citizens turn out to assist the officers of
the law in arresting those who will not behave themselves.

Clancy nodded, folded the letter, and put it away.
"Might come in handy."

"Then I suggest you get to work, Mr. St. John."
Crook rose, came around the desk, and shook Clancy's
hand. He had a firm grip and he looked Clancy squarely in
the eye, and Clancy knew that was a good sign. Then
Crook went to Soldado and extended his hand to him.

"It will take an Apache to catch an Apache," said
Crook.

Soldado seemed to understand. He shook Crook's
hand.

"*Enjuh,*" he said gravely, "good."

11

"I won't go," said Tom Gaines, truculently.

The young corporal was put off by the man's surly attitude, and he could smell whiskey on the civilian's breath, besides. The corporal silently cursed his abysmal luck for having been chosen for this dangerous mission. Why did he always get these crappy details? *Ride north as far as Mogollon and warn all the civilians that the Apaches are active in this area, and recommend in the strongest possible terms that they seek safety at the nearest army outpost.*

"Won't have no damn 'Pache skunks chase me off my range," sneered Gaines.

The corporal drew a long, calming breath. It was perfectly okay with him if this drunken idiot got himself cooked over an open fire, or skinned alive. Serve him right for being such a dunderhead. But then the corporal looked past Gaines, whose rancid-smelling bulk filled the adobe's doorway, and he saw the man's wife and two children. The girls were clinging to their mother's skirt, and they were plainly scared. The oldest, guessed the corporal, was maybe ten years of age, the other a couple of years younger.

They were pretty, with long pale blonde hair and the

brightest blue eyes. Just like their mother, who was the prettiest woman the corporal had ever seen. Now how was it that a worthless bum like Tom Gaines had such a pretty wife? She was scared, too—the fear was right there in her eyes. *She has every right to be afraid*, decided the corporal. *If she fell into Apache hands, she'd find out what hell was really like.*

"Be sensible, sir," said the corporal, determined to try one more time to persuade Gaines. "Think about your family."

"If I leave, my stock will scatter into the brush," growled Gaines. "Then what will I do? Nossir. I've worked too hard to walk away from it now."

"Sir . . ."

"I've spoken my last word on the subject. Now be on your way before I lose my temper."

I wish you would, thought the corporal, gritting his teeth. He was scared, too, and bone-tired, and he would have liked nothing better than to bloody this belligerent idiot's nose. It would make him feel better. But of course, he couldn't without provocation, and Tom Gaines wasn't quite drunk enough to instigate a ruckus. So it was time to move on. There were a few other homesteads between here and Mogollon, a few more civilians to warn. Hopefully they wouldn't be so damned mule-headed.

The corporal again looked beyond Gaines to the woman, touched the brim of his sweat-rimmed campaign hat. "Sorry, ma'am," he mumbled, and sadly turned away.

"Wait just a minute, Corporal," she said.

He swung back around. Gaines scowled over his shoulder at her. But there was a fierce determination in the woman now, and it came to the corporal in a flash that he had seriously misjudged her. She was no meek, slender reed to be blown this way and that by the whiskey-besotted gusts of Tom Gaines's harsh bluster. No, she had spirit, and an independent streak. A temper of her own, too. And she was not going to be pushed around.

"My children and I are coming with you," she said. "If you don't mind."

The corporal hesitated. Actually, escorting civilians hadn't been in his orders. His job was to warn them, convince them to move closer to the forts so that the army could provide them with protection. Getting there was their job. If he let the woman and her kids come along with him, he would have to forget about the folks up towards Mogollon and take these three straight back to the post.

"You ain't goin' nowheres," snarled Gaines.

"I most certainly am," she replied. "Obviously, you don't care what happens to Faith and Charity, but I do, and I will not put their lives at risk on account of your stubborn pride."

The corporal thought for an instant that Gaines would have a change of heart and take his family to safety. *Then I'll be free to carry out my orders—assuming I don't run smack into a passel of mad-as-hell broncho Apaches. In which case I'm deader'n last Thanksgiving's sage hen . . .*

"Then go, and be damned," muttered Gaines. "You've been achin' to leave me, anyhow. Just lookin' for the excuse."

"We made a terrible mistake," she said, then turned her attention to the corporal. "Will you help us, Corporal?"

How could he refuse? He would explain the situation to his captain—if he didn't take Mrs. Gaines and her children back, who would? Besides, he might not find anyone to the north. They might have already gotten the word and skedaddled. Which would mean he'd be risking his neck for no good cause.

He nodded. "I'd deem it a privilege, ma'am."

"I won't take long," she promised. "Just give me a few minutes to gather up some things. Would you hitch the mules to the wagon, Tom?"

"Do it your own self," grumbled Tom Gaines. He brandished a pocket flask and took a long pull.

"I'll take care of the wagon, ma'am," said the corporal. "Just don't bring much with you. We'll have to travel light and move almighty fast."

* * *

In less than half an hour they were on their way, heading due south, following a narrow trace. The corporal rode alongside the wagon. The children sat on either side of Laura Gaines as she handled the leathers. A few valises rode in the back, along with a small parfleche trunk. The corporal had the distinct impression that she had left her husband for good.

"How long will it take us to reach the fort, Corporal?"

"Should be there by noon tomorrow, ma'am."

"I want to thank you for what you are doing."

"I'm sorry I couldn't talk your husband into coming along."

"Do you think we'll run across any Apaches?"

"Hard to say, ma'am. They've been popping up all over the place lately." He glanced at the rifle on the boards beneath her feet. "You know how to use that long gun, do you?"

"I'm a fair shot, if I do say so myself."

The corporal nodded. He wasn't encouraged. If they did run into a pack of *bronchos*, they wouldn't stand much of a chance. Letting Mrs. Gaines and her girls fall into the hands of the hostiles was the one thing he could not allow to happen, and he resolved then and there to shoot them dead if worse came to worst. Shoot them, and hope God Almighty would make allowances. Because if he let the Apaches take them alive, he would burn in hell for sure. Of this the corporal was convinced. I'll have to kill them and save the last bullet for myself.

They made it through the day without any trouble, camped that night down in a dry gulch, without a fire. The night became quite cool, and the girls complained. Laura Gaines gently told them to shush and bundled them up in blankets. She had the common sense to know a fire was out of the question. The corporal shared his hardtack and salt pork and the water in his canteen.

When the girls were asleep, Laura said, "I guess you must be wondering how I could leave my husband like that."

"No, ma'am." It was an out-and-out lie, of course. The corporal was curious to know how such an intelligent, attractive young woman had ever gotten paired up with a no-account like Tom Gaines. But it wouldn't do to pry into the lady's personal affairs.

She sighed deeply. "I should never have consented to marry him. But my children needed a father, I thought, and . . . well, I was in dire straits. When their father died, we fell upon hard times."

"How did he die, if you don't mind me asking?"

"No one knows. He simply rode away one day, and never returned. No one could tell me anything. He never arrived at his destination. You see, he was a mining engineer. A decent man, a loving father, a good husband. He wouldn't have abandoned us. He loved us all very much."

"This land can kill you in a great many ways," said the corporal. "There ain't no telling what happened to him."

"You know, it's much more difficult to deal with that way," she said, and by her tone of voice, he could tell she was still hurting. "Not knowing, I mean."

He nodded, then realized she probably couldn't see the nod in the dark, and said, "Yes, ma'am."

"Tom was right. I was looking for an excuse." She sounded as though she felt guilty about leaving.

"What will you do now?"

"Oh I don't know, something." She said it in a casual, offhand manner, as though the future was of no concern to her, but it rang false.

"Well, I wouldn't worry," he said, in a lame attempt to be comforting. "Things will work out just fine for you and your girls, ma'am."

"Yes. Of course they will."

"You'd better try to get some sleep."

She lay down beside her daughters. The corporal sat there with his Spencer carbine across his knees and watched the night crawl by.

The next morning the Apaches struck.

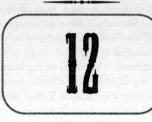

12

They let the wagon pass before springing the trap. The corporal had been campaigning against Apaches for five years, and occasionally he had made such barracks boasts as that he could smell one of the heathens a mile off even if the wind was wrong. But he rode right past six of them that morning, and they were concealed in a dry wash not twenty yards from the trace. Here the serpentine arroyo ran parallel to the wagon road for a spell, and the *bronchos*, having shadowed the wagon since the previous afternoon, agreed that the arroyo provided the best place for an ambush.

With bloodcurdling war cries designed to paralyze their prey with fear, the Apaches charged out of the arroyo as soon as the wagon had passed, seeming to sprout full-grown and bloody-minded from the womb of the earth itself. They rode hard, using knee pressure to guide their desert mustangs, firing their rifles as they thundered in pursuit.

One of the first bullets accounted for the corporal's horse. When his mount went down, the lithe cavalryman jumped clear, shouting at Laura Gaines to keep going.

Then, remembering he had promised himself that he would not let the woman and her daughters fall into Apache hands, he ran after the wagon, threw his carbine into the back, and vaulted over the tailgate himself.

The corporal knew there was no chance of outrunning the *bronchos*. Crouched in the rear of the wagon, he got off a few shots with the carbine, but it was hard enough to stay aboard the bouncing wagon, much less shoot accurately. His fire served to scatter the Apaches. Just as he realized that they were shooting at the mules in the traces, one of the animals made a strange sound and stumbled. The corporal yelled at Laura Gaines to stop the wagon. If one of the mules went down at full stride the resulting wreck would likely kill them all.

If the woman can shoot at all, we might be able to hold them off, he thought. But he entertained little hope.

Laura climbed the leathers, straining to stop the mules, and even as the wagon jolted to a halt, the wounded animal collapsed with a horrible wheezing sound, a bloody froth gushing from its mouth.

"Children, get under the wagon!" she said, picking up the rifle.

The sudden stopping of the wagon had thrown the corporal off-balance even though he had tried to brace himself. Sprawled in the wagon bed, he saw Laura Gaines standing in the box with rifle to shoulder. The rifle spoke. Raising his head, the corporal was pleased to see one of the Apaches somersault off his pony. But they were close now, very close. Bullets were flying, making strange sucking sounds as they passed. "Get down!" he yelled, and, rising, swept her to the ground. He tried to shield her fall with his own body. He hit the ground hard, and the wind was knocked out of him. At that moment the Apaches swept by on their galloping mounts. The corporal desperately rolled over on top of Laura Gaines. An Apache fired straight down into him.

Laura squirmed out from under the dying man. With his last ounce of strength he held out his Army Colt, and with his final breath, said, "Don't . . . let them . . . take you . . . "

Laura pried the revolver from the corporal's fingers. She understood and glanced at her two girls, who cowered beneath the wagon. The *bronchos* had overshot the wagon. Now they were turning their nimble mustangs to come back. She raised the pistol, fired once, twice, and accounted for a second Apache. Then she crawled under the wagon and gathered her two girls to her, pressing them tightly to her bosom. They were sobbing with terror. "Don't be afraid, my darlings," she whispered, and looked at the Colt in her hand.

Distant rifles spoke. A *broncho's* body slammed into the dust so close to the wagon that Laura jumped. Another Apache made a running dismount and crouched to peer under the wagon. Laura pointed the Army Colt at his face and pulled the trigger. The *broncho's* cruel leer dissolved in a bloody mist.

The two remaining Apaches rode away, making yelping sounds akin to the cries of the coyote. A horse thundered past the wagon after them. Another locked its legs and came to a dusty, skidding halt. Holding her breath, Laura watched the legs of the rider appear as he dismounted. Vast relief swept over her as she saw that the legs were covered with trousers and leather chaps, and there were boots, not *n'deh b'keh*, on the feet.

Sitting on his heels, Clancy St. John looked under the wagon and extended a hand.

"All clear, miss."

Now that it was over and her children were safe, hot tears streamed from her eyes to streak the pale powdering of dust on her cheeks. She knew the danger was passed, but at first she could not make herself crawl out from under the wagon and face such a cruel and capricious world.

"Come along," said Clancy, more forcefully. "Cry later. Right now we've got to get moving."

Laura Gaines composed herself. It helped that Clancy's stern tone of voice pricked her temper. The man might at least try to be a little more understanding, considering what they had been through. Of course, he had saved her life, and she realized she oughtn't to be so judgmental, not to say ungrateful, as to find fault with him.

As she emerged from beneath the wagon with Faith and Charity, the second rider returned from his brief pursuit of the two remaining Apaches. Laura glanced at him—and gasped as cold chills worked up and down her spine. Despite the white man's clothes he wore, this one was obviously an Indian, probably an Apache. Apache or not, Laura had cause to be scared out of her wits in the presence of any red man.

"Don't worry," said Clancy. "He's my son."

"Your son? But . . . but isn't he . . . ?"

Clancy nodded. "That's right. He's Chiricahua Apache. His folks were killed ten years ago. I took him in, raised him. You needn't be afraid of him."

She watched Soldado. He was paying no attention to her; rather, he was carefully checking each of the fallen Apaches to make sure, she supposed, that they were dead. He rode his horse in a circle around each of the *bronchos*, usually once, sometimes twice. He hadn't slipped his rifle into its saddle boot just yet; its stock rested on his thigh.

Laura turned back to Clancy—only to find the man was now in the process of cutting the one healthy mule out of its traces. Using a piece of harness, he deftly fashioned a makeshift, split-ear bridle, then used some "hard twist" from a coil of rope on his saddle to create some reins, which he tied to the bridle. A blanket rolled up behind the cantle of his Texas rig was transferred to the back of the mule. This done, he handed the rope-reins to Laura.

"I'll take one of the girls behind me," he said. "You take the other. Okay?"

She nodded. Clancy drew his Dance revolver and put a bullet in the brain of the downed but still suffering mule.

Soldado rode up, having concluded his examination of the dead. He nodded at Clancy, who glanced at Laura.

"You'll have to leave all your belongings behind, miss. We've got to travel fast and light."

"I don't care about that. But what of the corporal?"

"What about him?"

"He was a very brave boy."

"I'm sure he was."

"He deserves better than to be left out here for the buzzards."

"The dead lie where they fall."

She didn't argue, knowing that to do so would be fruitless. She got up on the mule and lifted Charity on behind her. Clancy hauled Faith up onto his saddle behind him and told her to hold on tight. In this way they rode south by west, leaving the road, with Soldado in the lead, his head turning constantly this way and that, scanning the desert for danger, with eyes that missed nothing.

13

They reached Fort Union without mishap. The outpost was encircled by a tent city filled with refugees. And wherever decent folks congregated, the human predators also flocked, regardless of the danger. There were plenty of cardsharps, soiled doves, and whiskey drummers to go around.

Laura Gaines viewed this throng of people with trepidation. Unlike so many who came to the frontier, she had found that isolation suited her solitary nature. She was a very private and introspective person, and she didn't like crowds. What was worse, she had two children to take care of and very little money—about twenty dollars in a little pouch tied to a thong and dangling from her neck, and which she kept underneath her blouse, between her breasts. What was she to do? How far would twenty dollars go towards providing food and shelter for Faith and Charity? Then, too, she feared for their safety. Whenever people came together like this, trouble was always a by-product.

Clancy St. John sensed her mental anguish. "Would you have no friends or family that might be here, miss?"

She shook her head. "I have no friends to speak of. As for family, my mother and father live in Missouri."

"Perhaps your husband will be along soon." She had told Clancy about Tom Gaines.

If so, she thought, *I shall be happy to see him—for a change.*

The inhabitants of the tent city were not permitted on the grounds of Fort Union, and the garrison's commanding officer, Major Heinemann, was doing his level best to keep his troops out of the tent city. It was a delicate situation, fraught with difficulty for all concerned. Clancy had a problem getting past the sentries. Laura Gaines and her children were only part of the problem; the guards eyed Soldado with blatant hostility.

"You'd best be getting used to seeing Apaches," snapped Clancy, "and learn to distinguish the friendly ones from those who'll cut your throat. There'll be a dozen or so Coyoteros along in a few days, and they'll be scouting for the army, which improves your chances of getting through the next campaign, alive, soldier."

"I don't need no dirty 'Pache lookin' out for me," said the yellowleg, who didn't like Clancy's tone.

Clancy looked at Laura. "This jackass reminds me of why I once swore never to work for the United States Army again."

But, in the end, they got past the sentries and were brought before Major Heinemann.

"I've been made aware of what you've been doing, Mr. St. John," said the major, "and I will make arrangements for the Coyotero scouts."

"Don't go to too much trouble on their account. They can take care of themselves. Just make sure your soldiers don't try to shoot them."

"We must devise some means by which to distinguish them from the hostiles. Perhaps we can issue uniforms ... "

"They may take to wearing the tunics, Major. But not the pants and boots."

"The tunics will suffice."

"I'd like you to wire General Crook at Fort Apache and ask him what he wants me to do now."

Heinemann shook his head. "Afraid I can't, at the moment. The Apaches keep the telegraph lines cut. I must rely on couriers to communicate with General Crook. So, for the time being at least, you are my guest, Mr. St. John."

"I hope you have room for Mrs. Gaines and her children."

"I'm sorry, but they will have to stay outside the fort."

"But she's lost everything . . . "

"I am truly sorry, but those are the rules, and I cannot make exceptions. Many people have lost their belongings, or worse, thanks to the Apaches." Heinemann glanced at Soldado, who was standing, as inscrutable and motionless as a statue, near the door. Clancy could tell the major didn't like having an Apache, even a friendly one, in his office, and the Irishman began to wonder if he had made a mistake in agreeing to scout for the army again.

"Now listen here," he said, fully intending to press the issue.

"Mr. St. John," said Laura. "Thank you for everything you've done, but I will get by without the army's help."

"Please understand," said Heinemann, "if I make an exception in your case, I would have to . . . "

"Thank you, Major." Laura turned back to Clancy. "And thank you, Mr. St. John. I owe you and Soldado more than I can ever hope to repay."

With that she left Heinemann's office.

Clancy found her in one of the tent "boarding houses," where some enterprising soul had laid out about thirty canvas cots beneath a big tarpaulin and was charging an exorbitant rate, thought Laura, considering that there was no privacy. Due to her financial situation, she had opted for one cot, thinking that at least Faith and Charity could stretch out side by side and get some sleep. Since sleeping on the ground was not allowed, she would sit up at the end of the cot. Even blankets, as it turned out, cost a dollar apiece per night. Laura was outraged to think that people could be so heartless and mercenary as to take this kind of advantage of others. But what could she do? She also had to think about food. Yet another frontier entrepreneur had set up a soup kitchen across the way; Laura could only imagine what a cup of thin gruel and a hardtack biscuit might cost.

She had just paid the man for the cot when Clancy arrived.

"You're not staying here, miss," he told her, in no uncertain terms. "Mister, give her back that money."

"I won't. She's paid for the cot. Cot's paid for, and that's that. Whether it's used or not makes me no difference."

Before the man could defend himself, Clancy had him by the front of his shirt. "Maybe I didn't make myself clear."

"Please, Mr. St. John," protested Laura.

Clancy seemed not to hear her.

The man gulped at the lump lodged in his throat. "You're clear," he muttered, and handed the money back to Laura.

Clancy let him go and turned to Laura. "Come along," he said, and left the tent.

He led her to a smaller tent that Soldado had just finished putting up. It stood a little apart from the rest of the refugee camp, but comfortingly close by the guarded perimeter of Fort Union. Inside, an oilskin had been laid out on the ground. There were blankets, pots and pans, a sack of flour, some sugar, tea, and coffee.

"What is all this?" asked Laura.

"For you and the children, miss," said Clancy.

"I don't . . . but where did it all come from?"

"The fort's sutler."

"You *bought* these things?"

"Not the tent. It's just a loan."

"I can't repay you . . . "

"No need. It's not much, really, but better than that other place, don't you think?"

"I really can't accept."

"Wish you would. For your children's sake. It's not charity. You can pay me back when you're able."

Laura stared at him. "Why this kindness, Mr. St. John?"

He flashed that winning Irish grin. "No strings attached. I just sold a herd of beeves, and I've got more money in my pocket than I know what to do with. And you'd do the same for me if the shoe was on the other foot, wouldn't you?"

"Well, yes . . . "

"If you want, Soldado and I will ride out and fetch your husband—if it isn't already too late."

"No. I won't have you risking your lives, again, on my account."

"Well, then, we'll be around for a spell, at least until I get orders from Crook, so if you need anything, just tell one of the sentries, and we'll get the word."

"Thank you, Mr. St. John."

"Don't mention it." Clancy touched the brim of his hat, smiled at Faith and Charity, and walked away. Soldado followed, nodding solemnly at Laura in passing.

In the days to come Laura never had to send word to Clancy—he came calling at least twice a day, and never empty-handed, always bringing food, so that she did not have to spend any of her money. Then, two weeks after their arrival at Fort Union, he brought her news of her husband. An army patrol had found him, dead.

"Apaches?" she asked.

Clancy nodded. She didn't ask for details and he offered none.

A few days later Clancy told her he would be riding out on the morrow. His Coyotero scouts had arrived, and they were ordered to hasten to Fort Apache, as Crook was ready to launch a strike against Cochise's stronghold in the Dragoon Mountains. She was sorry to see him go, but did not tell him so, for fear that he might misconstrue.

After Clancy had gone, a lieutenant brought her a pouch containing a hundred dollars in hard money. Clancy had told him not to deliver it until after he and Soldado and the Coyoteros had departed the fort.

Clancy soon learned that he was not the only "chief of scouts" employed by General Crook and endowed with that highfalutin but ultimately meaningless title. As far as the Coyoteros he himself had recruited, he was in charge, but that was it. Not that this mattered to him. His sole concern was to help end the Apache Wars as quickly as possible, so that innocent people like Maria and Luis could live their lives in peace.

Besides, he had no bone to pick about Crook's selections. There was Archie Macintosh, Canadian-born, father a Scotsman and mother a Chippewa Indian princess. Macintosh had worked for the Hudson Bay Company and then hired on as a guide for the United States Army in Idaho, where he happened to save George Crook's life, leading the officer to safety through a snowstorm. Macintosh was a drinker of Homeric proportions, but neither Crook nor Clancy held that against him. Every man had to have his vice, and drunk or sober, Archie Macintosh was forever keen of eye and judgment.

Another "chief of scouts" was the German-born Al Sieber. A veteran of the Civil War, Sieber had wandered west after Appomattox and tried his hand at prospecting, just as Clancy had done some years earlier. Yet a third was Merejildo Grivalja, a Mexican who at age ten had been captured by a raiding party of Chiricahuas. The Apaches tried to raise him as one of their own. But eight years later Grivalja escaped and proceeded to serve as guide and interpreter for the army. Clancy knew Merejildo well, and was of the opinion that no one knew better the ways of the Apache. Grivalja took grave risks in helping the yellowlegs, because the Chiricahuas considered him one of their own and a traitor, and hated him with red-hot intensity. Grivalja knew that if he was taken alive, he would be subjected to the most cruel tortures the Apache mind could devise.

But the civilian who had the greatest impact on the campaign against Cochise was not a scout at all. His name was Tom Jeffords. The Apaches called Jeffords "Red Whiskers," because of his rust-colored hair and beard. He worked for the Southern Overland express service, which ran stagecoaches between Santa Fe and Tucson. This was a risky business, and after losing a dozen drivers to Apache raiders, Jeffords had decided to have a word with Cochise, and hang the danger. He rode straight into the Chokonen camp, bold as new brass. Impressed by Jeffords's courage, Cochise spared his life. They became friends.

Just as Crook prepared to launch his campaign against Cochise, Brigadier General Oliver Otis Howard appeared on the scene. Pressured by peace lovers back east, President Grant had entrusted Howard with the task of persuading Cochise to come to terms. Howard had fought valiantly in the Civil War, losing an arm in battle. He was a fierce abolitionist, and having done his part to free the slaves, he believed his next mission was to save the Indian from certain extinction through futile warfare. Establishing the San Carlos reservation, he talked several small bands, Aravaipa and White Mountain Apaches, into moving there. But he had no luck with Cochise—until he convinced Tom Jeffords to help him.

Jeffords took Howard to the Chokonen hideout in the Dragoon Mountains, where he met the great Chiricahua leader. Cochise agreed to talk if Howard would return to Fort Bowie and declare a cease-fire. Howard agreed to this test of good faith. His orders forbidding any attack on Apaches in the vicinity of the Dragoons incensed Crook. But there was nothing Crook could do but wait. Howard enjoyed the President's imprimatur. Time, Crook felt, was his ally, for eventually it would become evident that to talk peace with the Chiricahuas was futile.

Back in the Dragoons with Jeffords, Howard engaged in lengthy negotiations with Cochise and the subchiefs who followed him. The one-armed general agreed to the Apache terms—the creation of a new reservation at Apache Pass, with Tom Jeffords as Indian agent.

The Chiricahuas were well-pleased with the reservation. In addition to containing the Dragoon Mountains and Apache Pass, it provided abundant springs and numerous canyons filled with game. Best of all, Jeffords, the new agent, was their true friend. He had their best interests at heart. He would not try to make farmers out of them. He would not make them wear the numbered brass tags which were used on other reservations to keep track of the inmates there.

But immediately Tom Jeffords had problems. The bureaucrats in Washington were incompetent, and criminally slow in responding to his many pleas for money and supplies to operate the Apache Pass reservation. The Indian Bureau seemed to be incapable of arranging to pay for or provide the pound of beef and pound of flour promised as the standard per diem for the Apaches.

Another problem proved to be the persistence of the Chiricahuas in their raiding south of the border. Cochise insisted that his agreement with Howard did not apply to Mexico, and Jeffords turned a blind eye to the repeated excursions of armed *bronchos* who slipped off the reservation and headed south to kill a few *Nakai-Ye*.

"There's nothing really that Cochise can do to stop

these raids, even if he wanted to," Jeffords told Crook. "We have a thousand Apaches, but less than half of them are actually Chokonen. They're the ones who follow Cochise without question. The others listen to Juh and Geronimo, and they believe they have a right to strike deep into Mexico."

"The governors of Sonora and Chihuahua would most heartily disagree," replied Crook dryly. "They have asked me for help in stopping the raids. Sonorans accuse General Howard of arming the Chiricahua and sending them into Mexico with his blessing. In six months the Apaches have killed a hundred Mexican civilians. Probably more that we don't know about."

"It's like this, General. Even a great chief like Cochise cannot order a man into battle. Likewise, he cannot absolutely forbid one of his warriors to fight. Each man makes that decision of his own free will, and each band has the right to make war if it decides to do so."

"I don't like the arrangement, and never have," groused Crook.

"I realize that, sir. But you must admit that in the past six months we've had no trouble to speak of *north* of the border."

"I believe it is just a matter of time. Seems to me we've merely given Cochise and the Chiricahuas a sanctuary from which they can raid with impunity, and when they're tired of killing Mexicans, they can come home and be fed and sheltered at our expense."

Jeffords scoffed at that. "I've had to pay for their beef out of my own pocket."

Crook seemed not to have heard him. "What's worse, when the trouble starts, I won't be as prepared to deal with the renegades as I was six months ago. I've lost most of my scouts. The Coyoteros that Clancy St. John went to great pains to recruit decided I was afraid of Cochise because I wouldn't attack him. They don't understand I was under orders from the President himself to give Howard a chance. They got tired of waiting and went home."

"As long as Cochise is alive, we won't need to worry," insisted Jeffords.

"You just told me he can't control the others."

"He cannot dictate to them. But most will abide by his wishes out of a profound respect for him. General, he is not the same man that he was ten years ago. At some point he accepted the fact that his people are doomed. That he could not win a war with the white man. Why do you think he agreed to live on a reservation? To prolong the inevitable?"

"At least he and I are in full accord in that respect."

"Problem is, Cochise will soon be dead."

"Eh? What do you mean?"

"He is ill," said Jeffords sadly. "In constant pain. He has told me the pain is in his stomach. It grows worse when he eats, and at times he can't keep anything except a little water down. Every day he grows weaker as the pain grows more severe."

"I'm sorry to say that I cannot share your grief at this development. Is this not the same Cochise who bragged that he had personally slain a hundred whites?"

Jeffords grimaced. "You don't understand, General. When Cochise dies, there will be hell to pay. Because then the Chiricahuas will turn to men like Victorio and Nana for leadership. And when that happens, I'm afraid this land will once again run red with blood."

15

"Cochise is dead," said Wiley James, Fort Union's sutler, as he poured Clancy another generous dose of Taos Lightning.

"And Crook is gone," lamented the Irishman. "Means we'll have hard times in these parts before too very long." He drank half the whiskey and proceeded to build a cigarette.

Watching him roll the smoke, James said, "I take it you ain't scoutin' for the army these days." He knew Clancy never smoked while he was working. It was nigh on impossible to hide from Apache renegades when you reeked of tobacco.

"Nope. Been sitting on my hands for months now."

"Then how come you spend so much dad-blamed time around here?" Wiley's eyes twinkled with merry mischief. He knew the answer. "Couldn't have anything to do with a certain yeller-haired widow woman, could it?"

Clancy looked at him askance. "What if it does?"

Wiley held up his hands. "Suits me right down to the ground, Clancy. If the two of you get hitched, I wish you'd take her and those little girls of hers and go someplace civilized, like Texas, leastways until things cool down in this neck of the woods. Now that Cochise and ol' Red Beard are both gone, hell's gonna be poppin' soon enough."

"You call Texas civilized?" Clancy shook his head. "No, I can't go."

"On account of Soldado?"

Clancy nodded. "This is his land. He wouldn't leave it, and I won't go without him."

"I seen him playin' with those Gaines girls. They act like he's their big brother or something. Never seen the like. But it don't sit well with some folks."

"They can go to hell."

"You're such an understanding sort of feller, Clancy St. John."

The sutler moved off down the bar to serve another customer, leaving Clancy alone with his thoughts.

He had the feeling that only he and his friend Wiley were worried about what the future would hold. General Howard's treaty with the Chiricahua had spawned a false optimism among the whites, in Washington as well as the Arizona and New Mexico Territories. Most of the refugees who had huddled in fear of Apache depredation in the tent city were by now back in their homes. Oh, there was still a handful of renegades out there burning up the *malpais*, a few "Wild Ones" who refused to live on a reservation. But for months the desert had been relatively peaceful. Clancy had watched his Coyotero scouts grow restless and disgusted and, finally, head for home, too. They knew there could be no lasting peace as long as men like Victorio and Geronimo lived. They knew war was inevitable. Clancy had to agree with them.

To make matters worse, General Crook had been transferred to the Department of the Platte. Gold had been discovered in the Black Hills of South Dakota, and the rush was on. Thousands were invading land sacred to the Sioux and the Cheyenne. Warriors led by Crazy Horse and Sitting Bull were taking up arms. Washington dispatched the flamboyant George Armstrong Custer to command the

Seventh Cavalry. His orders were to deal harshly with the Indians. Crook, the real Indian fighter, was to be Custer's support.

"Custer is an impetuous fool," Crook had told Clancy on the day of his departure. "Glory is all he's concerned about. I fought with him in Virginia, and believe me, I know. I led an attack that broke a Rebel brigade. Custer was there, but he didn't get his division into action until after the Confederates showed the white flag. Then he led a rousing charge, and captured a great many prisoners— who had already surrendered." Crook's words were soaked in sarcasm. "Of course, according to the press, their golden-haired Boy General had on that day won the war single-handedly."

"I wish Washington would understand that we need you here," said Clancy.

"I've tried to tell them the Apache Wars aren't over. But the fools won't listen. I'll be back, Clancy. They'll realize their mistake, sooner or later. You'll see."

To compound their folly, the Bureau of Indian Affairs sent the young and fervently religious John Clum to Arizona to take charge of the San Carlos reservation. Clum's orders were to shut down Jeffords's Chiricahua reserve at Apache Pass and consolidate all Apaches at San Carlos. This idiotic notion completely ignored long-standing tribal differences, but the plan was put into motion. Out of a job, Tom Jeffords protested the new policy. He didn't mind being fired, but he worried about the consequences of violating Howard's treaty with the Chiricahua Apaches.

At first, though, the Chiricahuas seemed to go along. They complained but did not go on the warpath. Taza and Naiche, the sons of Cochise, had been enjoined by their dying father from cooperating with Tom Jeffords. Heavy of heart, Jeffords had decided to encourage his Apache friends to go with Clum to San Carlos. He felt as though he were betraying the Chiricahuas by doing so, but he did it to prevent bloodshed.

Three hundred and fifty Chokonen and Chiricahua Apaches agreed to go to San Carlos. But some others did not. Led by Geronimo, they bolted, crossing the border into Mexico. The short-lived Chiricahua reservation was returned to the public domain.

The Chiricahuas' new home, on the salt flats where the San Carlos and Gila rivers met, was a poor and desolate land. It was the worst place in all of *Apacheria*. There was no grass and no game. The brackish waters of the two rivers spawned millions of mosquitoes, and soon the Apache inhabitants were stricken with malaria. The death rate was alarmingly high. Some of the Apaches muttered that the White Eyes were intentionally tainting the water to make them sick.

John Clum was another problem. He led a campaign against the consumption of *tizwin*, or corn beer, which his Apache wards made, destroying their stills and imprisoning every "moonshiner" he apprehended. He forced the Apache men to work as common laborers to build his quarters and the agency store, ignoring the fact that an Apache warrior believed such work was beneath his dignity. Clum also created a twenty-five-man Apache police force, as well as an Apache court so that the lawbreakers brought in by his police would be judged by their peers. This had the effect of turning Apache against Apache, and stirred up much hard feeling. Energetic but wrongheaded, Clum failed to recognize the trouble he was brewing. The Apaches had no respect for him. They called him "Turkey Gobbler."

It was Clum who looked Clancy up a few weeks later, locating the scout at the tent cabin where for six months Laura Gaines and her children had been living.

In the wake of the Howard treaty, Clancy had taken Laura back to the Gaines homestead. The few cattle Tom Gaines had popped out of the brush had returned to the wild, or been rustled. The adobe had been looted, the interior and all it contained burned. Miraculously, the trunk and valises abandoned with the wagon on the road to Fort Union were recovered intact. With few belongings, little money, and nowhere to go, Laura lingered at Fort Union, along with a dozen or so other civilians. Clancy and Soldado had constructed the tent cabin—walls made of scrap lumber with tent canvas for a roof. Laura had tried to earn some money by mending clothes for the soldiers of the garrison.

She was an attractive woman, and some of the soldiers began to court her, which troubled Clancy, who consequently spent a lot of time at the tent cabin, hoping his presence would discourage the amorous yellowlegs. He wished he could take Laura away from here, perhaps back to his own place. But he didn't have the nerve to ask her if she would go with him. And besides, Maria's memory troubled him when he thought about taking up with Laura.

When John Clum arrived, he found the Irishman sitting on a blanket on the ground in front of the tent cabin. Soldado sat nearby, with Charity on his knee.

"Mr. St. John," said Clum. "I need your help. It concerns Geronimo."

Clancy squinted up at Clum. The young man remained so ignorant of frontier etiquette that he remained mounted while speaking.

"What about Geronimo?"

"He must be brought to justice. In the past month ten men have been murdered, and a hundred mules and horses stolen—all by Apaches raiding out of Mexico."

"Get somebody else."

Clum was startled by this brush-off. "Tom Jeffords won't do it. He says he's retired. Gone off to his ranch. Al Sieber's out in California. Mary Grivalja is in Mexico and won't respond to my summons."

"Maybe you should stop calling him Mary. His name is Merejildo. You need to learn to treat people as your equal, even if they aren't the same color as you are, Mr. Clum."

"Listen to me. Geronimo was seen in New Mexico, near Ojo Caliente, with stolen horses. I have been ordered by the Bureau to arrest him and bring him back to San Carlos, to be tried on charges of murder and robbery."

"Really? What about Juh and the others? Them, too?"

"I only have evidence against Geronimo."

Clancy sighed. There was no denying that Geronimo was a bad one, and that more innocent civilians—like Maria and Luis—would probably die horrible deaths as long as the Bedonkohe raider roamed free. He realized he shouldn't let his dislike for the high-and-mighty Clum—and for what Clum was doing to the Apaches in his charge—color his judgment.

He glanced at Soldado, and switched to Spanish. "What do you think?"

"They will never put a rope around the neck of Goyahkla," was Soldado's solemn reply. "But maybe we can kill him. For her sake." Soldado stroked Charity's golden hair. Charity responded by hugging his neck.

"What did he say?" Clum asked Clancy.

"We'll ride with you," said Clancy. Rising, he noticed that Laura had emerged from the tent cabin. "We'll be gone for a spell," he told her. "Can't say for how long."

She nodded.

"You watch out for those soldier boys," he said, flashing a grin to lighten the mood.

She touched his arm. "Please do come back safe, Clancy."

The emotion in her voice and the anxiety on her face surprised him, even as his heart quickened, for it was clear to him, for the first time, that Laura Gaines really cared what happened to him.

"Don't worry about that," he said, and went to fetch the horses.

Soldado moved to follow him, but Laura detained the Apache.

"Don't let any harm come to him, Soldado. Promise me. I—I have a bad feeling . . . "

Soldado's dark, inscrutable gaze seemed to bore right through to her soul. Then Charity latched onto his leg. He pried the little girl loose and handed her to Laura. He nodded once and moved on. The nod was all Laura needed.

She realized then that she hadn't needed to elicit a promise from Soldado to look after Clancy St. John. The young Chihenne was even more fond of the Irishman than she had become.

16

Geronimo sat on a log on the banks of Ojo Caliente and watched dragonflies skim across the surface of the sacred spring. The day was stifling hot, but the shade of the alder trees cooled him. Not that he paid much attention to the heat. Hunger or thirst, heat or freezing cold, these things were of little consequence to Geronimo. From his youth he had trained himself to pay no attention to physical discomfort.

Ojo Caliente lay in a side canyon that branched off from the Canada Alamosa. The creek which was nourished by the spring rambled eastward through a deep notch. Rugged crags loomed on every side. Swallows and hawks winged through the air. Once this canyon had been rich in deer and antelope. But the coming of the white men had changed all that. The spring, though, was still sacred to the Apaches. Its waters were known to cure many ailments.

But even the sacred water cannot cure the sickness in me, brooded Geronimo. *The sickness of revenge.*

This place made him think back to happier childhood days spent at his birthplace on the Middle Fork of the Gila River, in the Bedonkohe *rancheria* near the hot springs, where he had played with other children in the shade of tall sycamores and cottonwoods, with the towering canyon walls reaching to the sky. There, he had explored the ancient cliff dwellings of the Mogollon Mountains, just as here he was acquainted with all the caves in the rocks above, where the swallows nested.

His childhood training had been rigorous. At the age of eight he had risen before the sun every day to run to the top of a mountain and back again. If he did not return before the sunrise he was severely punished. In the winter he had to break through the ice on the surface of the river and plunge to the very bottom. He learned to be quick by catching birds with his bare hands. The culmination of his physical training was a four-mile run, without stopping, carrying a mouthful of water which he was not permitted to swallow.

He was also taught *enthlay-sit-daou*, the art of immobility. Geronimo became so adept at this ability to blend into his environment that his followers believed he had the power to actually make himself invisible. *Enthlay-sit-daou* also meant being unshakably calm and courageous in a crisis, and no one could deny that Geronimo was that.

Though for centuries the Apaches had been at war with the Spaniards and then the Mexicans, the Bedonkohe had lived in peace in their secluded canyon, and Geronimo was eighteen years old before he saw action. The Bedonkohe had strong ties with the Nednhi, who lived far to the south in Mexico's Sierra Madre. Geronimo's best friend was a Nednhi—Juh, who had married Ishton, Geronimo's beautiful sister. Geronimo, in turn, married Alope, a Nednhi maiden, when he was seventeen. He spent a lot of time in Mexico with the Nednhi. And even though the Mexicans were offering a bounty on Apache scalps, a number of Bedonkohe traveled south in the spring of 1851 to visit the Nednhi *rancheria* in the Sierra Madre. On the way they stopped near the Mexican town of Janos to trade. While Geronimo and most of the other men were in Janos, four hundred Sonoran soldiers attacked the

Bedonkohe camp, killing twenty women and children and taking more than sixty into slavery. None of the captives were ever seen again. Geronimo's mother and wife were among the dead.

From that day on Geronimo's heart ached for vengeance. No matter how many raids he led, or how many of the *Nakai-Ye* he killed by his own hand, he could not seem to quench that flaming desire for retribution.

One day not long after the Janos massacre, he wandered alone into the desert, consumed by grief. He heard a voice call out his name four times. Four was a sacred number. Then the voice said, "No gun will ever kill you. Your aim, with arrow or bullet, will always be true. You will become a great leader, and your people will look to you for their salvation."

For twenty years Geronimo waged relentless war on the Mexicans. He used only the bow and arrow, the knife, and the lance made from the stalk of the sotol. He killed dozens of Mexicans, yet his thirst for revenge remained as fierce as ever. Many times he survived situations where survival seemed impossible, and his people began to say he possessed special powers. Geronimo believed it was so. He was absolutely fearless; if one knows he cannot be killed in battle, he need have no fear. He became a famous healer, using a ceremony which included many chants and the use of the eagle feather, an abalone shell, and pollen from the tule, called *hoddentin*, to summon healing spirits which would invade the body of his patient and drive out the evil.

Geronimo's power continued to grow, so that nowadays the people said he had the gift of clairvoyance. Somehow he knew of events which occurred many miles away. Those who followed him had seen indisputable evidence of this power too many times to have doubts.

Sitting on a log beside the sacred spring in the alder shade, Geronimo knew that disaster was about to strike.

A rider galloped into camp. There were eighty men, women, and children in Geronimo's band, and most of them gathered eagerly around the messenger, wondering what news he brought, but he broke through the crowd and sought out Geronimo.

"*Nantan betunney-kahyeh* is at the agency, *jefe*," announced the rider. "Twenty *reducidos* ride with him."

Geronimo nodded. So John Clum was the one who had come, accompanied by some of his Apache police. Only twenty? Surely Turkey Gobbler did not seek a fight, with the odds stacked so steeply against him.

"He wants to talk to you, *jefe*. He asks that you come to the agency. He has *nato* and *tu-dishishn* for you."

Geronimo grunted. Tobacco and the fragrant "black water" the whites called coffee to sweeten the bait.

"When did he arrive at the agency?" Geronimo asked the spy who had been posted to watch that rectangle of adobe structures a scant half mile from Ojo Caliente as the crows flies.

"In the night, *jefe*."

Geronimo nodded. He had suspected as much. "And how did he give this message to you?"

"He sent a *reducido* out with a white flag."

"So you never went near the agency?"

"No, *jefe*."

Geronimo stood up. "Take word back to the agency. I am coming in to talk with the Turkey Gobbler. Alone."

"Alone? But, *jefe*, it might be a trap."

"Of course, it is a trap."

"Why, then, will you go alone?"

"In time you will understand why I do this."

"But they might kill you, *jefe*."

"How can they? What happened to your faith in my powers?"

"Their bullets cannot harm you, I know. But they might put a rope around your neck."

"No. I am not destined to die, yet. For now this is the best way. For many sleeps we have been on the run. The people are tired and hungry. You and the others will go peacefully back to San Carlos and wait."

"San Carlos?" The *broncho* spat his contempt. "I would rather die in battle than rot in San Carlos."

"We will fight, but this is not the time. Soon all the Chiricahua Apache will rise as one against the White Eyes. Don't worry, I will be there to see that day."

The warrior believed Geronimo. Did his *jefe* not have the power?

"*Ugashe*," said Geronimo, *go*. "And deliver my message to *Nantan betunney-kahyeh*."

The warrior swung lithely upon the back of his desert mustang. "On that day, *jefe*, will we win the battle?"

"No. We cannot defeat the *Pinda Lickoyi*. They are too many, and we are so few. But we will make them pay in blood for every foot of *Apacheria* they steal. And we will give our children and our children's children a story they can tell with pride forever."

17

John Clum's heart sank as he watched Geronimo ride into the agency. "He's alone," he said in dismay to Clancy St. John, who stood nearby in the shade of the agency headquarters porch. "I was hoping to bring in the whole bunch."

"He knows that," remarked the scout.

"How could he?" Under cover of darkness, sixty of Clum's Apache police had slipped into the agency, and were at this very moment concealed in the commissary building fifty yards away. The twenty policemen with whom Clum had openly entered the agency the day before were formed in parallel ranks in front of the headquarters building.

Soldado, standing with Clancy, said something in Apache, and the Irishman nodded.

"What was that?" asked Clum. "What did he say?"

"He says Geronimo knows these things without seeing."

"Poppycock," scoffed Clum.

Clancy shrugged. "Then how else do you explain his coming in alone?"

"It doesn't matter. I will have to settle for arresting Geronimo. Cut off the head of the snake, so to speak."

"I expect the rest of his bunch will beat us back to San Carlos."

"Oh? You also have the gift of clairvoyance, Mr. St. John?"

"Call it a wild guess."

Geronimo steered his pony between the ranks of Apache police, stopping within spitting distance of the porch. Dismounting, he stood at the head of his horse with the reins in his hand and a rifle cradled in his arms. He spared the policemen a single, contemptuous glance, then fixed his dark, penetrating gaze upon John Clum.

"Sergeant Najita," said Clum. "You will kindly act as an interpreter."

Najita, a squat Mimbreno outcast, stepped forward from one of the lines of Apache police. Since Geronimo did not speak English and Clum knew very little Spanish, Najita, who was fluent in both languages, would translate.

"Geronimo, you are a liar and a thief," said Clum. "You broke the Howard treaty, you have murdered whites, you have stolen many cattle and horses."

Clancy shook his head. Clum was talking to Geronimo as though the Bedonkohe leader was a recalcitrant child. Would Turkey Gobbler ever learn not to be so patronizing?

"You talk brave," replied Geronimo. "But I don't like your words. You should be careful, or you and your Apache police will remain here at Ojo Caliente forever, as food for the lobos. You White Eyes came to the Chiricahua reservation and broke the peace. You told us we had to give up the land we had been promised would remain ours forever. You said we had to go live at San Carlos, where many people die from sickness and starvation. San Carlos is the worst place in the world. I have not killed any White Eyes. Only the *Nakai-Ye*. Goyahkla has always been at war with the *Nakai-Ye*, and always will be. If I have stolen so many cattle and horses, why are my people hungry?"

"You sold stolen horses right here at this agency," said Clum. "You deny that?"

Clancy was watching the thumb of Geronimo's right hand, which rested on the hammer of his .50 caliber Springfield. It occurred to him that the Bedonkohe renegade might have come here to die, or that Clum's words might prove so inflammatory that the unpredictable and volatile Apache might take action regardless of the odds against him.

"I traded a few Mexican horses for meat and cartridges," replied Geronimo.

"You and your followers must go to San Carlos. You will no longer raid against the Mexicans."

"I do not belong to you," said Geronimo. "I am not your dog, that I need your permission to go where I might."

"From now on I am afraid you will." Clum raised his left hand to touch the brim of his hat.

This was the prearranged signal. The sixty Apache police concealed in the commissary building burst out into the sunlight, while the ranks on either side of the porch quickly formed a circle around Geronimo, their rifles aimed at the renegade. Clum took a few steps towards Geronimo, intending to relieve him of his rifle. But Geronimo gripped the weapon tightly, and the hate that blazed in his eyes was so intense that it stopped Clum dead in his tracks.

Soldado moved faster than thought. Inserting himself between Clum and Geronimo, he grabbed the Bedonkohe's rifle with one hand.

"No," he said, in the Apache tongue. "You will die."

"Their bullets cannot harm me," said Geronimo.

"They will kill you."

"If so, what concern is it of yours?"

"I do not want to see any more Apache blood shed."

"Who are you?"

"Kayitah, son of Kaywaykla, of the Chihenne."

"You are a slave of the *Pinda Lickoyi*," hissed Geronimo.

Soldado did not flinch from Geronimo's savage gaze, nor did he let go of the Springfield. Then, with a cold smile, the Bedonkohe released the rifle.

"Sergeant Najita," snapped Clum, "put the prisoner in irons."

As Geronimo was led away, Clum returned to the porch and looked at Clancy with a self-satisfied smile on his face. "We have accomplished the first and only bona fide capture of Geronimo the renegade, Mr. St. John."

"They'll say it took eighty men to do the job," said Clancy dryly.

"Who will?"

"The Apaches. You've made a big hero out of Geronimo, Clum. I'm afraid he's outwitted you."

Clum scoffed at the idea. "I expect that soon enough Geronimo will hang for his crimes. Then we'll see what they think of their hero, when he's dangling from a gallows."

"When that happens, you'll make him into a martyr," said Clancy. "You people never learn, do you?"

He turned his back on Clum and walked away.

They were two-days ride from the San Carlos agency when a yellowleg detail from Fort Bowie met them. Clancy and Soldado were still with John Clum and his Apache police, even though the Irishman was by now thoroughly soured on the whole business. Still, he wanted to make certain that Geronimo got to San Carlos alive. The Apache police were leery of the Bedonkohe leader, and Clancy was afraid the fate which had befallen Mangas Colorado might befall Geronimo, too. If that happened, the Apache Wars could very well heat up again, and more innocent people would surely die. Clancy was getting sick of war, especially this kind of war, where there were no noncombatants.

Clum and the lieutenant in charge of the detail rode off a ways by themselves, to talk out of earshot of the others. The soldiers gathered round to have a look at Geronimo. Clancy kept one eye on them and the other on Clum and the lieutenant. He wondered what was going on. Yesterday Clum had sent a rider to Fort Bowie to inform General Kautz, Crook's replacement, that he had captured Geronimo and was bringing his prisoner to the agency. Clancy figured the army would want a piece of Geronimo.

But Clum was not inclined to share his glory. The capture of Geronimo was his crowning achievement, and he didn't want the army to have anything to do with it.

Even at a distance, it was obvious Clum didn't like what he was hearing from the subaltern. He argued with the lieutenant for some time. Finally they rejoined the column.

"What's the matter?" Clancy asked the Indian agent.

"That is none of your concern, Mr. St. John," replied Clum, red-faced and scowling.

Clancy was amused. He assumed that Clum had just found out he was going to have to share Geronimo with the United States Army after all.

That night he found out how wrong he was.

They camped beneath a few scrawny cottonwoods lining a creek that, this time of year, was bone-dry. The lieutenant and his detail kept to themselves and did not mingle with the Apache police. Geronimo was chained to a tree, and a policeman stood guard over him. Soldado and Clancy remained close by to keep an eye on the prisoner. But when Clancy saw Clum leave the camp, wandering along the creek and puffing furiously on his clay pipe, the Irishman left Soldado to maintain the vigil alone and caught up with the Indian agent.

Now, with the lieutenant absent, Clum was more communicative. "It's Kautz, Mr. St. John. He has been trying to undermine my authority and sully my reputation ever since he arrived here. He is plainly jealous of my success. That is the problem in a nutshell, sir. But I am not beaten yet. I shall telegraph the Commissioner of Indian Affairs as soon as we reach San Carlos. This is an outrage. An outrage, I tell you."

"Clum, you can talk a lot and not say anything. Just exactly what is the outrage?"

"They are trying to disband my Apache police. Kautz claims they are ineffective, that we have been unable to keep the Apaches on the reserve. So Kautz has asked for and received instructions from Washington to assume the responsibility of patrolling San Carlos. My police will be stripped of all powers and returned to the general population of the agency."

"Life won't be easy for them once that happens," predicted Clancy. "The other Apaches have come to resent them."

"Oh, I don't care about that. This is between me and General Kautz. The Apache police are my creation, and that is why Kautz is trying to have them disbanded."

"So you're just worried about yourself and not the police, is that what you're saying?"

Clum fired a dark look at the Irishman. "I don't believe I care for your tone of voice, mister. You're free to go your own way, and frankly, I wish you would."

"Soldado wants to make sure Geronimo gets to San Carlos alive. So do I. Then we'll go."

"You are implying I cannot guarantee Geronimo's safety."

"I'm not implying anything. I'm saying it straight out."

Infuriated, Clum turned on his heel and walked away.

Clancy rejoined Soldado. After giving the situation a lot of thought, he turned to the young Chihenne and said, "I think you'd better slip away tonight."

Soldado's expression was faintly quizzical, but he said nothing.

"I have a gut feeling there's going to be trouble at the agency," continued Clancy. "I really can't explain it . . . "

Soldado studied Clancy's face for a moment, then shook his head. "I stay."

Exasperated, Clancy said, "You're more mule-headed than I am, and that's saying something."

When they arrived at the San Carlos agency the next day, an entire company of soldiers from Fort Bowie was there to greet them. Geronimo was tossed into the guardhouse. As Clancy and Soldado prepared to take their leave, Clum summoned all the Apache police and spoke to them from the porch of his house. The soldiers stood on the alert, prepared for trouble from the police. But the Apaches accepted the news Clum had for them with typical stoicism. Clancy felt sorry for them. A handful had let the power Clum invested in them go to their heads, and lorded it over the reservation Indians. But the majority were simply doing what they thought was best for their people, believing that the troublemakers like Geronimo made things worse for the rest. Yet all would suffer, thought Clancy, as a consequence of the excesses of a few. A couple of bad apples and the whole barrel was thrown out.

The lieutenant who had met Clum the day before walked up to Clancy and Soldado, followed by three troopers brandishing carbines.

"Where do you think you're going?" the officer asked Soldado.

"He's going with me," said Clancy. "He's my son."

"Your son? He's a lousy Cherry Cow. You're free to leave, mister, but he's staying." The lieutenant glanced at Soldado. "Get down off that horse."

Clancy's hand moved to the Dance revolver on his hip, but he froze as the troopers turned their Spencers on him. The lieutenant drew an Army Colt and, pointing it at Soldado, repeated his order to dismount.

"You bastard," rasped Clancy. "He is my adopted son. He's been with me for fifteen years."

"All Apaches are to live on the reservation. No exceptions. Those are General Kautz's orders."

Clancy swung down out of his saddle and grabbed the lieutenant's pistol, cursing a blue streak. One of the troopers stepped in and hammered him in the back with the butt of his carbine. Clancy went down, wheezing for air. Soldado lunged out of his saddle and bore the trooper to the ground. One blow with a quick, hard fist and the soldier lay bloodied and unconscious. The other two troopers backed up, leveling their carbines, but Soldado held out both hands. "No shoot," he said calmly. "No shoot." He turned to Clancy, helped the Irishman to his feet. Again Clancy clutched at the Dance, but Soldado stopped him.

"No," said the Apache. "You go. I stay."

"The hell you will."

"I stay."

"Soldado . . . "

"*Ugashe*. You go."

"You belong with me."

"I belong here, with my people. You marry yellow-haired woman. Leave this land. Forget Soldado."

Clancy stared at him. Soldado was serious. He was going to stay at San Carlos. He didn't have to; he could jump the reservation as easily as the next Apache, yellow-leg patrols notwithstanding. But that was not his intention. Why? Clancy had no earthly idea. Soldado was inscrutable, as always. Perhaps he was tired of living in the white man's world.

"Get going, mister," rasped the lieutenant.

Clancy got on his horse. He looked down at Soldado, feeling confused and empty and old.

"*Yadalanh*," said Soldado.

Apache for good-bye—the good-bye of friends who would never see each other again.

Clancy nodded and rode away. He refused to let himself look back.

Soldado watched him go, a glimmer of sadness breaking through his stoic mask.

"Come on," said the lieutenant, giving Soldado a prod with the Army Colt. "Get over there with the rest of your kind."

19

"*Anciano*," said Soldado, with the most profound respect, "I have spilled Apache blood."

The *diyi* was blind, the milky cataracts over his eyes almost as white as the hair which framed a time-ravaged face, hair long enough to drape his shoulders. His skin resembled old leather, brown and creased, etched deeply by a lifetime of hardship and self-denial.

His name was Tahdaste, and he was the foremost living medicine man among the Chihenne Chiricahua. Soldado remembered him from those happy childhood days at Warm Springs. Even then Tahdaste had looked ancient. He wheezed when he drew breath, and tottered when he walked, and was thin as a rail and bent as a broken reed. Yet he seemed to conquer the years with ease.

He was a man of great power, but it was not his medicine that had brought Soldado to his jacal. Tahdaste was the wisest man among the Chihenne, perhaps among all the Apaches. Even the great Mangas Colorado had turned to him for advice on numerous occasions. Now Soldado had come seeking the same thing, and more.

"Who were they?" asked Tahdaste. His voice

sounded like pebbles grinding together. "Why did you take their lives?"

Soldado knew the *diyi* did not want to know the names of his victims; it was forbidden to speak the names of the dead.

"The first were Nednhi Chiricahua, followers of Juh. They killed the woman who raised me as her own."

"The *Nakai-Ye* woman."

"*Anh*. She was *Nakai-Ye*. But she loved me as though I were her own flesh and blood."

"Did you love her as deeply?"

"In time, yes."

"You have killed other Apaches?"

"*Anh*. They were trying to take the lives of a white woman and her two *dayden*."

"It is bad that children must suffer and die."

For a moment neither man spoke. Soldado glanced about him at the smoky interior of the medicine man's jacal. They were alone. Tahdaste had survived his entire family, even his sons and grandsons, who had all perished in battle or from disease.

On Soldado's part, there was no more to be said. He had made his confession, given his excuses—the latter only because Tahdaste had expressly asked him why he had slain Apaches. Now his fate lay in the *diyi*'s hands. It was up to the medicine man whether he would be banished from the Chihenne forever or accepted back into the fold. Even if he were accepted, there would be conditions. Many would still resent him for living among the *Pinda Lickoyi* and fighting alongside them against the Apaches, but none would go against Tahdaste if the *diyi* gave his blessing and welcomed him home.

"We made war against one another long before the *Pinda Lickoyi* came," said Tahdaste, finally. "Before the *Nakai-Ye*, even. You took the lives of the men who murdered a woman who was a mother to you after your own mother was slain by the soldiers. Are you to blame that she was *Nakai-Ye*? The heart of a child knows no difference between Apache and Mexican. His young eyes can see no

importance in the color of the skin. Vengeance is an honor-
able pursuit. As an Apache, you were required to revenge
her death. As for the others you killed, there is no shame
attached to saving the lives of innocent children, no matter
what their race."

"Thank you, *anciano*."

"I remember you, Kayitah. Your heart is good. I am
glad you have returned to your people. I welcome you
home."

And so he lived once more among the Chihenne, or rather
what was left of them—a few hundred souls trying to survive in the hellhole called San Carlos, alongside the remnants of various other Chiricahua bands, as well as the
Mescaleros and Coyoteros. Once again he was Kayitah, but
the name always rang false in his ears. He continued to
think of himself as Soldado, born a Chihenne Apache,
raised by a Mexican woman, the adopted son of a white
man, who had lived most of his life in limbo, belonging
neither here nor there, a victim of a wicked fate, a freak of
human nature, which is the most capricious nature of all.

He tried to make the best of a difficult situation. It
wasn't easy going, but then he had known it wouldn't be.
Still, he had no regrets. He had done what he'd had to do.
Not just to save Clancy St. John's life, though that was a
large part of it. But also because he had come to the
painful realization that he would never truly fit into the
world of his white father. Clancy had known this, too, but
would never have forsaken him. So it had been left to
Soldado to make the move.

The first step was to destroy the white man's clothes
that he wore, adopting the himper, breechcloth, leggings,
and desert moccasins of the Apache. There were some who
scoffed and said this alone would not make of him a true
Apache; his sojourn among the *indah* had been too long,
they claimed; it had corrupted his heart and soul. Others
were more forgiving, more willing to live and let live. He
had been but an *ish-ke-ne*, a little boy, when his parents

were killed and he was taken away by the *Pinda Lickoyi*. He could not be held accountable for that.

In time the Chihenne, with a few exceptions, accepted him. No one could deny that he was brave, good at heart, and wise beyond his years. The *nahlins*, the unwed Chiricahua maidens, and even some young women from the other bands, all had eyes for him, for he was tall and slender and very good-looking. But he was always absent when the *goo-chitalth*, the virgin dance, was held. Clearly he was not interested in taking a wife. In fact, he spent much of his time in a self-imposed solitude. He developed no close friendships and kept his own counsel. He was the lone wolf, who maintained a brooding silence.

In spite of this, he gradually became one of the spokesmen of the San Carlos Apaches. It was a testament to the trust he managed to earn that the others relied on him to deal with the new agent, the man who had replaced John Clum. Turkey Gobbler had resigned in a huff shortly after the disbandment of the Apache police and the arrival of the military at San Carlos. Although the new agent seemed honest enough, there remained a chronic shortage in food and medical supplies. The Apaches were indifferent farmers, and the malarial barrens of the reservation proved wholly unsuited to agriculture, anyway. The agency never had sufficient funds to purchase enough beef to feed the more than two thousand Indians in its charge.

Then, in the summer of 1877, quite unexpectedly, this situation was improved when, on two occasions, Clancy St. John drove a couple hundred head of cattle to San Carlos and sold them for the ridiculously low price of one dollar apiece. He could have gotten fifteen to twenty dollars a head at any mining camp or army post. But as he explained to the agent, he wanted to do his part to keep the peace on the southwestern frontier. The Apaches would not long remain at San Carlos if they were haunted by the specter of starvation.

On neither of these occasions did Clancy see Soldado, who disappeared every time the Irishman came.

Soldado was also one of the Apaches who lobbied vigorously for the release of Geronimo. The Bedonkohe leader languished for months in the agency guardhouse while the whites tried to decide what to do with him. The Apaches refused to put him on trial in their own court. Clum had then offered to turn Geronimo over to civilian justice in Tucson, promising to provide sufficient evidence to insure a conviction on charges of murder and robbery. To Clum's surprise, Tucson declined the privilege. Clum was convinced that if Geronimo was tried, convicted, and hanged, the Apache Wars would be over forever. The people of Tucson knew better. They did not want to be the target of Apache revenge.

With the help of others, like Juh and Eskiminzin, Soldado convinced Clum's replacement that executing Geronimo would be a grievous mistake. So it was that eventually the Bedonkohe leader was released from the guardhouse, after four months in irons.

The peace-loving Apaches kept a wary eye on Geronimo. Deeming him an inveterate *teiltcohe*—troublemaker—they did not want to let him make more problems for them.

But trouble came from another source. In the autumn of 1877, Victorio and three hundred Chihenne men, women, and children stole a herd of horses and bolted San Carlos.

20

The Chihenne had settled on the tract of land at San Carlos that the agency assigned to them. This placed them in close proximity to the White Mountain band, who feared the Chihenne. This fear made them bad neighbors. One day a White Mountain man killed a Chihenne. Victorio became the willing instrument of swift Chihenne retribution; he killed the White Mountain man and his entire family. A few days later he and many of the Chihenne "jumped" the reservation.

Victorio managed to elude army pursuit for more than a month. He led his people by a roundabout route back to their beloved homeland near the sacred spring of Ojo Caliente—all but a handful who fled south, crossing the Mexican border to seek refuge in the Sierra Madre. Near Ojo Caliente stood Fort Wingate, and Victorio sent two envoys to see the post's commanding officer. The Chihenne did not want war, the envoys said. They wished only to live at Ojo Caliente and be left alone. If the white man tried to force them to return to San Carlos, where they had to live elbow-to-elbow with their enemies, they would fight and die to the last man.

The colonel turned out to be a very broad-minded and reasonable fellow. He let the Chihenne remain at Ojo Caliente, and even provided them with beef. For nearly a year Victorio's people were left alone. The colonel at Wingate argued that there was no good reason not to leave them there. What purpose could be served by sending them back to San Carlos?

For eleven months the Bureau of Indian Affairs procrastinated; then the orders came down—the army was to return the Chihenne to the San Carlos reservation.

The colonel at Fort Wingate didn't approve of this decision, but he kept his opinions to himself. Orders were orders. He was a good soldier. Gathering his men, he marched on Ojo Caliente.

When he got there, Victorio and ninety warriors had vanished into the mountains.

The rest were taken back to San Carlos. All the Chihenne, including Soldado, who had remained on the reservation with a hundred and fifty of his band, were kept under close scrutiny by the army. They were, in effect, under house arrest. The army feared that Victorio would try to set his people free.

All that winter Victorio and his *bronchos* raided up and down the Rio Grande. More than a dozen whites lost their lives.

Because of the bad blood between the White Mountain and Chihenne bands, it was decided to relocate the latter to the Mescalero reservation near Fort Stanton. The Chihenne were pleased. The Mescalero reservation was located on a high plateau with grassy meadows and stands of Ponderosa pine—an infinitely more pleasant place than San Carlos.

Learning of this, Victorio's *bronchos* began to long for family and friends. In twos and threes they deserted Victorio and gave themselves up. By the summer of 1879 the last of the Chihenne raiders—Victorio and twelve others—surrendered to the authorities at Fort Stanton.

But peace proved fleeting. During the Chihenne rampage, a man had been killed near Silver City, and local offi-

cials indicted Victorio in absentia on a charge of murder.
That summer several men from Silver City went on a
hunting trip which happened to bring them near the
Mescalero reservation. One of these men was the judge
who had issued the warrant for Victorio's arrest. When he
heard this, Victorio fled into the mountains. A number of
bronchos went with him. They were absolutely loyal to
Victorio and were determined to protect him from white
justice.

A few months later, Colonel Luther Hatch and the
Ninth Cavalry arrived at Fort Stanton. Hatch and his regiment of black cavalry—hard-as-nails "buffalo soldiers"—
had just come from campaigning against the Comanches in
Texas. Now they were under orders to hunt down Victorio
and his renegade Apaches.

"Lieutenant Lane, reporting for duty, sir."

Colonel Hatch looked up from the territorial map
spread out across his desk and gave the young shavetail
standing before him a quick once-over. Lane was covered
with trail dust, but he still managed to cut a fine figure in
his uniform. He was a slender man, broad in the shoulders,
with a strong square-jawed face, alert blue eyes, and short-
cropped blonde hair.

"Oh yes," said Hatch, leaning back in his chair with a
weary sigh. "Lieutenant Hudson Lane. Graduated top of
your class at West Point, didn't you, Lane?"

"Yes, sir."

"I would have thought you'd warrant a better posting."

"I requested service out here, Colonel."

"I see. Looking for some action. Well, I expect you'll
get plenty. How do you feel about Negro soldiers,
Lieutenant?"

"I hear they are hard campaigners, sir."

"You're damned right they are. They're the best
damned soldiers I've ever had the privilege to command.
You'll find out what I mean when we get into a scrape with
the Apaches."

"If you don't mind my asking, sir, when do we start out after Victorio?"

Hatch smirked. "Don't be in too big of a hurry, Lane. Do you know anything about the Apaches?"

"No, sir. Only what I've read."

"Forget all that garbage. I don't know much about them, either. But we had better learn, and damned fast. Time after time a handful of Apaches have gotten the best of our troops. Run circles around them and then fought them to a standstill. These are no ordinary Indians, Lieutenant."

"I understand, sir."

Hatch leaned forward. "General Crook used to be in command down here. He employed Apache scouts. When he left, that practice was largely discontinued by his successor. I believe we should reintroduce it. There is a man named Clancy St. John. He lives in Tucson now. Your first assignment for the Ninth, Lieutenant, is to go to Tucson and talk to this man. Persuade him to serve as my regimental chief of scouts on the campaign against Victorio. Tell him he will be in charge of a company of Apache scouts, whom he will handpick."

"Yes, sir."

"You won't have an easy time convincing St. John to join us, Lane. There is bad blood between him and the United States Army. But, be that as it may, I want him. He's the best scout in the business. So don't come back without him."

21

When Hudson Lane stepped into the gunsmith's shop on Tucson's main thoroughfare, he saw a man seated at a work table at the rear of the long narrow room. Passing between cases and racks filled with every variety of firearm, Lane approached the man. This gave him a few seconds to carefully scrutinize Clancy St. John. He was immensely curious, never having met a living legend.

What he saw was a burly, middle-aged man with craggy features and a dusting of gray in his sandy-colored hair. Clancy was bent over a rifle, securing the breech plate with a screwdriver, and peering through a pair of wire-rimmed spectacles as he worked. He did not look up as Lane approached, and the young lieutenant wondered if the man was afflicted with deafness, in addition to poor eyesight. Reaching the vicinity of the work table, Lane cleared his throat.

"What do you want?" asked Clancy. Still he did not look up from the rifle, and Lane realized he had been too hasty in his judgment—Clancy wasn't hard of hearing. He was merely indifferent to Lane's presence, or his reason for coming.

"Lieutenant Lane, sir. Are you Mr. Clancy St. John?"

"What if I am?"

"General Hatch sends his compliments. He . . . "

"Hatch?" Now Clancy straightened and looked up, peeling the see-betters off his face and tossing them on the table with a measure of disgust. "Hatch." Lips pursed, he shook his head. "Can't say that I've heard of the man. Hard to keep track of the generals around here. They come and go so fast. But then, I don't read the newspaper, either."

"General Hatch is commanding officer of the Ninth Cavalry."

"The Ninth? Buffalo soldiers?"

"Yes, sir."

"Well, they gave a good account of themselves against the Comanches, I hear."

"They are first-rate soldiers."

"Hmm." Clancy picked up a rag that reeked of gun oil and began to wipe down the rifle.

"Isn't that a Winchester 73?" asked Lane.

"That's right. She's a beauty, isn't she? Carbine, .44 caliber, forty-grain bullet, the first really good center-fire repeating rifle. A man left it with me a few weeks ago. Said the firing mechanism needed repair. He was a gambling man, of the professional sort, and he said he'd won this rifle in a recent game of five-card stud. He never came back for it."

"Why not? What happened to him?"

"He has recently taken up permanent residence at our local bone orchard. Seems a cowboy thought he was hiding an ace up his sleeve. Turned out not to be an ace, but rather a single-shot hideout, an over-and-under derringer. I understand the cowboy is buried right alongside the cardsharp."

"Does that kind of thing happen often in Tucson?"

"All too often." Clancy's smile was a wry smirk. "And to think I moved here because I thought my family would be safer in town. There's no place safe west of the Mississippi, is there, Lieutenant?"

"One day there will be, sir."

"Hmm. You soldier boys will see to that, won't you?" Clancy sounded skeptical. "West Point, aren't you?"

"Yes. But how did you know?"

"You stand there like you've got a ramrod attached to your spine. I've known a few West Pointers in my time. They might do in a civilized war, but they can't cut the mustard out here."

Lane stiffened. "You judge me without even knowing me, Mr. St. John."

"You're all alike. All cut from the same blue cloth. Oh, there are a few exceptions. Crook, now he was an exception."

Lane wasn't sure he followed. "Sir, General Hatch has sent me to ask . . ."

Clancy held up a hand. "Don't waste your breath, Lieutenant. The answer is no."

Lane began to fume. He was tired, hungry, and dirty, and he was in no mood to be treated so cavalierly, even by a living legend.

"Mr. St. John, I've traveled three hundred miles to come here and see you, and by God you will hear me out."

Clancy was amused and surprised. "You're absolutely right, Lieutenant. I'm being rude. It is a fault I have long been aware of but haven't yet been able to overcome. Go on and say your piece."

"Sir, General Hatch has been ordered to suppress the current Apache uprising led by the Chiricahua Apache called Victorio. To best accomplish this task, the general feels he should employ Apache scouts. He would like for you to be chief of those scouts."

Though God only knows why, thought Lane. Clancy St. John might have been big doings twenty years ago, but Lane saw nothing in this beaten down old man to warrant such confidence.

"Apache scouts?" Clancy chuckled, a raspy sound. "Well, well. Maybe your General Hatch isn't so bad after all. But I'm afraid I can't help you, Lieutenant. My scouting days are over. I'm nigh on fifty years old. I put this ramshackle old body of mine through a lot of abuse in my early days, and I'm paying for it now. I get up in the morning so stiff in the joints and back I can hardly pull my boots on, sometimes."

I can believe that, thought Lane, uncharitably.

"Besides," continued Clancy, "I promised my wife I wouldn't ride off to war anymore. It's a promise I intend to keep."

"I know it will be a great inconvenience, sir, but you'll have to tell General Hatch yourself. I have orders not to return without you."

"Well, you're over a barrel, aren't you, Lieutenant?"

"I'm afraid I am."

Clancy smiled, rose from the work table, and put a hand on Lane's shoulder. "You'd better come along with me, son."

"Where are we going?"

"My house. You'll have dinner with us. You can get cleaned up, and though I don't have a spare bed to offer, I can at least provide a roof over your head tonight. We'll put our heads together and try to hash out a solution to your predicament. What do you say?"

"Thank you. I gratefully accept."

"Good, good. You're pretty smart, for a West Point man."

Clancy and his family lived in an adobe house at the edge of town. It was small, but comfortable, with three rooms, two of which were bedrooms, and the third containing the kitchen in the rear, a dining table, and a couple of chairs gathered round the stone fireplace.

Lane found Clancy's wife a very becoming woman who looked much younger than her years, and she was gracious in her welcome, considering that his presence at the table for dinner was a last-minute thing, and she'd had no warning.

The lieutenant sat down to a meal the likes of which he had not enjoyed since leaving his home in Ohio upon receipt of the orders that posted him to Fort Stanton. Thick, juicy beefsteak was accompanied by white potatoes, roasted ears of corn, sourdough biscuits, lemon pie, and good, strong Arbuckle coffee. Lane ate so much he felt obliged to apologize for being such a glutton. Laura St. John just laughed. "I take it as a compliment to my cooking," she said.

"She's too good of a cook," lamented Clancy as he patted his belly in mock despair. "I'm starting to develop a noticeable paunch. Realized just the other day that I couldn't see my toes anymore."

"I suppose you'd like to go back to living off hardtack and salt pork," was Laura's good-humored riposte.

"Would you care for more pie, Lieutenant?" asked Faith.

Lane glanced at Laura's oldest daughter and felt extremely self-conscious. Sixteen-year-old Faith was the spitting image of her mother, which meant she was a winsome lass indeed, with golden hair and a honey-and-cream complexion that Lane decided must be quite rare in this country. She was slender, but the way she filled out her dress in certain places made it abundantly clear that she was no longer a child.

"No, thanks," he said.

"More coffee, then?"

"No, thank you." Lane felt the heat in his cheeks. Faith had been gazing raptly at him all through dinner, scarcely able to take her eyes off him.

"Leave the poor man alone, Faith," said Laura.

Faith pouted. "I'm just trying to be a good hostess, Mother."

"She's in love," said Charity. "Or thinks she is." Faith's younger sister was also golden-haired, but her tresses were cut short and in a perpetual state of disarray. Throughout dinner she had occasionally tugged at her dress in such a way that Lane surmised she was more comfortable in a shirt and trousers. In fact, he pegged her as something of a tomboy.

"Hush your mouth, Charity," hissed Faith.

"But don't worry, Lieutenant," continued Charity, blithely ignoring her fuming sister. "She falls in love with just about every young man she sees."

"Oh!" Faith reached over and pinched Charity on the arm as hard as she could. "You little brat! I do not!"

"Girls!" Laura rose, plate in hand. "Help me clear the table."

Lane glanced at Clancy, saw that he was amused by the girls' antics. "Let's go outside for a smoke," suggested the Irishman, and Lane nodded, relieved.

They stepped out into the cool purple twilight. The first stars were twinkling in a blue velvet sky, and an early moon loomed large over a distant rank of black peaks. Faintly, from the center of town, came the tinny jangle of a hurdy-gurdy piano.

"I can see why you moved to town," said Lane. "You have a wonderful family, and you would not want any harm to come to them."

A bleakness filled Clancy's eyes as he rolled a smoke. "My first wife was killed by Apaches. I was gone at the time. Used to run a few cattle. Still would, were I a single man. But when I married Laura, I gave that up. Found I couldn't bring myself to go out of sight of the house. As you can imagine, that made working cattle damned hard to do."

"By the looks of things, I'd say you are prospering here. Your business seems to be thriving."

"I make ends meet. Tucson is a rough-and-tumble town, and every man goes heeled, so a gunsmith keeps occupied."

Lane thought Clancy sounded less than enthusiastic about his chosen vocation. *Could it be*, mused the perceptive lieutenant, *that Clancy St. John misses the old way of life?* Even if he did, Lane doubted it would make any difference; Clancy had given his word to Laura, and he wouldn't break a promise.

"Of course, some folks might argue that Tucson is no place to raise a family," continued Clancy wryly. "It's a wild and woolly place. Hell with the hide off, as they say. But most of the hardcases who'd shoot you for looking at them wrong would never dream of harming a woman or child."

Lane said nothing, listening to the distant pulse of nighttime Tucson as it quickened, the saloons going full blast now that the sun had set on another workday.

"Lieutenant," said Clancy, "I can't go back with you. You'll have to give my regards to General Hatch and tell him I respectfully decline. If you don't mind lying a little to save your hide, you can tell him I broke both legs, or have a bad case of the gout."

"Yes, sir." Lane noticed that Clancy was gazing— longingly?—out at the desert.

Early the next morning Lane ate breakfast and went down to the livery to fetch his horse. Returning to the St. John house he met Faith outside.

"Will you write to me?" she asked breathlessly.

"What?" Lane was caught completely off guard by the question.

"Please say you will write." She clutched his arm. Her touch sent a jolt of electricity through him.

"I will."

She beamed. "And I shall write you back," she promised, then stepped away from him and feigned a profound interest in the far reaches of the dusty street as Clancy emerged from the house, carrying the Winchester 73. He handed the rifle to Lane.

"I would like you to do me a favor, Lieutenant."

"Yes, sir."

"There is a Chihenne Apache named Soldado. I believe you will find him on the Mescalero reservation. Would you give him this for me?"

"Of course."

"He and I go back a long way," said Clancy, by way of an explanation. "You'd do well to make him one of your Apache scouts, if he'll go along. I don't know if he will. Been a long time. But he's a good man to have on your side. I know of none better."

"I'll make certain he gets this rifle." Lane shook Clancy's hand. "Thank you and good-bye."

"So long, Lieutenant."

Lane mounted up and, with a last, bewildered glance at Faith, rode out of Tucson.

22

Hatch's orderly found Hudson Lane hunkered down by a fire which he shared with a couple of other Ninth Cavalry subalterns. Not a word had passed between the officers for some time. They were listening to some of the buffalo soldiers singing. About a dozen were standing or sitting near a big fire yonder, singing "Swing Low, Sweet Chariot" in harmony. They sang well together. The Ninth was, as one trooper had told Lane, the "singin'est outfit in the whole army." Lane didn't mind at all. The sound soothed frayed nerves. Problem was, the ballads also made him a little homesick. This border bivouac seemed like a long way from anywhere.

"General wants to see you, suh," said the orderly.

Lane nodded, dumped the coffee dregs out of his tin cup and rose, wincing as his saddle-sore body complained. Today had been his turn to lead a patrol on a fruitless fifty-mile round-trip excursion along the border to the east.

Hatch was seated at a wooden camp table, balanced on a flimsy folding chair. Moths fluttered with suicidal abandon against the chimney of the lantern which cast a mustard yellow sheen on the report the general was writing. He dipped his pen in an iron inkwell and scratched another sentence as Lane approached. When Hatch finally looked up from his labors, Lane snapped off a brisk salute. With a sigh Hatch nodded and slacked back into the wood-and-canvas chair.

"Well, Lane, I've just received a report that the two mountain howitzers I requested six weeks ago will be here sometime tomorrow."

"That's good news, sir."

A smile twitched the corners of Hatch's mouth, beneath his sweeping mustache. "You don't sound too excited."

"May I speak frankly, sir?"

"I expect all my officers to be candid with me. As long as they don't step over the line into insubordination, of course."

"No, sir. I'm just wondering, sir, what good the howitzers will do. The Apaches are in Mexico. And as far as we know, they'll stay there until we're both retired from the service."

It seemed to Lane that they had been camped here on the border since the Creation, even though it had only been three weeks. Victorio had fled into Mexico, though not before stabbing at them with a series of sudden hit-and-run attacks. Nothing in Lane's training at the military academy had prepared him for this kind of fighting. At West Point, cadets studied all the great pitched battles of history—Agincourt, Hastings, Austerlitz, Waterloo, Gettysburg. But pitched battles were not the Apache way. To them there was no shame in retreat. It was just part of the deadly and—to Lane—very frustrating game they played, and played with consummate skill. How could one fight a will-o'-the-wisp?

Then, just as the column finally closed in on Victorio and his *bronchos*, they had slipped away, crossing over into Mexico. Hatch was left with no recourse. He could not pursue the hostiles onto foreign soil. There was word that the United States government was at this very moment negotiating what they called the Hot Trails Treaty with the Republic of Mexico. By the terms of this diplomatic instrument, the U.S. Army could enter Mexico if in hot pursuit of the Indians, and the same privilege was accorded the Mexican Army. The accord was expressly designed to deal with the Apache problem.

"Maybe not," said Hatch. "I have information that Victorio is hard-pressed by a large force of *federales* under the command of a General Joaquin Terrazas. He is, by all accounts, one of Mexico's best Indian fighters."

"Sir, from what I've been able to learn since I've been out here, not even Terrazas could flush Victorio out of the Sierra Madre."

"Ah, but Terrazas seems to have cut the hostiles off from that sanctuary."

That pricked Lane's interest. "Then Victorio may turn north."

Hatch nodded. "He may very well be forced to cross back into the United States. Remember, he threatened to murder the families of our Apache scouts."

Lane remembered all too well. Victorio was a sly and ruthless bastard. The Apache scouts had proven themselves worthy. Though the Ninth had yet to come to grips with the *bronchos*, Victorio, on the other hand, had been unable to shake off the pursuit, and this relentless hounding had finally driven him across the border. He knew the army had their Apache scouts to thank for that. Unfortunately, Victorio and his renegades had murdered more than a hundred American citizens before leaving the territories. God only knew what damage he had done in Chihuahua these past three weeks.

Lane gave all due credit to the scouts. Most of them had stuck it out, in spite of Victorio's threat. Lane figured Victorio was just waging a little psychological warfare; he personally did not think the Apache leader had the where-withal to do what he threatened to do. Victorio was too busy running for his life to slip up to San Carlos and kill the scouts' families.

"You don't really think he would go through with that, do you, General?" asked Lane.

"Victorio is known to be a man of his word. Of course, I've sent a warning to San Carlos, and the garrison at the agency is on full alert." Hatch wearily flexed his shoulders. "Still, I wouldn't put it past that red devil to try. He knows these scouts of ours give us a big advantage in the long run. If he could kill a family or two, all our scouts would desert. And I wouldn't blame them, frankly."

"They may not wait for that, sir. If Victorio comes north, they might rush back to San Carlos to protect their loved ones."

"I'm sure that's what Victorio will be counting on."

"Well, sir, there's at least one scout we won't have to worry about. Soldado. He has no family."

"This is what I want you to do, Lieutenant. Take a twenty-man detail and ride east. Leave first thing in the morning, and escort those howitzers back here. I have a gut feeling that Victorio is close by, with Terrazas hot on his heels."

"Yes, sir."

"And Lane—take one scout with you."

Lane bent his steps for the campfires of the Apache scouts. He knew exactly who he wanted as a scout.

There was something about Soldado, something Lane couldn't quite put his finger on, that convinced him the Chihenne was a man to be trusted. Soldado seldom spoke, and gave nothing away in regards to his true feelings, but there was a candor and directness about his gaze and attitude that was as good as gold when it came to buying Lane's trust. Besides that, Clancy St. John trusted him.

Lane thought back to that day, three months back, when he had found Soldado at the Mescalero reservation, locating the elusive loner's jacal in a thicket several miles from the main Chihenne *rancheria*. He had presented Soldado with the Winchester 73 and explained the circumstances which had brought him so far to do so. Soldado had merely nodded his thanks. But he had held that repeating rifle in his hands as though it were some kind of holy object, and upon hearing Clancy's name, the Apache's stoic mask had crumbled, betraying a deep emotion, if only for an instant, leaving Lane thoroughly intrigued. What was the connection between Soldado and Clancy St. John?

He could find no one who could enlighten him on that score. And he had not bothered asking Soldado, sensing that the Chihenne would not have told him anything.

Thoughts of Clancy St. John caused Lane to reflect on the man's oldest daughter. Faith's beautiful features, amber curls, the touch of her hand on his arm—all these memories, burned into his mind, kept haunting him. He had written her twice, steeling himself not to expect a reply, and indeed he had not received a letter back. This proved to be a keen disappointment, even though he told himself that no mail could catch up with him on this campaign. Not that it mattered. No, of course, it didn't.

Then why couldn't he stop thinking about her?

The mountain howitzers were being transported west out of El Paso, accompanied by a small detachment. Too small, as it turned out.

On the second day out from the Ninth Cavalry's encampment, Lane and his troopers spotted a black pillar of smoke rising into the morning sky, dead ahead. Somehow Lane knew it wasn't some isolated farm or ranch house fallen prey to Apache raiders. No, the detachment from Fort Bliss that he had been dispatched to meet had come to a bad end.

He wasn't prepared for how bad it turned out to be.

The bodies of the soldiers had been stripped and horribly mutilated. A couple had been lashed to the wheels of their caissons, presumably while they were still alive. There they had suffered until the ammunition exploded in the fires the Apaches set. There would be no finding all the pieces of those poor bastards. The howitzers had been rendered inoperable, and a quick inspection confirmed to Lane that they were beyond salvaging.

Somehow he managed to swallow bile and maintain the dignity expected of an officer, until his troopers were engaged in burying the dead. The corpses were wrapped in blankets and shallow graves were scraped out of the hard ground with knives and the butts of Spencer carbines.

When he was sure his men were too busy with their grue-some work to notice, Lane stumbled behind a patch of man-tall ocotillo, dropped to one knee, and puked his guts out.

After a while he lifted his head and saw Soldado standing there watching him. Lane's stomach was clench-ing involuntarily, but he had nothing left to vomit. A sud-den burst of irrational anger gripped the young lieutenant. It was an anger fueled in large measure by stark terror; the tortured remains of the soldiers had gone a long way towards completely unmanning Lane.

"Why?" he croaked. "Why do they do that?"

Soldado remained silent. His features betrayed noth-ing.

"Answer me, damn you!" rasped Lane.

Soldado shook his head. He seemed confused, as though he didn't understand what Lane was talking about. "They . . . are Apache."

"Well then damn all Apaches to hell," snapped Lane. "The world will be an infinitely better place when the last goddamned Apache is dead. Every last man, woman, and child of your bloody people should be eradicated. Wiped from the face of the earth."

The stinging lash of these bitter words had no visible effect upon Soldado. He just stood there, the Winchester 73 cradled in his arms, watching Lane rant.

Breathless, his spleen vented, Lane felt suddenly weak. "We will return immediately to the regiment," he said dully.

"I follow Apaches," said Soldado. "Make sure they don't circle back."

"Yes, you do that," sneered Lane. "Do whatever the hell you want. Just stay away from me."

Lane walked away. Taking the canteen from the sad-dle of his horse, he rinsed his mouth with a brackish swig. As he watched Soldado mount up and ride south, following the *broncho* trail, Lane realized he would never trust Soldado, or any other Apache, again. You could not civilize a wolf, no matter how hard you tried. Sooner or later the wolf would turn on you. It was in his nature.

23

Whenever being cooped up inside his shop got to be too much for Clancy St. John to bear, he took a stroll down Tucson's main street, an excursion that invariably delivered him to the threshold of the Pearl Saloon. Of Tucson's many watering holes, the Pearl was Clancy's favorite. For one thing he knew the barkeeps, and more to the point, they knew him, and were wise enough never to try palming off on him some of the watered-down panther piss they often succeeded in peddling to less-discerning patrons. Clancy was guaranteed an honest-to-God shot of nerve medicine at the Pearl. He found he needed one at least once a day, usually late in the afternoon. The forty-rod smoothed out his hackles and gave the day a rosier hue. Most of all, it served to calm the stormy seas of his discontent, which had been raging fiercely in his soul since the visit of Lieutenant Hudson Lane.

    Usually the Pearl was empty, or nearly so, in the afternoons. After sundown the cowboys came in from the outlying ranches, and of course where the cowboys congregated one would always find the percentage girls and a cardsharp or two. This time, though, Clancy saw that he would have to share the bar. Three men were bellied up to the mahogany, knocking back shots of Taos Lightning like it was water.

They were a scruffy-looking lot. Clancy recognized one of them: Buckshot Reilly. The big, burly, bearded son of a bitch had his sawed-off, double-barreled greener on the bar within quick and easy reach. This was Reilly's weapon of choice. He didn't often use buckshot, but rather kept the scattergun loaded with his own lethal mixture of horseshoe nails, broken glass, shards of stone or crockery, and rock salt. If the blast didn't kill his victim, the rock salt in the wound would make the poor bastard wish he were dead.

Seeing Reilly made Clancy's stomach muscles knot, and his hand brushed his right hip, an involuntarily reflex action. But there was no Dance revolver at his side today. He generally did not go about town heeled. Some folks declared that an unarmed man in Tucson was a fellow bent on suicide. But after years on the malpais, the wild and woolly streets of Tucson held nothing worth being afraid of, in his book.

Reilly spotted him standing just inside the saloon's batwing doors. "Clancy St. John! Ain't it a small world? Come to think on it, I do recall hearing you'd got yoreself hitched and moved into town. The little lady done civilized you, eh?"

"Hello, Reilly. The wind must've been wrong, else I would have smelled you a block away."

Behind the bar, Sam, the apron, turned very pale, and his eyes flicked nervously back and forth between Clancy and Reilly as he edged slowly away.

Reilly's grin tightened. His gimlet eyes glittered like black diamonds. "I don't rightly unnerstan why you take such a powerful dislike to me, Clancy. I ain't never done nothin' to you or yours, that I can recall."

"I just can't abide scalp hunters. To me, they're lower than a snake's belly."

"We don't want no trouble in here," said the barkeep. He clearly expected some. On the frontier, many men had been killed for lesser insults than the ones Clancy had just conveyed to Buckshot Reilly.

But the scalp hunter was in a rare good mood. He chuckled. It sounded like dead, windblown leaves skittering across hard ground.

"Ain't gonna kill you, Clancy, though Lord knows you sure are askin' for it. I've got important business elsewhere, so I cain't afford to spend any time in the Tucson hoosegow. You see, the state of Chihuahua is offering two thousand pesos for every Apache scalp turned in to the proper authorities. That's man, woman, or child. They don't care. Neither do I, for two thousand pesos. How do you like them apples, Clancy boy?"

"I think it stinks."

But Clancy wasn't surprised. Victorio's recent activities south of the border had the Mexicans in an uproar. Bounties on Apache scalps was a tried-and-true formula down there. The price, though, had never been so high.

"Come on, Clancy," said Reilly. "Let me buy you a drink. Let's bury the hatchet for once, just for old time's sake. I'm in a mighty generous mood today. Must be on account of how rich I'm gonna be before long."

Clancy had known Buckshot Reilly for fifteen years—and never liked the man. Reilly had gotten his start out here as a hunter, just like Clancy. Since then he had branched out into manhunting. He'd brought in some of the territory's most notorious bad men. All dead, and like as not shot in the back. Nobody made much of a fuss over that, since his victims were owlhoots. Back in the days when Cochise had run wild, Reilly had started hunting Apaches. They didn't have to be *bronchos*, either. Rumor had it that Reilly sometimes visited the reservations and killed a few "tame" Indians. He also took Yaqui and other Indian scalps, secure in the knowledge that the Mexican authorities would not distinguish them from Apache topknots. Even Mexicans weren't safe from Reilly and his scalp-hunting crew; if they thought they could pass your hair off as Apache, you were fair game.

"No thanks," said Clancy, and turned sharply on his heel to leave the Pearl Saloon.

He paused on the sun-warped boardwalk, as the long afternoon shadows slanted across the yellow, rutted hardpack of Tucson's main thoroughfare and contemplated paying the town marshal a visit. The local law dog and his deputies were good men, committed to cleaning up Tucson. A tall order, but then they were tall men. Chances were the marshal would like to know a two-legged snake like Buckshot Reilly was here. He would probably run Reilly and his crew out of town. But Clancy decided not to go running to the badge toter like a school yard tattletale. Besides, Reilly would be leaving soon enough, and he would make no trouble in Tucson. It was out in the badlands where Reilly made his trouble.

Deep in thought, Clancy walked home. He was moody all through dinner, scarcely touching his food, and speaking nary a word. After dinner he stepped outside to build a smoke. Leaving the cleanup chores to Faith and Charity, Laura joined him. The sun had set, and a cool purple twilight blessed the desert.

"What's bothering you, Clancy?"

"It's nothing."

"Of course it's something. You know I can read you like a book. Are there to be secrets between us now?"

He told her about Buckshot Reilly.

"From what I've heard, Victorio is down in Mexico. I agree that scalp hunting is a despicable business, but I don't see that Reilly can do much harm."

"You don't understand. I'm not worried about the *bronchos*. It's the innocent people whose scalps Reilly will pass off as belonging to wild Apaches."

"What do you want to do about it, then?"

"I don't know. Follow him, I guess. Find out what he's up to."

"You, alone? Isn't that dangerous?"

Clancy nodded. "Might be. But what does it matter? I'm not going to do it."

"Now you just listen here to me, Clancy St. John,"

she said sternly. "I never asked you to make that promise. I would never do that. Never try to keep a man I love from doing what he thinks needs to be done. You made the promise of your own free will. To be perfectly honest, I think you did it to ease your conscience, because of what happened to Maria."

Clancy smiled fondly at her. "There's no fooling you, is there?"

"I sincerely hope not." She smiled back, reached out to take his hand. Her touch quickened his pulse and reminded him of what a lucky fool he was, and of what he stood to lose if his luck ran out. "You do what you think is right. I just have one question. Why do you have to be the one to stop Buckshot Reilly?"

He pondered that one for a spell. "I guess because I can. And because I'm sick and tired of innocent people getting caught in the middle of all this. I'd like to live long enough to see real peace come to this land, so that folks can get on with their flamin' lives, and not have to wonder if they'll be alive to see tomorrow's sunrise."

Her eyes brimmed with pride. "There's a big wide streak of decency in you, Clancy St. John. That's one of the reasons I love you so, I guess. Now you come in to bed. You'll need to get an early start tomorrow, if you're going to pick up Reilly's trail."

24

When the word came from Washington, it passed from a telegraph terminal to a series of heliograph stations and thence to General Hatch, whose Ninth Cavalry had been impatiently whiling away the weeks as they straddled the border.

The Hot Trails Treaty with Mexico had been signed.

In theory, American forces could violate Mexican sovereignty only if in immediate, "hot" pursuit of hostiles. Hatch's buffalo soldiers hadn't actually laid eyes on an Apache *broncho*, despite numerous, far-ranging patrols. But the howitzers had been hit five days earlier, and Hatch figured the trail of the Apaches responsible was warm enough to serve his purpose. So the Ninth struck camp and moved south.

Terrazas was pressing Victorio hard, and yet for some reason that forever remained a mystery, the Apache leader was reluctant to seek sanctuary in the traditional Nednhi stronghold of the Sierra Madre. Victorio decided instead to return to the United States. Only then did he learn of Hatch's approach. He tried to slip past the Ninth Cavalry, but he was not as mobile as he might have been. Seventy-five women and children accompanied his sixty warriors. Their horses were starving. They were perilously low on ammunition. Hatch's Apache scouts discovered the *bronchos*, and the buffalo soldiers rode hard to cut Victorio off from the border. Now Victorio had no other recourse; he would retreat into the rugged Sierra Madre, a range of steep cliffs and deep canyons, high mountain meadows and dense stands of virgin pine.

In the past, those foolhardy enough to pursue Apache raiders into the Sierra Madre had met with disaster. Victorio was hoping that those who now persecuted him would think twice before venturing into the fabled Nednhi stronghold.

But he never reached the Sierra Madre. At a place called Tres Castillos, the Apache "Wild Ones" found themselves trapped between the *federales* of Terrazas and General Hatch's Ninth Cavalry.

On October 14, 1880, Hatch summoned Lieutenant Hudson Lane to his tent.

"It was the intention of General Terrazas to attack at sunset today," Hatch informed his young subaltern. He spread a map out on his field table and pointed at it. "Our scouts and the Tarahumaras who scout for Terrazas indicate that the *bronchos* have thrown up a breastwork of rocks here, with this hill at their backs."

"That's a highly unusual tactic for Apaches, sir."

"Exactly. It is clear to me that they intend to stand and fight to the death."

"They don't stand a chance. They're outnumbered fifty-to-one."

"Right. I've persuaded Terrazas to postpone his attack by twenty-four hours."

"We won't be involved in the action, sir?"

"No. This is Mexican soil. Mexican troops will do the fighting. In a very courteous but firm manner, Terrazas thanked us for doing our part to corner the Apaches—and then assured me that there was absolutely no reason for us to linger."

Lane felt the tension of a long and arduous campaign

drain out of him. It was over. Victorio and his *bronchos* were doomed. The Ninth Cavalry could go home, virtually without firing a shot. This was not the way it was supposed to end.

"However," said Hatch, "I respectfully disagreed with the general. There are seventy-five women and children with Victorio. Terrazas has agreed to give me that twenty-four hours to get those noncombatants out."

"What?"

"You heard me, Lieutenant. Al Sieber and one of our Apache scouts have agreed to enter Victorio's camp under a flag of truce and try to reason with him, persuade him to let the women and children go. I am offering a firm guarantee of their safe return to San Carlos. I want an officer to accompany Sieber, and I picked you."

"Me?" Lane was stunned.

"I won't lie to you, Lieutenant. The *bronchos* are trapped, and there's no telling what they might do. This could be quite dangerous for you. So I'm not making it an order. If you would rather not volunteer for this duty, I'll find someone else."

"No, sir, it's not that."

"Then what?"

"Nothing, sir. I'm just curious—why did my name come to mind in connection with this assignment?"

"My other officers have all spent some time campaigning against hostile Indians. They have developed certain prejudices, as a result. I'm counting on you to be a little more . . . compassionate, shall we say."

Or maybe, mused Lane, *he's thinking that if he is to lose an officer, it ought to be his least experienced one.*

The irony of the situation did not escape Lane. He doubted there was an officer or enlisted man in the Ninth who cared less than he about what happened to the Apache "noncombatants." After witnessing the aftermath of the slaughter of the detail escorting the mountain howitzers from Fort Bliss, Lane had decided that the world would be a better place to live if every Apache in it were exterminated. But Hatch was unaware of his true feelings in this regard. Lane had left all animosity out of his report on the incident, sticking strictly to the facts. The irony now was that Hatch intended to send an Apache hater to save Apache lives.

"Well, Lieutenant, what's it going to be?"

Lane couldn't refuse. If he did, Hatch might think him a coward. *Even if I tell him the truth about how I feel and why, he might think it is merely an excuse to squirm out of a dangerous job.*

"I'll go, sir."

"Good. Here comes Sieber, and the scout who will accompany you."

Lane turned to see the small, wiry German-American clad in dusty range clothes walking towards them, with Soldado at his side.

Victorio was nearly sixty years old when Hudson Lane first laid eyes on the great Chiricahua chief. His people called him "The Conqueror." He was a man of unswerving will and unstinting dedication to his cause, which was to wage unrelenting war upon the enemies of his people.

His long, wavy black hair was streaked with gray, and his stern bronze features were deeply lined, but there could be no doubt that this was a physically powerful man, despite his advanced age. There was nothing in his attire to distinguish him from the other warriors; he wore a plain brown himper, breechcloth, and desert moccasins. A rifle lay across his lap as he sat cross-legged on a frayed woolen blanket and listened to what Al Sieber had to say.

The white scout sat facing Victorio, with Lane and Soldado standing behind him. Flanking Victorio was old, crippled Nana, and the legendary woman warrior called Lozen, Victorio's sister. In her youth, Lozen had been a maiden of great beauty. Though pursued by many determined suitors, she had never married. She could outrun any Apache male, and was their equal in shooting, horsemanship, and fighting. "Lozen is always at my right hand,"

Victorio had said. "She is strong as a man, braver than most, and a shield to her people."

It was said that Lozen had the power to locate the enemy, the way some could divine a hidden source of water. Chanting a prayer to Ussen, she would stand with arms outstretched and slowly turn in a circle. When the palms of her hands tingled and began to change color, she knew she was facing the enemy.

Now in her forties, Lozen dressed like a man, but there was no mistaking her for one. Though slender, there was about her the strength and ferocity of the panther. Lane knew that if the Apache women and children did leave Tres Castillos, Lozen would not be among them. Her place would be at her brother's side, fighting to the last breath.

Lane was understandably nervous. On the rocky slope above them, and in the rocks around them, Victorio's *bronchos* watched the parley, and the lieutenant realized that his life, along with Sieber's and Soldado's, rested in Victorio's hands. Victorio would have nothing to lose by killing them. He knew he was doomed to die here, that there was no escape, and if he wanted all his people to perish with him, which was a possibility, he needed give only a signal and there would be three less *indah* to deal with.

Al Sieber spoke to Victorio in the Apache's own tongue, so Lane had no idea what passed between the two. He could only stand there and try to look untroubled, even though dozens of *bronchos* were staring at him in a very unfriendly manner. Standing beside him, Soldado was, as always, impassive. It occurred to Lane that as much as the hostiles hated him and the uniform he wore, their animosity must run even deeper towards Soldado. For Soldado was one of the "blue wolves," an army scout, and considered by all of the "Wild Ones" as a traitor to his kind.

Finally—it seemed to Lane like an eternity—Sieber looked back at him and nodded. "He's going to do it, Lieutenant. He will let the women and children go. He was reluctant at first. Said the *Nakai-Ye* want to kill all the Apaches, even the women and the children, and he has some doubts that we will be able to get them out of Mexico unharmed."

"Tell him he has our word."

Sieber smirked. "That wouldn't pull much freight with him. The word of a white man doesn't mean spit to an Apache. Why should it? We have a history of breaking our word."

"Then why is he going along with this?"

Sieber shrugged. "Because he figures the women and the little ones will have at least some chance this way. They'll die for certain if they stay."

Lane glanced about him at the *bronchos*. "Why are they doing this, Mr. Sieber? Always before, the Apache has surrendered when cornered. Why are these men so determined to die? They know they can't win."

"For one reason, surrendering to the Mexicans isn't the same as surrendering to us. Those *federales* would likely line them all up in front of a firing squad and be done with it."

Victorio spoke up, and Lane realized that even if he did not speak English he could understand it. This time he spoke in Spanish. At West Point, Lane had demonstrated a talent for learning foreign languages, becoming fluent in French and German, and since his arrival in the Southwest, he had applied himself to the study of Spanish, so that now he could follow what Victorio was saying without too much difficulty.

"We will die free and unconquered," said Victorio gravely. "Mangas Colorado would have preferred to die in battle. Cochise, as well. Our people will not mourn our passing. Instead, they will be proud. By dying here we will be spared the humiliation of imprisonment and slavery." Victorio's dark and piercing gaze fixed on Soldado. "For this we thank Ussen."

The meeting concluded, Lane started back for the Ninth Cavalry's position with Sieber and Soldado. At sundown a detail of buffalo soldiers would come to the bottom of the hill and escort the Apache women and children to safety. This would give the *bronchos* a little time to say last farewells to their families.

"You look somewhat confused, Lieutenant," observed Sieber, as they rode stirrup-to-stirrup.

"I can make no sense of this," confessed Lane. "Apaches use hit-and-run tactics. They don't stand and fight. They give up when things get too hot for them. They live to fight another day. They don't die like . . . like heroes. Victorio could have surrendered to the Ninth a week ago."

Sorrow lurked behind Sieber's smile. "Take care, Lieutenant. You might start admiring them."

Lane shook his head. There was only one way he could reconcile what Victorio and his men were doing with his own unflattering notions about the Apaches. They were not heroes. In death they escape justice for their crimes. And in death, they became martyrs, provoking other Apaches to war and glory. In effect, General Hatch had pledged himself to the safekeeping of the next generation of "Wild Ones," inspired by what was about to happen here at Tres Castillos to follow in the bloody footprints of their fathers.

25

With the benefit of hindsight, Hudson Lane decided he should have known General Hatch would saddle him with the unpleasant duty of commanding the detachment that was to escort the Apache women and children back to San Carlos. Being the Ninth Cavalry's newest subaltern, Lane could expect to get most of the dirty, thankless tasks. And this certainly qualified as one of those.

Risking the immense displeasure of Mexican General Terrazas, Hatch had made up his mind to linger in the vicinity of Tres Castillos for a day or two. He would not take part in the action against Victorio unless invited to do so by Terrazas, but as he explained to the Mexican commander, his assignment was to make absolutely certain that Victorio's raiders were permanently dealt with, so that they posed no further threat to American citizens in the Territories of Arizona and New Mexico. That being the case, he would not turn around and go home until he was sure Victorio did not slip out of Terrazas' trap.

Lane's command consisted of twenty-eight men. More than enough to handle seventy-five half-starved and trail-weary women and children. Most of the Apaches did not even have horses, these having been killed to provide the young ones with food. Hatch spared two dozen mules so that at least the children would not have to walk all the way back to the reservation, a distance of more than four hundred miles. He also provided two wagons filled with rations for the hungry Indians. As soon as he was north of the border, Lane was to dispatch a rider to the nearest army outpost bearing Hatch's written request for sufficient wagons to convey the Indians the rest of the way. In addition, Lane was authorized to confiscate all other means of conveyance necessary to this end. Lane was resigned to the fact that it would take at least a month to get the Indians to San Carlos. They were in no condition to make very good time.

Two Apache scouts, Soldado and Najita, had also been assigned to Lane. General Hatch feared they might be molested by Mexican civilians, who would prefer to see every last Apache exterminated. So Lane kept his buffalo soldiers on the alert and had his two scouts constantly afield looking for any sign of impending trouble.

It was mid-October, and the days were still warm, though the nights cooled considerably. The Apaches plodded along in the dusty heat without complaint. Lane's soldiers showered them with every possible courtesy. These people had suffered many months of hardship following their men on the warpath, and now they had been forced to leave their husbands and brothers and fathers in the sure and certain knowledge that they would never see them again. Their stamina and stoicism under the most trying of circumstances was admirable. Even though he tried to harden his heart against them, Lane felt compassion for their plight.

Three days after leaving Tres Castillos, a rider from General Hatch caught up with them. Terrazas had attacked the Apache position at sunset on the fifteenth. Fierce fighting raged well into the night. Though tremendously outnumbered, Victorio and his *bronchos* held on until midmorning of the following day. Had they not been so desperately short of ammunition, the Apaches might have held out even longer. Finally, though, they were overrun. Seventy-eight Apaches, including Victorio, were slain. All of the dead were scalped for the bounty. There was debate as to who had actually killed the legendary Victorio. At the time no one could know that the Chihenne would insist that Victorio had, in the end, taken his own life rather than give the *Nakai-Ye* the satisfaction of killing him.

A few of the *bronchos* managed to escape under cover of darkness. Among these were Nana and Lozen. But there were not more than twenty survivors.

Lane was faced with a dilemma. Should he tell the women and children? He asked his scouts for their opinions. Najita was opposed to telling them; in their grief, he said, they might make trouble. Soldado disagreed. The news would come as no surprise to these people. They were prepared for the worst. Lane agreed. The news was dispensed. Lane expected a great wailing and gnashing of teeth, but the Apaches received the grim tidings without so much as a whimper, and if they shed a tear, they did so without Lane seeing.

That night Soldado paid Lane a visit. Najita came along to interpret, being able to translate Soldado's Spanish into English. Soldado was aware that Lane could understand some Spanish, but what he had to say was very important, and he wanted to make certain Lane fully comprehended.

"Once you asked me why the Apache tortures his enemies," said Soldado. "Do you remember?"

"I am not likely to ever forget that day," replied Lane.

"When I was very young," said Soldado, "a woman in my *che-wa-ki* was believed to be a witch. She was suspended by ropes between two trees, and left hanging there for many days, until she confessed. Then a fire was built beneath her, and she was burned to death. Such a thing is not considered cruel by my people. It is necessary, to drive the evil out of this world."

Lane opened his mouth to voice a hasty opinion that this was barbarism at its worst. Then he recalled that his own kind had done the very same kind of thing, and worse, for centuries. What difference was there between what Soldado had just described and the Spanish Inquisition, or the Salem witch-hunts?

"To endure pain bravely is the mark of character," continued Soldado, speaking through Najita. "Early in our lives we are taught to accept pain as a fact of life. If a man is evil, he will not be brave under the knife. So the evil must be driven out of his body before he dies, or it will remain in this world and inhabit the body of another. If the man is brave under the knife, he will be honored, even though he is the enemy."

"If you truly believe that," said Lane, "then you would torture your enemies, wouldn't you, Soldado?"

Soldado nodded. "I would. If I had any enemies."

Lane was incredulous. "You're saying that you don't? If Mexicans attacked us tomorrow, would you not try to kill them?"

"Yes, to protect these people."

"Then those Mexicans would be your enemies, which makes them evil."

Soldado shook his head. "If the *Nakai-Ye* were my enemy, I would ride with Victorio and Nana."

"I see," said Lane, plainly dubious. "Such distinctions are so fine that I must confess they are lost on me. But obviously, you are sincere in what you say. Unfortunately, I cannot accept it."

"I do not have to accept the ways of the white man, and you do not have to accept the ways of the Apache. But we must try to live together. If we do not, the killing will go on."

Lane sighed. "I see your point. But I am afraid you may be naive in your idealism. It could be resolved in another way. All the Apaches could perish, or be subjugated. Then my people would not have to learn to live with others whose ways we do not understand or accept. In the past we've not been very good at that sort of thing, anyway. I hope it doesn't end like that, but you have to admit that it's possible."

* * *

Several days later, as they neared the border, Lane was very surprised to see Clancy St. John appear out of the heat shimmer. Clearly the Irishman had been many days on a hard trail. His horse was lathered and weary, and Clancy himself was dusty, gaunt, and bearded. He looked like a man who hadn't slept in a week.

"What in God's name are you doing here?" asked Lane.

"I've come to warn you, Lieutenant. Buckshot Reilly and twenty scalp hunters are waiting in ambush about a mile north of here."

"Scalp hunters?"

Clancy nodded. "I've trailed Reilly and his outfit all the way from Tucson. They want these women and children, and they're willing to go through you and your soldiers to get them."

"I find it hard to believe they would dare attack troops of the United States."

"I'm just giving you the facts," said Clancy, exasperated. "You can believe what you want." He threw a quick look around. "Is Najita your only scout?"

"No. Wait a minute—how did you know Najita was with me?"

"Because I just saw him less than an hour ago, in Reilly's camp. He's in with the scalp hunters, Lieutenant, thick as thieves."

26

"Way I see it," said Clancy, "Buckshot Reilly will send in a few men to shoot up your column. Then they'll ride like the devil's clinging to their coattails. Reilly will be hoping you'll send most of your men after them. If you do, he'll hit you with the rest of his crew."

Lane shook his head. "I still can scarcely believe he would attack the United States Army . . . "

"Do you think that blue uniform makes something special out of you and your men, Lieutenant? Reilly figures on collecting two thousand pesos a scalp. That's a lot of money over yonder." Clancy nodded in the direction of the Apaches.

Lane bristled. "What do you suggest we do, Mr. St. John?"

Clancy laughed. "Well, I'll be. A West Point man asking me for advice? Maybe there's hope for you yet, son. How many men with you? Twenty-five? Thirty?"

"Twenty-eight, with two scouts. Well, one, now."

"Who's the other, besides Najita?"

"Soldado."

"I'll be damned. Where is he?"

"He rode off to the southeast a couple of hours ago. We saw some dust, and he went to investigate. Thought it might be some Mexicans."

"Mexicans are the least of your worries now. Well, at least he'll be safely out of the ruckus. Though you couldn't ask for better to watch your back. Okay, Lieutenant, this is what we'll do . . . "

It happened just as Clancy supposed it would.

A mile further on, four men appeared suddenly out of a dry wash and sent a flurry of shots into the column. One of the buffalo soldiers, a sergeant, went down with his dying horse. The Apache women dragged their children from the backs of the mules they were riding and carried them to the ground, to shelter the little ones with their own bodies. Before any of the buffalo soldiers could get off a shot, the four scalp hunters were galloping away on fleet ponies, throwing some lead over their shoulders. One uttered a taunting rebel yell.

Clancy was the first to reach the sergeant. The non-com's horse was dead. The sergeant was on his feet, ruefully trying to reshape his crushed campaign hat.

"You hurt?" snapped Clancy.

"Nope. But I'm madder'n hell. Doan relish walkin' the rest of the way to Fort Bowie, suh."

"You might not have to. A dead scalp hunter has no need of his horse."

The sergeant grinned. "See your point."

Lane arrived as the sergeant was stripping his saddle from the dead horse.

"Sergeant, you and ten men will remain with the Apaches. I will take the rest and pursue those fellows. I recommend that you take Mr. St. John's orders in every particular, if he has any to give while I'm absent."

"Yessuh, Lieutenant. Bring me back a hoss, if you can."

Lane smiled. "I'll do my best, sergeant." He glanced at Clancy and nodded. Then he turned his horse sharply to

call out orders to the other men. In short order he and seventeen of the Ninth Cavalry's finest were in hot pursuit of
the four scalp hunters.

"You got any advice?" asked the sergeant.

"Matter of fact, I do," replied Clancy cheerfully. "We
need to get these people down into that dry wash, pronto."

Squinty-eyed, the sergeant cocked his head to one
side. "You and the lieutenant are cookin' sumpin' up, ain't
you?"

"Let's just hope it works."

Clancy steered his horse in among the Apaches.
Speaking their language, he instructed them to seek refuge
in the dry wash where the scalp hunters had been concealed
only moments before. As the Apaches moved in that direction, herded by the remaining buffalo soldiers, Clancy
scanned the malpais. To the north, in the direction of a low
rise, a cloud of dust plumed above the desert flats. *Here
comes Buckshot and his murdering scum,* mused Clancy grimly.

When he was certain that all the Apaches were down
in the wash, Clancy rode down to join them. Dismounting,
he drew the Henry repeater from its saddle boot and
turned to the sergeant.

"Guess you'd like to know what's going on," he said.

"I'd be obliged, Mr. St. John. I surely would."

"About twenty scalp hunters are going to be here
before you know it. They aim to murder these women and
children and collect from the Mexican government for
their scalps."

"Over my cold dead body, suh."

"That's their plan. Thing is, they don't know that we
know they're coming."

"We'll give them a right warm welcome."

Clancy nodded. These buffalo soldiers struck him as a
tough bunch. Good men to tie to in a scrape.

"Post a man at either end of the wash," he told the
sergeant. "They can hold our horses and keep the Apaches
from scattering, too."

He walked through the crowd of Apaches, telling
them to keep their heads down and to stay together, no

matter what happened. Then he climbed to the rim of the wash. The sergeant and his troopers joined him, spreading out on either side of him along the rim. Already they could hear the thunder of hard-running horses.

They didn't have long to wait. Moments later the scalp hunters appeared, riding hell-for-leather straight towards the dry wash. Clancy spotted Buckshot Reilly in the lead. He rose up with the rifle to his shoulder and fired. He missed Reilly and hit the horse instead. The horse went down, head over heels, and Reilly sailed through the air. The buffalo soldiers started shooting. The crackling volley of Sharps carbines plucked several scalp hunters from their saddles. The rest scattered to left and right, returning fire. The trooper to Clancy's right cried out. Clutching his chest, he toppled backwards, rolling down the bank of the dry wash to sprawl dead at the bottom. Clancy fired the Henry repeater as fast as he could work the action. A scalp hunter steered his horse to the very edge of the wash through a hail of hot lead and shot at the trooper at point-blank range. Clancy picked him off with the last bullet in the repeater. Throwing the Henry aside, Clancy drew his Dance revolver and searched for more targets in the swirling dust and powder smoke.

Some of the scalp hunters had dismounted. From the cover of the desert scrub they answered the fire of the buffalo soldiers with telling effect. In a matter of minutes half the cavalrymen were dead or wounded. Clancy could sense the tide of battle swiftly turning against him and the Ninth Cavalry. To a man Reilly's cutthroats knew how to shoot. They had all cut their teeth on a gun barrel. *If Lane doesn't get here quick, it will be too bloody late . . .*

Even as this grim thought crossed his mind, he saw Lane and the rest of the detachment sweeping in from the south, flanking the scalp hunters, flushing out those concealed in the clumps of saltbush and ocotillo. Guns blazing, they accounted for five or six of Buckshot Reilly's crew. The rest of the scalp hunters gave up the fight and scattered.

Sliding down to the bottom of the wash, Clancy

reloaded his pistol and long gun, then decided to break one of his rules and build a smoke. His hands were steady, but his nerves were shot to hell. It had been a close-run thing.

Lane checked his horse and looked down at the scout.

"Are you okay, Mr. St. John?"

"I've just made up my mind that I'm too damned old for this kind of work."

Lane smiled faintly and rode on.

After indulging in the roll-your-own, Clancy climbed wearily out of the dry wash and prowled through the scrub, checking among the dead scalp hunters. He did not find what he had hoped to. Apparently, Buckshot Reilly had escaped. That came close to ruining Clancy's day. Neither was there any sign of Najita, the Apache traitor.

An hour later, Soldado arrived. He was surprised to see Clancy. As for Clancy, he didn't realize how much he had missed the Chihenne until he saw him again.

Lane moved a few miles north of the dry wash before stopping for the night. Sitting around the cherry flicker of a small campfire with Soldado put Clancy in a nostalgic mood. He thought fondly of the old days, when he and Soldado had popped wild cattle out of the brush, or sat outside the adobe with Luis in the purple twilight while, inside, Maria sang *"Pajarito Barranqueno"* or some other little ballad as she cooked. She'd had a sweet voice. Clancy missed those times. It wasn't that he was unhappy in Tucson with Laura and the girls. Far from it. But Soldado was like a son to him, and his life was not as complete as it had seemed back in the good old days. Of course, he shared none of this with Soldado. In fact, they did not say very much at all to one another. It was enough to share a campfire, and take pleasure in the other's company.

Lane came by to inform Clancy that one of the four buffalo soldiers wounded in the scrape with Reilly's hardcases would not live out the night.

"I'm truly sorry to hear that," said the scout. "They are damn fine soldiers, Lieutenant. Did anyone see any sign of Najita?"

Lane said no. "You saved many lives today, Mr. St. John. Not a single Apache came to harm."

"Well, that's something. I don't think Reilly will try to tangle with you again, so in the morning I'm heading back to Tucson. I didn't know I could miss that shop so much. Reckon from now on I will leave the fighting to younger men. Today was my last hurrah."

Lane nodded. "That's good, because I would hate to see Mrs. St. John widowed a second time."

"When you get the chance, come pay us a visit, Lieutenant. I know a certain young lady who has a strong hankering to see you again."

Lane actually blushed. "I'll do that, thank you."

Clancy glanced at Soldado. "And you know my door is always open to you."

"I know, *dagotai.*"

Clancy's heart swelled with pride.

It was the first time Soldado had called him father.

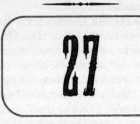

27

His name was Nochedelklinne, but he was better known among all the Apaches as "The Dreamer." He was a medicine man, and in the summer of 1881 he began to preach a vision, and teach the Apaches a special dance. In this dance, men and women performed a slow, solemn step in rows, like spokes on a wheel, around The Dreamer who stood in the center and sprinkled the dancers with *hoddentin*, a powder made from tule and possessed of magical powers.

The Dreamer claimed that in his vision he saw all the *Pinda Lickoyi* depart *Apacheria*. When this came to pass, the great chiefs now dead—Mangas Colorado, Cochise, Victorio—would come back to life. One night, Juh and Geronimo attended The Dreamer's meeting. In the half-light before dawn, The Dreamer climbed to the top of a hill and, chanting, lifted his arms to the heavens. At that moment those who watched from the bottom of the hill saw the ghostly forms of Mangas, Colorado, Cochise, and Victorio rise slowly from the earth at the crest of the hill where The Dreamer stood. Then, just as slowly, they sank back down into the ground. From that night onward,

Geronimo firmly believed in The Dreamer. So did a quickly growing number of Apaches.

The whites at the San Carlos agency and nearby Fort Bowie became alarmed at the size of The Dreamer's following. The San Carlos Indian agent frantically requested additional troops, believing that the medicine man was sowing the seeds of revolt. Ten years earlier, among the Paiutes, a "ghost dance" had presaged an outbreak of violence.

But the San Carlos agent and others like him completely misunderstood The Dreamer's message. According to the medicine man, the Apaches did not need to take up arms against the White Eyes. In fact, the Apaches did not have to lift a finger. Ussen would see to it that all the whites left *Apacheria*.

Near the end of the summer of 1881 The Dreamer held several dances at Cibecue Creek, a day's ride north of the San Carlos agency. A few days later a contingent from Fort Bowie arrived on the scene. Eighty soldiers and twenty Apache scouts commanded by Colonel Eugene Carr had come to arrest Nochedelklinne. A dozen Apache warriors surrounded The Dreamer, prepared to fight, for they were afraid of what might happen to the medicine man while he remained in army custody. Who could forget the fate that had befallen Mangas Colorado, shot to death and then decapitated by his yellowleg captors? But The Dreamer just smiled and assured Colonel Carr he would go peaceably.

Escorting their prisoner, Carr and his men rode south along Cibecue Creek. They soon discovered that a large group of Apache warriors were shadowing them. The Apaches made no hostile moves, but their presence frayed the nerves of Carr's troopers. Finally, a captain steered his horse across the creek. He rode straight at the Apaches and yelled at them, ordering them to go away. The Apaches did not go. Suddenly a shot rang out. It was never clear whether an Apache or a soldier fired that first shot. But both sides proceeded to sling lead across Cibecue Creek. The captain who had brashly confronted the Apaches was one of the first to die. Colonel Carr rode up to the detail assigned to guard The Dreamer.

"Kill the medicine man!" he snapped.

Nochedelklinne was promptly gunned down, his body riddled with bullets.

Carr's troubles were just beginning. Many of his Apache scouts abruptly deserted, and some even joined the other Apaches to fight the soldiers. A few of the troopers later swore they recognized Lozen, the famous woman warrior and Victorio's sister, who had somehow escaped Tres Castillos. They said it was she who rode brazenly through Carr's lines and drove off many of the soldiers' horses.

The fight raged until sundown. Then the Apaches melted away under cover of night, taking their dead and wounded with them. Colonel Carr lost seven men and fifty horses. His own horse had been killed under him. He and his command limped back to Fort Bowie.

"The flamin' idiots," muttered Clancy St. John. "You'd think the army would have learned its lesson after hanging John Brown after that business at Harper's Ferry."

Lane nodded. "They made a martyr out of that medicine man. God knows what will come of what happened at Cibecue Creek."

"Soldado—was he there?"

"No. In fact, no one has seen him for months. I think he's in Mexico, looking for Najita and those scalp hunters. So far I don't think he's had any luck."

"I wouldn't give a plugged nickel for Najita's chances of surviving the year."

"The problem is, Soldado has been listed as a deserter. It's Cibecue Creek again. When those scouts went over to the other side, I'm afraid they've turned everyone against this experiment of using Apaches for scouting. They captured and convicted five of the scouts who were with Colonel Carr. Sent two of them off to Alcatraz with life sentences."

"Life sentences?" Clancy grunted. "Locking an Apache up in a cell is a death sentence, Lieutenant."

"Three others are being held at Fort Grant, destined for the gallows."

"Damn. Who are they, do you know?"

"Dead Shot, Skitashe, and the one called Dandy Jim. If you want my opinion, sir, what happened just proves what I've suspected all along. An Apache can't be trusted."

"And that remark just proves that you aren't as smart as I thought you were."

Lane stiffened, but a sharp retort died stillborn on his tongue. He had come all this way to visit the St. Johns. More specifically, to see Faith again. This was his first furlough since arriving in the Southwest Military District, a ten-day leave, and he didn't want to ruin it by getting into an argument with Clancy over the merits of Apache scouts.

Faith's letters had made him aware that Clancy had sold his Tucson gun shop and bought a small spread east of town. Figuring that Victorio's death at Tres Castillos had pretty much finished the Apache Wars, the aging Irishman had deemed it safe enough to move his family out of Tucson so that he could pursue the life he preferred to gunsmithing. Hiring several *vaqueros* to help him, he had built a comfortable adobe house near a year-round spring, and flushed a couple hundred head of wild cattle out of the scrub to start up a herd, marking them with his shamrock brand.

Having just eaten dinner, Lane and Clancy were sitting on the porch, enjoying the cool autumn night. Over in the small bunkhouse one of the Mexicans was strumming a guitar. Inside the house, Faith and Charity were helping their mother clean up. Lane thought, *I'd much rather be sitting here with Faith*. But Clancy had wanted to know all the details about Cibecue Creek.

"Well," said Lane, "I can only speak from experience regarding the reliability of Apache scouts. Najita's treachery might have cost me my life, and the lives of my troops."

"Not to mention the lives of seventy-five Apache women and children."

"Yes, of course."

"Why do you think Soldado is trying to track Najita down?"

"I predict the Apache scouts will be disbanded."

"That's the army's loss," replied Clancy bluntly, flicking his spent cigarette away and watching the orange spray of embers on the hardpack. "The killing of The Dreamer will result in many more deaths. Mark my words, Lieutenant. Before the month is out, Geronimo will jump the reservation, and a lot of *bronchos* will ride with him, and the whole bloody business will start all over again."

"Geronimo?" Lane shook his head. "He's all washed up. Last few years he's been content to sit at San Carlos and get fat on government beef."

Clancy laughed. "I've yet to see an Apache get enough government beef to get fat on."

Faith appeared on the porch. As far as Lane was concerned, her smile illuminated the night. He shot to his feet.

"Miss St. John, would you care to sit down?"

"Actually, I was thinking of taking an evening stroll. Would you care to accompany me, Lieutenant?" Her eyes sparkled. "Father, is it all right with you if we walk down to the spring?"

"You think you'll be safe?" asked Clancy.

"Oh, you know perfectly well there aren't any bad Apaches within a hundred miles of here."

"It's not Apaches I'm worried about," said Clancy, smiling wryly as he glanced at Lane.

"Fiddlesticks," said Faith. Taking Lane by the arm, she led him off the porch. "Hudson is the perfect gentleman—aren't you, Hudson?"

"Well, I . . ."

But Faith was walking him briskly away from the house, rendering pointless any weak assurances Lane might have made to a skeptical Clancy St. John.

They walked past the corral and the bunkhouse, to the trees and big rocks that marked the location of the sweet-water spring. Lane didn't say anything. His tongue was tied in a knot. Faith walked very close at his side, so that occasionally her hip and breast brushed against him, igniting a fire of passion in Lane that he knew was ill-advised. And yet he was powerless against it, so that when they reached the spring, and the trees closed ranks to conceal them from the house, Lane took Faith in his arms and kissed her. She let him, but only for an instant, and then pushed him away.

"Really, Lieutenant Lane," she said, breathlessly feigning shock. "You know what Father would do to you if he knew you took such liberties."

"Yes, I know. He would rip my head off with his bare hands. But I don't care."

"I care. How would you become a famous general if my father ripped your head off?"

"A general?" Lane laughed. "I'll be lucky to make captain before it's time for me to retire."

She pouted. "I would much prefer to be married to a general than a captain."

"Well, I . . . married?" Lane's heart flip-flopped in his chest. "Would you really marry me, Faith?"

She smiled and coyly lifted a shoulder. "Perhaps. But I'm only eighteen, and my mother wouldn't dream of letting me marry right now. In a year or two I might marry you, Hudson. But you will have to be at least a major by then."

"If you'll give me a kiss every now and then, I might be motivated to try," he said.

She draped her slender arms around his neck, and as she kissed him, she pressed the full length of her body against his.

Coming up for air, Lane gasped, "I love you, Faith."

"Mmm," she said, and kissed him again.

Up at the house, Clancy was rising to go inside when out of the corner of an eye he caught movement in the deepening shadows of the night. Whirling, he saw Soldado emerge from the darkness at the end of the porch. The Apache wore breechcloth, leggings, and desert moccasins. A blue kerchief was tied around his head. There was an Army Colt in the gun belt strapped to his waist. He carried the Winchester 73 in one hand and a gunnysack in the other.

"Soldado!" breathed Clancy. "Dammit, son, you took ten years off my life. And at my age I can't afford ten years. I mistook you for a Wild One, sneaking around like that."

The ghost of a smile just barely touched Soldado's gaunt, bronze face.

"Come inside," said Clancy. "Laura would love to see you again. Not to mention Charity. It's been—how many years since you've seen them?"

Soldado shook his head. "I cannot."

"Lieutenant Lane is here, too. He told me you'd been listed as a deserter. But I don't think he would try to turn you in. For one thing, I wouldn't let him."

"No. I go back to Mexico. I come to warn you, *dago-tai*."

"Warn me? About what?"

"Reilly. He say he kill you."

"Where is that son of a bitch?"

"I do not know."

"Where did you hear this?"

"Najita."

"You found him, then."

"Yes. He tell me. Before he die."

Soldado opened the gunnysack and pulled something out—Clancy couldn't see what it was, at first, and stepped closer. When he realized that Soldado was holding Najita's head, his fingers tangled in the matted hair, Clancy's blood ran cold.

"Mother of God," he gasped.

Soldado's eyes glittered with a cold and fierce flame.

"I take this to San Carlos. A warning to all who would betray their own people for gold."

"Some Apaches might say you betrayed your people by scouting for the army, Soldado."

"I know what they say."

"Be careful, son. Bad things have happened while you've been away. They've hanged some Apache Scouts. Dead Shot and a couple of the others. And soldiers killed

The Dreamer up on Cibecue Creek. God only knows what will happen next."

Soldado nodded gravely. He put Najita's head back in the gunnysack. "I go," he said. "*Yadalanh, dagotai.*"

"*Yadalanh.*"

Soldado vanished like a wraith into the night.

As Clancy walked inside, Laura took one look at him and asked, "What's wrong, dear? You look like you've seen a ghost."

"It was Soldado."

Charity was sitting at the table—in a heartbeat she was on her feet and bolting out the door. She called out Soldado's name, ran a little ways out from the house, and called again. Faintly she heard a horse at the gallop. The sound quickly faded away.

Stepping out onto the porch, Clancy called her back. He was surprised to see tears on her cheeks.

"He could have at least said hello," she sobbed, as she stormed past him to go inside.

28

A few days after Soldado's nocturnal visit, one of the *vaqueros,* who had been to Tucson on a piece of business for Clancy, rode hell-for-leather into the ranch yard to announce that Geronimo had jumped the San Carlos reservation.

He had heard the news in town. Juh had gone with Geronimo, and Naiche, the son of Cochise. At least two hundred men, women, and children had followed, some of them Nednhi, and quite a few Chokonen. Naiche was chief of the Chokonen now that his brother Taza was dead. Although Naiche and Juh were legitimate chiefs of their respective bands, everyone knew that Geronimo, who had not been born chief of any band, was the leader of the renegades. The Chiricahua knew that in times of trouble he was the most resourceful, the most cunning.

Apparently it was the arrival of several companies of soldiers at the reservation, on the day when the Apaches were to collect their rations, that had triggered the breakout. Increased activity by the army following the incident at Cibecue Creek alarmed the Apaches. Wild rumors abounded. It was said that all the Apaches were going to be shipped off to prison in chains. Or that the whites were planning to hang a hundred Apaches in retribution for the deaths of Colonel Carr's soldiers. The appearance of so many grim yellowlegs on rations day had convinced Geronimo that it was time to run. He had been one of The Dreamer's adherents. And, too, he had been at Cibecue Creek.

Clancy deduced that, as with all such news, one had to account for exaggeration, and he told Hudson Lane that he doubted if even a hundred people had followed Geronimo out of San Carlos.

"The actual number matters little," said Lane. "Even if Geronimo was alone, there'll be full-scale panic among the civilians. Which means a flying column in pursuit and every fort in the district sending out patrols. And *that* means all leaves will be canceled. I'd better be getting back."

He cursed his luck. The past few days had been the most wonderful and exciting in his life. Since childhood he had dreamed of becoming a soldier, and single-mindedly spent every waking hour since long before his admission to West Point in that pursuit. But suddenly the life of a soldier had lost its allure. He wanted to stay with Faith, to be with her always. Leaving her wrenched at his heart.

On the other hand, Faith did not seem at all heartbroken about his departure.

"I would have thought you'd be sorry to see me go," he told her, when they had a few precious moments alone.

"Oh, Hudson, don't pout. It's so unbecoming. Of course, I'll miss you terribly. But don't you see? Thanks to Geronimo you will have an opportunity to do something so heroic that they'll just have to promote you."

Lane grimaced. "Faith, darling, I was on the campaign against Victorio, and I assure you there is nothing even remotely heroic about it. If the Ninth Cavalry is involved, it will just mean that I will be in the field for weeks, maybe even months, with no hope of seeing you until it is all over and, in all likelihood, little chance of even getting a letter from you."

"Don't fret, Hudson, darling. I'll be waiting here for you." She gave him a lingering kiss, full of passion and promise.

She had told him not to tell Clancy or her mother about their romantic plans for the future, and he had promised not to, but, as he said his good-byes to Clancy and the whole family on the porch, he impulsively forgot the promise and said, "Mr. St. John, I have a feeling you don't really like me, but I must tell you I intend to marry your daughter."

All eyes swung to Faith. Recovering from her shock, she cried, "Hudson! How could you!" and fled into the house, leaving an uncomfortable silence in her wake.

Then Laura, with flawless cordiality, said, "Hudson, we've enjoyed your visit. Please do come again." She followed Faith inside.

Lane was horrified. What had he done? He couldn't bear to leave Faith so upset with him. But Clancy St. John was standing there like a big, scowling, red-headed bear, and Lane didn't give much for his chances of getting past the Irishman if Clancy didn't want him to.

"I apologize, sir," said Lane stiffly, bracing for the storm. "I know this must come as a shock to you."

"You could say that."

"But Faith and I love each other. We want to be married."

He thought he recognized pity on Clancy's craggy features.

"Lieutenant, I love both those girls something fierce. But Faith and Charity are as different from one another as two people can be. Faith is eighteen, and headstrong, and I've never been able to keep her from doing whatever she wants to do. So I probably couldn't stop the two of you from getting hitched."

"No, sir. You could not."

Clancy smiled. "Never let it be said that Clancy St. John stood in the way of true love. Problem is, Faith is too young to know what she really wants. I've seen her desire something so bad one day I thought she would die from not having it. But then the next day dawns and she is wanting something else entirely."

Lane darkened. "If you're trying to tell me Faith isn't really in love . . . "

"I'm trying to tell you that I would take things real slow and easy, if I were you. Marriage isn't something you should rush into. I know it's hard to keep your wits about you when you're head over heels in love, but I suggest you try. I'd hate to see either one of you young people get hurt."

Clancy's patronizing tone of voice served only to irritate Lane. His movements quick with anger, he turned to his horse and swung into the saddle.

"Faith is going to be my bride, sir, and that's all there is to it."

Before Clancy could respond, Lane pulled sharply on the reins to spin his horse around and kicked it into a canter.

Clancy shook his head as he watched Lane go. The lieutenant was dead wrong. He did like the young man— though he wasn't quite sure why that was so. And it was Lane who stood to be hurt most. Clancy loved Faith, but he knew her for what she was—a flighty and flirtatious girl who would break many a man's heart before she was done. God only knew why she had turned out that way. He wasn't surprised that a dashing young officer like Hudson Lane had caught her fancy. There wasn't much to choose from in these parts. But it was infatuation, not love. Of that Clancy was certain.

Now, the feelings Charity had for Soldado—that was a horse of an entirely different color. This had sure been a week of surprises. Biggest surprise of all was finding out that sixteen-year-old Charity loved Soldado. Clancy wondered how that could have happened. A few years ago Charity had been a little girl sitting on Soldado's knee. Since those days at Fort Union she had seen very little of the Chihenne Apache. Yet there could be no denying the way she felt. Unlike Faith, Charity had always been a very level-headed child who knew her own mind. But she was such a tomboy that Clancy hadn't given a moment's thought to the possibility that she might succumb to a young woman's passions. Thing about Charity was that once she set her mind to having something, wild horses wouldn't drag her off the course she had set.

Just as Clancy was sure Lane's relationship with Faith would end up in heartbreak, he believed the same to be true for Charity and Soldado, though for different reasons. For one thing, Soldado had changed, and Clancy didn't think it was for the better. Not that Clancy blamed Soldado. No, he blamed himself, mostly. Soldado was a man trapped in a limbo between two worlds, that of the Apache and of the white man, and he did not fit into either. Clancy wondered if he had been wrong to take Soldado away from his own people. He had simply wanted to make certain that little Kayitah had a chance to live. But what kind of life did Soldado have now? He was an outsider. And it was beginning to show.

Colonel Joe Warren had been right. Warren had told Clancy that, in his opinion, Clancy had taken the Apache youth into his home to assuage his own guilty conscience. *I was guilty*, mused the Irishman. *As guilty as Ezra Bascom and his soldier boys for the Warm Springs massacre.* And now, because of what had become of Soldado, he suffered even more guilt.

I should have left him. Might have been better had he died beneath a cavalryman's saber.

29

For a week following Soldado's clandestine visit, Clancy worried about Buckshot Reilly. He didn't doubt for a moment the veracity of Soldado's information. Reilly was the type who would seek vengeance. Clancy had cost him a lot of money by warning Lane's buffalo soldiers in time to save the women and children from Victorio's band. Reilly would seek payment in blood.

With a man like Reilly, Laura and the girls were fair game, too. Laura was a courageous woman, and a fair shot with a long gun, and Clancy knew she would insist on standing at his side, come what may. He recognized as well that it was only fair that she know the danger that she and her daughters were in. On the other hand, he did not want to alarm them. It was his job to protect his family from the evils of the world. He had failed once in that respect. He could not, would not, fail this time.

Until he could decide how best to do that, Clancy kept Laura in the dark. He tried to act as though nothing was out of the ordinary. He and his *vaqueros* went about their work well-heeled as a matter of course; a gun was as much a tool of the cowboy's trade as a length of hard twist and a branding iron. Apart from diamondbacks and javelinas and other dangerous critters, there were two-legged varmints to look out for. The territories had become chockfull of outlaws since the war.

After Lane's departure, Clancy went about his business, but he always contrived to keep at least one *vaquero* near the main house, or stayed close to home himself. There was plenty of work to do near at hand. For a while no one suspected that anything was amiss. Clancy carried the burden alone. It proved to be a tremendous ordeal. He got edgy, jumping at shadows, and before long he was wishing Buckshot Reilly would just come on ahead and get it over with. Waiting was definitely the hardest part. And patience had never been Clancy St. John's long suit.

He couldn't help but wonder how Reilly would go about trying to kill him. Likely the scalp hunter would bring along a few friends. Reilly wasn't the type to call a fellow out and face him down, *mano a mano*. No, he'd bring some help. Maybe two or three men, but not more than that. To round up twenty cutthroats just to deal with one man would reflect poorly on Reilly, and might cause some folks to question his backbone. A few extra gun hands along to handle the *vaqueros*—that was what Reilly would have in mind. And when he struck it would be sudden, an ambuscade. That was Reilly's way. He knew no other. Hit and run, like an Apache. Reilly had learned guerrilla tactics in Missouri during the late, unlamented war; as a young man he had ridden with the likes of Bloody Bill Anderson.

The days turned into weeks, dragging by. Laura began to sense that something was wrong. Clancy had known all along he would not be able to keep the truth from her forever. He didn't sleep well, or eat well, either, and he was as nervous as a long-tailed cat in a room full of rocking chairs. Worse still, Clancy had a contract to deliver a hundred head of cattle to a nearby army outpost. That would require that he absent himself from home for at least two days. He would need both *vaqueros* to handle that many beeves, and he couldn't leave Laura and the girls to their own devices for forty-eight hours.

Finally, one night after dinner, when the girls had gone to bed, he told Laura that he wanted them to stay in Tucson while he was away. Laura had friends in town. She could visit them, and be welcome. Faith could pick out that new dress he had promised to buy her with the proceeds from the sale of the cattle. He rattled on, prolonging the inevitable, because he could read Laura like a book, and knew right off she wasn't buying it.

When he ran out of breath, she cocked her head to one side and said, "So now why don't you tell me the truth, Clancy?"

He sighed. "It's Buckshot Reilly."

"The scalp hunter? What about him? What has he done now?"

"It's what he is planning to do. He wants my hide. Blames me for costing him all that bounty money. Soldado told me, the night he came by. If Soldado says it's so, I reckon it is."

"Yes." Brows knit, Laura pondered the news, then reached across the table and put her hand over Clancy's. "You must go to Tucson and tell the sheriff."

"This is my problem, Laura."

"Oh, don't be so mule-headed! Pride goeth before the fall, Clancy St. John. When will you learn there is no shame in asking others for help."

"What can the law do? Lock Reilly up?"

"Why not?"

"Because that won't solve the problem. They can't keep him behind bars forever. And when he got out—no matter how long it took—he'd come looking for me. This won't be finished until one of us is dead."

"I wish you hadn't gotten involved in his business in the first place," said Laura, distraught.

Clancy bristled. "I don't regret that, not for one minute. Reilly and his bunch wanted to murder seventy-five women and children, Laura."

"I'm sorry. You're right. Clancy, let's leave this place. Let's go far, far away. So far away that Buckshot Reilly will never find us."

"Go? Where?"

"I don't know and I don't care. As long as we have each other, we'll make do."

"But this is our home, Laura."

"We'll build a new home. We can do it. There is nothing, really, holding us here. Nothing we can't have somewhere else."

"I don't want a new home."

"Is it . . . Soldado?"

Clancy shook his head sadly. "No. Somewhere along the line I lost him. This has nothing to do with Soldado. I just won't run. Running away from problems is no solution. Besides, you never can tell with Buckshot Reilly. If he's got it in his head to see me six feet under then he'll follow us to the ends of the earth to get the job done. I don't fancy living the rest of my life looking over my shoulder. I'm sorry, Laura. This is the way it has to be. Tomorrow I'll take you and the girls into town. Then I'll drive those cattle to the fort and come back here and wait for Reilly to show his ugly face. You must promise me that you will stay in Tucson until I come for you. Shouldn't take all that long for him to make his play."

Laura was afraid for him, but she put on a brave face. "Will the *vaqueros* stay with you?"

"I'll leave that up to them. They have a right to know what they'll be up against, don't you think? But, given the choice, I believe they will stick."

"But you'll send them away, too," said Laura, in a small voice. "You know you will. Because they're just boys, really, and this isn't their fight, either. You'll face Reilly all alone. And like as not get yourself killed. I wish . . . "

"Yes?"

"I wish Soldado was here. You wouldn't send him away. You couldn't. He wouldn't go. You say you've lost him, but I know Soldado would die for you, Clancy."

Clancy squeezed her hand. "You'd better get some rest, dear. We leave at first light."

30

Geronimo and Juh and their followers made for Mexico. Juh was the leader of the Nednhi band of the Chiricahua Apache, and his home was the Sierra Madre. He had convinced Geronimo that the mountains would be the only place they could find safe haven.

They traveled fast, hounded by several companies of United States cavalry. Their path took them near the town of Tombstone. John Clum lived there now. He formed a posse of thirty-five men, including the Earp brothers—Wyatt, Morgan, and Virgil. Clum told his fellow vigilantes that they must give no quarter. This time, declared the erstwhile Indian agent, he would deliver Geronimo in a wooden box, with a paper lily on his chest. Clum was immensely proud of the fact that he had captured Geronimo once before, and he was confident he could do so again.

But Clum and his men never saw a single Apache.

The cavalry's flying columns fared little better, engaging in a few skirmishes with small groups of *bronchos* that Geronimo dispatched to slow the yellowlegs down.

The Apaches killed every Anglo and Mexican in their

path. They stole horses, guns, and ammunition. That autumn was marked by unusually heavy rainstorms, but the bad weather did not seem to slow the renegades. Crossing the border, they bloodied a force of *rurales* before dashing to safety in the Sierra Madre.

In the northern portion of the mountain range was Juh's Stronghold, a place the Apaches called Pahgotzinkay. The Indians believed this natural fortress was protected by mystical powers that would not permit any *Nakai-Ye* or *Pinda Lickoyi* to ever set foot upon it. This was a high plateau accessed by a single narrow trail zigzagging up a sheer cliff. The Nednhi put great faith in these mystical powers, but that hadn't prevented them from taking additional precautions. Boulders were rigged so that they could be rolled down upon the trail. Once, Mexican troops had tried to ascend the trail to storm the Stronghold. Their bones still littered the canyon floor.

The plateau offered numerous streams, abundant game, plenty of graze for the horses, and stands of towering pine trees. Here, said Juh, with confidence, they could live forever free and in peace.

They were soon joined by old Nana and the handful of survivors of Tres Castillos, who had somehow managed to remain at large since that disaster. Lozen, the woman warrior, sister of the great Victorio, also arrived at the Stronghold. Now there were nearly two hundred warriors in the band, and as many women and children. Never since the glory days of Cochise had the renegades been so strong. They were Nednhi, Chihenne, a few Chokonen, and Bedonkohe—all Chiricahua Apache.

Nana and the others were weary of war. They were quite content to remain in the Stronghold and leave their enemies alone. Not Geronimo. Even in the winter months, Geronimo led daring raids against nearby Mexican villages. He could never forgive the *Nakai-Ye* for the Janos massacre, in which his wife and child had been murdered. Cochise had sworn he would kill a hundred *indah* for each of his family slain; Geronimo put no such limits on his own brand of relentless vengeance.

The United States Army decided to wait until late spring to launch a campaign against Geronimo. But the Bedonkohe leader was the first to strike in the year 1882. While Nana stayed in the Stronghold to watch over the women and children, Geronimo rode north with Juh and Lozen and sixty *bronchos*. This time they stole no horses, killed no civilians. No one even knew the "Wild Ones" were north of the border until, as he drew near the San Carlos reservation, Geronimo cut the agency's telegraph line.

In San Carlos, several hundred Chihenne remained. Their *jefe* was named Loco. No one doubted Loco's courage. In his youth he had battled a grizzly bear and killed the fierce creature with only a knife, though not before the bear scarred Loco's face and made him a cripple for life. But that had been a long time ago. Loco was old now, and he was tired of the warpath. Besides, he knew resistance against the White Eyes was futile. He was content to remain on the reservation.

Geronimo was obsessed with the idea that Loco's Chihenne should join the Sierra Madre renegades. On a cool, clear April morning, he and his *bronchos* swept into Loco's *rancheria*. Geronimo's orders were that every last Chihenne was to be taken out. Those who would not or could not go were to be put to death.

As they departed San Carlos, Geronimo swung by the agency and gunned down a white employee there.

"Now you have no choice but to join us," Geronimo told Loco. "The *Pinda Lickoyi* will blame you and your people for the white man's death. You can never return to San Carlos."

A grim Loco knew that this was so. Geronimo had condemned his people to the renegade life.

The United States Army reacted swiftly. Finding his route south to the border blocked by yellowleg patrols, Geronimo swung east. Among Loco's people were a great many women and children; they suffered terribly from the arduous pace Geronimo maintained. Geronimo showed no sympathy for them, threatening to kill anyone who fell behind or slowed the others down.

To feed the Chihenne, Geronimo attacked the ranch of a white sheepherder. The white man was away, having left the ranch in the hands of his Mexican foreman. The foreman and some of his workers had wives and families living on the ranch. The women were forced to cook a meal for the renegades. Geronimo promised the foreman that he would harm no one, as long as they cooperated. But later he changed his mind. Some of the *bronchos* who rode with him tried to talk him out of the murder he contemplated. Geronimo would not listen to their entreaties. All the Mexican sheepherders, their wives, and their children were bound and then methodically butchered.

A few days later a ranch near Tombstone was attacked. Three white men were killed. A small child was taken up by the ankles and slammed into the side of the house until his brains were splattered all over the whitewashed adobe. A sixteen-year-old girl was taken captive. Her body was later discovered. Several *bronchos* had raped her, and then stabbed her to death with their knives.

Once across the border, Geronimo slowed the pace. For some reason he was confident the cavalry would not pursue him into Mexico. He was wrong. For once Geronimo was caught by surprise. His power to see events occurring many miles away failed to alert him to the presence of a column riding hard and closing fast. The running fight that followed lasted through the day. Many Chihenne were killed, most of them women and children. Only darkness saved the rest. Next morning, inexplicably, the soldiers turned north to recross the border. The Apaches breathed a sigh of relief.

Their ordeal was not over, however. The very next day they walked right into a trap laid by a large force of *federales*. Geronimo was inclined to leave the women and children to their fate, believing that he and his *bronchos* could escape while the *Nakai-Ye* were busy with their butchery. But Juh and Naiche and Lozen would not hear of it. Again the battle raged until sundown. Again the Apaches slipped away under cover of night. This time they left more than seventy dead.

Finally, Geronimo and the survivors reached the Stronghold.

The savage violence of Geronimo's breakout and subsequent raid stunned the American people, who had labored under the mistaken impression that the last of the Indian wars had been fought and that the western frontier had at long last been made safe. The army realized that of all their Apache adversaries—Mangas Colorado, Cochise, Victorio—Geronimo would prove to be the worst of the lot. Here was a man without honor, who cared nothing for the lives of others, not even those of his own people.

Duly alarmed, President Chester A. Arthur sent the only general who seemed capable of dealing with the likes of Geronimo. The Apaches called him *Nantan Lupan*— Chief Tan Wolf—because he preferred civilian khaki garb to his army uniform. And he still rode a mule named Apache rather than a horse.

In 1882, General George Crook returned to the Southwest Military District.

31

The first thing George Crook did upon arrival at Fort Stanton was pitch his tent a mile from the stockade, grab his English-made shotgun, and go hunting with his aide and personal Boswell, John Bourke. Bringing back several sage hens, he invited the officers of the garrison to join him for lunch. Assigned as aide to General Hatch, Hudson Lane had the great good fortune to be present. The meal was laid out on a table beneath an awning in front of Crook's tent.

"Gentlemen," said Crook, after all had finished eating, and the brandy and cigars had been passed around, "When I left this district seven years ago, I said I would be back. I knew then that the Apaches would be the last of the tribes to surrender to the inevitable. Back when President Grant sent me out here, his decision raised a storm of protest. Even Sherman opposed my appointment. The protest against me this time has been even louder. I'm told that nearly a hundred officers have petitioned the President. They say I am dishonest, and an imbecile. They claim my actions on the Rosebud were nothing short of disgraceful. Well, perhaps I am an imbecile, but I do not believe I am a dishonest person. I will always be candid with you gentlemen, sometimes brutally frank, and I expect to receive the same courtesy."

Lane reviewed in his mind what he knew about the Battle of the Rosebud. Ordered to support George Armstrong Custer in the campaign against the Sioux led so ably by Crazy Horse and Sitting Bull, Crook had been out-witted by the former Sioux leader a few days prior to Custer's debacle at the Little Bighorn. Though outnumbered three-to-one by the soldiers, the Sioux prevented Crook from uniting with Custer's Seventh Cavalry for the final confrontation which ended in such disaster for the United States. Crook steadfastly denied he had been whipped at the Rosebud. But, objectively, there could be no denying it. Still, Lane was not alone in considering Crook one of the best Indian fighters in the army. The Rosebud was his only defeat, the only blemish in a long and illustrious career. True, Crook was eccentric, but then the great ones often were.

"As a demonstration of the frankness which I have pledged," continued Crook, "I tell you here and now that after many years of dealing with numerous Indian tribes I have come to the conclusion that these frontier wars have been largely the consequence of our own deceit and incompetence. In other words, I think the Indians—and particularly the Apaches—have legitimate complaints against us. Had we treated them equitably from the outset, we could have avoided considerable bloodshed.

"The debacle at Cibecue Creek is a classic case. I intend to investigate the situation at the San Carlos agency which precipitated that fight. But I think I can tell you right now, gentlemen, what I will discover. I will find that government rations and medicines earmarked for the Apaches were sold to nearby mining camps, resulting in huge profits pocketed by corrupt traders and Indian agents. I will find that the few cattle the Apache actually do receive are so poor that you couldn't fry a skinny jackrabbit in the fat you'd get off one of them. Furthermore, I daresay I will find that if the Apaches had wanted to, they could have wiped out Colonel Carr's command, down to the last man. I will also find that this medicine man they called The Dreamer actually posed no threat."

Lane glanced around the table. He could sense that many of the officers present were not pleased that their new commander was obviously sympathetic to the enemy. Lane himself thought it was bad form for Crook to denigrate Carr and his soldiers, especially those who had lost their lives at Cibecue Creek.

"You're probably right, sir," said Hatch, "at least about the plight of the Apaches. I've held all along that the army ought to take over the administration of the reservations. Too many of the civilians affiliated with the Bureau of Indian Affairs are as crooked as a mule's hind leg or, at the very least, totally incompetent."

Crook nodded. "I agree. The army could do a much better job. But the politicians in Washington will never agree to it. I've never known them to voluntarily give up power."

"Since the general wants honesty," said another officer, "I believe an investigation at San Carlos to be a fruitless endeavor, and a waste of time. What's done is done. Our job is to defeat Geronimo. We should focus all our energy to that end."

"Indeed. There are approximately six hundred renegade Apaches with Juh and Geronimo in the Sierra Madre. Less than half that number are fighting men. Against that small force we can field—what? Five thousand troops?" Crook leaned forward with a wolfish smile. "But I say to you, gentlemen, do not underestimate these Apaches. We have as our foe the tiger of the human species."

"The problem," said Hatch, "is that by the terms of the Hot Trails Treaty we can only enter the Republic of Mexico if we are in the immediate pursuit of hostiles. And Geronimo is, by all accounts, having too much success wreaking havoc in Sonora and Chihuahua to bother crossing the border onto American soil. We almost had him last time, when he took Loco's people out of San Carlos. That was a disaster for the Chiricahuas, General. Geronimo may have learned his lesson, and, if so, we are out of the picture entirely."

"I intend to carry out a major campaign against Geronimo," said Crook, " and I do not intend to wait for the hostiles to raid into the United States, as you did with Victorio, General Hatch."

"But how will you do that, sir, without creating an international incident?"

"Soon I will take a little trip to Guaymas, to confer with the Mexican officials there. But I have a couple of things to do here, first. The civilians claim these reservations are simply refuges for the hostiles. There is a kernel of truth to their claim. Apache *bronchos* jump the reservation, raid to their hearts' content for a few weeks, then surrender to the agency when the pursuit gets too hot. I've heard an ugly rumor that the people of Tombstone are talking about forming a vigilante force and riding on San Carlos to gun down every Apache they can find. I don't need to tell you gentlemen what disastrous consequences would follow such an action. We have almost six thousand Apaches in various reservations. We certainly do not need them all on the warpath, do we? So we must take steps to defuse the situation. We must make sure that no Apache leaves the reservation without written permission. We must crack down on the production of *tizwin*. Drunken men of any race tend to ponder too much the inequities of life while under the influence, and who has more inequities to ponder than the Apache? All recalcitrant Apaches must be incarcerated. It is foolish to insert the troublemakers into the general population. And finally, that is why I will conduct my investigation of the San Carlos agency, gentlemen—because if we begin to treat the peaceful Apaches fairly, they might just remain peaceful."

"John Clum was right about one thing," said another officer. "Geronimo should have been hanged years ago."

Crook shook his head. "No, sir. He is no criminal. He is a soldier, fighting for his cause."

"Soldiers don't butcher innocent civilians, General."

"Don't they? Consult history, sir, and I believe you will find that the Apache is not the first to wage war on the civilian population. I would prefer Geronimo dead on the field of battle. But mark my words—one way or the other, we will destroy the Chiricahua threat. You see, I would like to retire and devote myself full-time to hunting and other pleasurable pursuits."

"This is hunting," said Hatch, "and Geronimo is the biggest game of all."

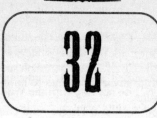

32

"Kayitah, now known as Soldado," said Tahdaste, "I have been waiting for you."

Soldado was amazed. The blind medicine man had identified him before he had spoken a word. Silently, he had slipped into the *diyi*'s jacal, Colt revolver cocked and ready, and somehow Tahdaste had instantly known him. The *anciano* had great powers indeed. But not enough, it seemed, to save the Chihenne. Soldado had returned to the reservation only to find his people gone. They had left many of their belongings behind, so obviously their departure had been made in great haste. What could have happened? Soldado did not have a clue, except for the many army patrols which he had easily eluded to enter the reservation.

"Where have you been, Soldado?" asked the medicine man, seated cross-legged and hunched over by a small fire crackling in a ring of blackened stones.

"In the land of the *Nakai-Ye*," replied Soldado.

Winter had come, in earnest. The day before, the first heavy snow had fallen. Today the sky was overcast. A northern wind cut to the bone. The fire did not produce

enough warmth. It consisted of a handful of twigs and pine
straw. Tahdaste had a ragged woolen blanket, army issue,
draped over his shoulders. Soldado wondered how long the
medicine man had been here, all alone in the deserted *che-
wa-ki*, without food or firewood. Holstering the Colt, he sat
across the meager fire from Tahdaste.

"With the *Netdahe?*" asked the medicine man.

"No, *anciano*. I do not ride with the Wild Ones. I have
been searching for a white man. A scalp hunter."

"Your voice tells me you have not yet found this
man."

"No, I have not. I have looked for many sleeps, in
vain."

"This man you seek—you wish to kill him, as you
killed Najita."

"I do, *anciano*. He is a wicked man."

"There are many wicked men loose upon the world
these days," sighed Tahdaste. "Some are *Pinda Lickoyi*.
Some are *Nakai-Ye*. And some are Apache."

Soldado leaned forward. "Tell me, *anciano*. What happened here?"

"Geronimo came. He forced all the Chihenne
Chiricahua to go with him to the Sierra Madre. You have
not heard of this?"

"No. I have been very far to the west."

"Geronimo had those who would not go killed, as well
as a few who were too sick or frail with age to make the
journey."

Soldado was shocked. "Geronimo did this?"

"He is mad, that one."

"At least you were spared, *anciano*."

"Geronimo wanted to kill me, too. But he was afraid
that his warriors would object."

"How long have you been here alone?"

Tahdaste shook his head. "I lost count of the nights.
The soldiers came. They buried the dead. They said to
me, come to the agency, where you will be safe. But I said
no, I will wait here."

"Wait here? Why?"

"For your return, Soldado. Later, another soldier came. He said *Nantan Lupan* had sent him."

Crook! Chief Tan Wolf was back. He had returned, as he had said he would many years ago. The White Eyes had sent their best warrior to fight Geronimo.

"This soldier said *Nantan Lupan* wanted to know where you were. I told him I did not know. He asked if you might be with Geronimo, and I said he could not know you very well if he could ask that question. I said that whatever Soldado did, he did for the good of his people. This is not true of Geronimo. He does not care about his people, only about revenge."

"What does *Nantan Lupan* want with me?"

"The soldier did not say. Perhaps he did not know. But we both know, Soldado."

"*Anh.*" There could be but one reason. Crook wanted him for a scout in his campaign against Geronimo. Chief Tan Wolf would not hesitate to drop the charge of desertion against him.

"What will Soldado do?" asked Tahdaste.

"First I will find something for you to eat, and gather some wood for your fire. Then, tomorrow, I will take you to the agency."

"The soldier told me many Chihenne died on the way to the Sierra Madre. My heart is heavy. I fear none will return."

"I will do what I can, *anciano.*"

"I know you will. Does this mean you will fight with *Nantan Lupan* against the *Netdahe?*"

"I do not know," admitted Soldado grimly. "But I promise you this. Geronimo will pay for what he has done to my people."

"It is your duty," said the medicine man gravely, "to avenge your people. Even if that means you must kill an Apache."

Three days later, not long after sundown, George Crook had an unexpected visitor. A long day of preparing for his trip to Guaymas, to negotiate with the Mexicans about letting him and his army cross the border, had exhausted him. He had just stretched out on his field bed with a long groan and a book of English verse when a sentry threw back the tent flap.

"General Crook?"

"What the hell do you want, soldier?" snapped Crook, more than a little irritated by the man's intrusion.

"Someone here to see you, General."

"What? Who is it? No, by God, I don't care who it is. Unless it's the President of these United States, send him away. Tell him to come back in the morning. But he had better make it real early, because I am leaving at sunrise."

"Sir, I, uh . . . "

Fuming, Crook swung his legs off the bed and rose to glower from his full height at the sentry. Even in his stocking feet, with "see-betters" perched on the end of his nose, he could strike terror in the heart of the most hardened trooper.

"Dammit, man, are you just plain deaf? I do not want to be disturbed. Is that clear?"

The soldier just stood there, white as a sheet, his Adam's apple bobbing like a cork, and it suddenly occurred to Crook that the man was terrified. Not of Crook, but of dying. Crook could tell the difference. He glanced at his pistol on the folding table, almost within reach. Then the soldier lurched forward and sideways, and Crook stared at the Colt revolver in the Apache's hand.

He didn't recognize Soldado at first, because Soldado was clad like a *broncho*: plain cotton himper, breechcloth, and desert moccasins.

"Who in the blazes are you?" growled Crook. Though he was scared, he refused to show it.

"You know me. I am called Soldado."

Hiding fear was one thing; Crook couldn't conceal his vast relief.

"By the eternal, Soldado, you gave me a start! I thought for a moment that Geronimo had added the art of assassination to his bloody repertoire. You have an unorthodox way of paying a call on a man. Why did you slip past the pickets and jump this poor fellow?"

Was there just a hint of a smile on Soldado's lips? Crook couldn't be certain.

"I am not ready to die," replied the Apache.

Crook chuckled. "Yes, I see, and I think you have a valid point. You have also demonstrated the incompetence of some of my troops." Crook impaled the sentry with a steely gaze. "Very well, Private. That will be all."

"But, sir . . ." The sentry stared at the gun in Soldado's hand.

"It isn't me he might shoot," said Crook. "It's you, if you make a hostile move. But thank you, mister. Since you are so concerned for my safety, perhaps you could do a slightly better job of guarding me in the future."

"Yes, sir," mumbled the soldier, mortified. He slipped out of the tent like a whipped pup.

When he was gone, Soldado cautiously moved away from the tent flap and holstered the Colt.

"Good to see you again, Soldado," said Crook, sitting on his cot. "How is Clancy St. John?"

"Still alive. I think."

"Something the matter?"

Soldado nodded. "Scalp hunter called Reilly. *Mal hombre.*"

"Does this have anything to do with Clancy saving Victorio's women and children?"

Again Soldado nodded.

"I heard about that," said Crook. "Splendid piece of work. I always liked that ornery Irishman. Well, if Clancy's in trouble, why the hell are you here and not with him?"

"My people, the Chihenne."

"Oh, I see." Crook could tell his words had struck a nerve. Even Soldado's capacity for stoicism could not conceal the fact that he was squirming on the horns of a painful dilemma. Clancy St. John needed him. But so did the Chihenne. It was bound to happen, mused Crook. Soldado's mixed loyalties had come back to haunt him.

"If I know Clancy," said Crook, "and I think I do, I wouldn't worry too much, Soldado. There's a man who knows how to take care of himself."

Soldado was not comforted. "You want Soldado for scout, *Nantan Lupan*?"

"Right to the point, eh? As a matter of fact, I do. In a few weeks I intend to launch a campaign against Geronimo. I've been trying to resurrect the Apache scouts. Been a damned difficult proposition, too. Can't find very many willing to sign on. Part of the problem is Geronimo. Folks are just plain scared to go against that one. And, too, the business at Cibecue Creek, and the executions of Dead Shot and the other scouts, left a bad taste in everyone's mouth. But, be that as it may, I generally get what I want, sooner or later. And I want Apache scouts. I need Apache scouts, if I'm to penetrate the Sierra Madre and come out again with my scalp where it's supposed to be. Have you been there, Soldado?"

"I been there."

"I am told Geronimo and his bunch are holed up in a place called the Stronghold, and that there's only one way to get in. A Mexican contingent tried to storm the place a good many years back and were virtually wiped out. Nobody's tried since then."

"*Es verdad.*"

"Is there no other way into the Stronghold?"

"I do not know. But I find out."

"Then you agree to serve as my scout?"

"*Dah,*" replied Soldado, no. "I go now. Not wait."

"You plan to wage a one-man war against Geronimo and his Wild Ones? What chance will you have?"

"I must try. Will your soldiers' bullets know a *broncho* from one of Loco's Chihenne?"

Crook sighed. "I see what you mean. Frankly, though, I wouldn't give two bits for your chances of getting in there to take your people out."

Soldado moved towards the tent flap. "When you come, *Nantan Lupan*, I will be there. I will be watching."

Crook rose, stuck out his hand. "Best of luck to you,

Soldado. I should be in the Sierra Madre by the time the snows begin to melt."

Soldado gravely shook the proffered hand.

They stepped out of the tent together. The sentry snapped nervously to attention.

"Private, escort this man beyond the picket line," said Crook. "Make damned sure he doesn't get shot. Do it for your sake, if not for his."

"Yes, sir," gulped the sentry.

33

As the days accumulated with excruciating slowness into weeks, and the weeks into a month, and then two months, Clancy St. John began to wonder if Buckshot Reilly would ever show.

The waiting was bad enough. Infinitely worse was being separated from his family. He went into Tucson once a week, usually on a Sunday. After going to church with Laura and the girls, he would stay for dinner and then be on his way. He did not dare stay overnight, giving in to his loneliness and his need for Laura, for fear that the one time he did would be just the moment Reilly picked to appear. While he was with Laura part of him would want to stay and part of him would want to go, because he knew he was a human lightning rod, and sooner or later the lightning would strike.

At first Laura and the girls stayed with friends, but when it became apparent that the separation would be a lengthy one, Clancy set them up in Mrs. Howell's boardinghouse. Laura tried to make the best of the situation. She never complained. She didn't have to. Clancy could tell she was as miserable as he. Risking her husband's wrath, she went to the sheriff and told him the whole story, and the sheriff rode out to the ranch one day to call on Clancy and nearly got his head blown off by mistake. Unable to talk Clancy into staying in town, the sheriff promised to use his connections to try and find out where Buckshot Reilly was holed up. The sheriff knew a great many people in the Arizona and New Mexico Territories, and he made numerous inquiries, but all to no avail. Reilly could not be found. He hadn't been seen in the territories since his attack on the buffalo soldiers. This came as no surprise to Clancy. He had figured all along that the scalp hunter was somewhere down in Mexico. Clancy thanked the sheriff for his efforts, and made the badge toter promise to keep a close eye on Laura and the girls.

Soon after transporting his family to Tucson, Clancy paid his *vaqueros* the wages due them and sent them packing. He told them the truth—they had been loyal and hard-working employees and it wasn't fair to keep them in ignorance and endanger their lives. Both men begged him to let them stay. Clancy would not hear of it. He would not have their blood on his hands. Telling them to ride back through in the spring, he saw them off.

For the first week or so of the vigil Clancy stayed close to home. After a while he began to suffer from cabin fever. The walls closed in on him. He began to take a ride every day, swinging a wide loop around his property, looking for a sign. He was glad when the first snow came. It made tracking a lot simpler. Except there was no one to track.

A fortnight prior to Christmas Clancy was on the verge of giving up on Reilly altogether. Maybe something had happened to the son of a bitch. He led a violent life. Perhaps he had met with a violent end. Or maybe he had changed his mind about seeking vengeance and engaged in a more profitable enterprise. Whatever the case, Clancy was nearing the end of his rope. He considered his options. He could bring Laura and the girls back to the ranch, or he could sell the place and take his family far away from here, as Laura had first suggested.

That Sunday, as was his custom, Clancy saddled up and was on his way to Tucson at first light. He went to church with his family, ate dinner with them, and then spirited Laura off alone to tell her of his decision. She was overjoyed. He went looking for the sheriff who, as a friend, agreed to handle the details of selling Clancy's cattle and land and forwarding the proceeds.

"I have no idea where we'll end up," Clancy told him. "California, maybe. But when we stake a claim somewhere, I'll let you know."

"And if I see Buckshot Reilly," said the sheriff cheerfully, "I'll put a couple of slugs in him as a present from you."

"I think if he was coming, he would have by now."

"Bend your steps over to the Pearl, Clancy. We'll have one drink, for old times."

Clancy agreed. One drink led to another, and then another. By the time Clancy arrived at the boardinghouse to say his good-byes to Laura, the long shadows of the late afternoon reached across the dun-colored streets of Tucson.

"I'll be back tomorrow," he promised, "or the next day at the latest. I'll load up what I can in the wagon and leave the rest."

"You're sure you want to leave this country, Clancy?"

"I'm sure. Reilly's not going to show, so it's not like I'm running away."

"I was thinking about Soldado."

Clancy just shook his head. He kissed her, hugged Faith and Charity, and rode away.

Night had fallen by the time he reached the ranch house. There was an early moon, and by its soft silver light he could clearly see the sign of horses in front of the adobe. Three men had ridden right up to the house and dismounted.

"Christ," muttered Clancy—and jerked the reins to turn his horse.

A rifle cracked from the direction of the bunkhouse, its muzzle flash a spurt of yellow flame in the darkness.

Clancy gasped as the bullet hit him in the shoulder with the impact of an ax handle swung hard. He came out of the saddle and landed poorly. Numb with shock, facedown in the snow, he almost passed out, fought against the wave of wound sickness that washed over him. *Get up! Get up or die!* He struggled to his feet. His left arm hung uselessly at his side. He staggered like a drunken man, clawing at the Dance revolver in its holster. Someone was loping towards him, rifle in hand, from the bunkhouse. Dragging the Dance clear of leather, he raised the pistol. It seemed incredibly heavy. Before he could steady his aim, a man emerged from the house and struck the gun from his grasp and hit him in the face. Clancy sprawled backwards into the snow. The moon and the stars in the winter sky began to spin. Then they disappeared. As he plummeted down into a bottomless pit of blackness, Clancy dimly heard a man chuckling, a sound like dead windblown leaves skittering across hard ground.

Buckshot Reilly.

Clancy's final thought was that he had kissed Laura for the last time.

When he came to, Clancy was in the house, tied to one of the chairs at the table near the fireplace. Buckshot Reilly sat across from him, his scattergun on the table. One of Reilly's men stood behind Clancy's chair. Clancy could see a third man through the doorway to one of the bedrooms. This man was ransacking the place, looking for something worth stealing.

As soon as Clancy raised his head, the man behind him jammed the barrel of his pistol to the back of his neck and cocked the hammer. Clancy smiled bleakly at Reilly.

"Buckshot, you must be mighty scared of me. Sure you brought along enough help?"

"You're the one who ought to be scared," replied the scalp hunter. " 'Cause tonight's your last night among the living."

"Tell your boy to put his pistol away. You didn't hang

around here waiting for me to come to just to put a bullet in me."

Reilly chuckled. He nodded at the man behind Clancy, who backed off, moving to one side so that Clancy could just see him out of the corner of his eye. He kept the sidegun pointed at the Irishman, though.

"I heard what happened to that Apach' named Najita," said Reilly. "Your boy Soldado did a number on him. Then he come lookin' for yours truly. Didn't find me, though. I ain't one to be found if I don't want to be. So I says to myself, Buckshot, that son of a bitch Clancy St. John probably knows you're coming for him. Najita knew, and I figured he must have talked. Apaches sure know how to make other folks talk even when they don't want to, and Najita had a yellow streak running right through him. Thought you might have some help, Clancy. That's why I brought these boys along. And you sure needed help, hoss. Was a whole lot easier than I thought it would be to get the drop on you."

"I must be getting old," said Clancy, "to let scum like you get the best of me."

"Well, you ain't gonna have to worry about gettin' any older."

Clancy spat across the table into Buckshot Reilly's face. Reilly shot to his feet, overturning the chair he had been sitting in. Wiping the spittle from his bearded face, he glowered at Clancy. Then he drew a knife from his belt.

"I'm gonna skin you alive, you bastard. You cost me a lot of money, and I ain't the forgivin' kind. You're gonna beg me to kill you before I'm done."

"Go to hell," said Clancy.

"You first," sneered Reilly.

Clancy brought both legs up and kicked the table over. Then he rose and backed up, smashing the chair he was tied to into the stones of the fireplace as hard as he could. The impact sent jolts of searing anguish through him from the gunshot wound in his arm. But the chair shattered into so much kindling, and suddenly his arms were free. The man who had stood behind him with the pistol got off a single shot. The bullet plowed into Clancy's thigh, but it didn't stop the Irishman. Clancy dived over the table which now lay on its side. He collided with Reilly as the scalp hunter stooped to retrieve the scattergun. Reilly was thrown backwards. Clancy got the scattergun, came up on one knee, and let go both barrels at the man with the gun. At such close range he couldn't miss, even holding the sawed-off shotgun with one hand. The loads picked the man up off his feet and hurled him backwards into the wall. He flopped forward onto the floor, dead. Clancy whirled, swinging the empty scattergun with his one good arm, using it like a club to hammer Reilly back down as the cursing scalp hunter tried to get up.

The third man had rushed in from the bedroom. Clancy hurled the scattergun at him and dived for the pistol, which had slipped from the dead man's grasp. He reached it just as the third scalp hunter fired. The bullet caught Clancy in the side. He rolled over and got off one shot. One shot was all he needed. The third man's head snapped back as Clancy's bullet drilled his skull and exploded out the back in a spray of blood, brains, and bone fragments.

"Clancy, you son of a bitch!" roared Buckshot Reilly as he poured six shots from his revolver into the Irishman.

Reilly stood there in a swirl of acrid powder smoke and stared at Clancy's lifeless body. Then he retrieved his scattergun and, on the way out, smashed a burning kerosene lamp against one wall. By the time he was mounted up, the interior of the house was ablaze. Reilly watched it burn for a moment with sullen satisfaction stamped upon his features. Finally, he turned his horse south and rode for Mexico.

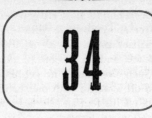

34

As it turned out, General Crook did not need to formulate a secret protocol with the Mexican government to expand the parameters of the Hot Trails Treaty. Early in the spring of 1883, Apache raiders struck across the border into New Mexico Territory. Nearly thirty whites were slain, among them a prominent judge, whose six-year-old son was abducted by the Apaches. The fate of this lad, Charley McComas, became a *cause célèbre* throughout the United States. Charley was never seen or heard from again. It was rumored that he had been brutally murdered, and the hearts of the American people were hardened against the Apaches.

In Tombstone, John Clum declared that the raid was Geronimo's handiwork. A group of vigilantes who called themselves the Tombstone Rangers rode for San Carlos, armed to the teeth, bent on vengeance, and determined to kill every Apache they could find. Most of the civilians in the Southwest had decided that no distinction should be made between the *reducidos*—the "tame" Apaches content to live peacefully on the reservations—and the *teiltcohes*, or troublemakers. As far as the Rangers were concerned, permanent peace could only be achieved after the last Apache was dead. A majority of Americans were inclined to agree. The United States had run out of patience.

Fortunately, the Tombstone Rangers caused very little damage. They took some potshots at an old Apache and then lost their nerve and hightailed it for home. In Washington, the Bureau of Indian Affairs began to consider transporting the Apaches out of the southwestern territories altogether, perhaps to Florida, if only to prevent bloodshed.

Chatto, not Geronimo, had led the raid. He was Geronimo's protégé, but all agreed he was too arrogant and impetuous for his own good. The raid was carried out against Geronimo's better judgment. The Bedonkohe leader had heard that *Nantan Lupan* was once again in command of the yellowlegs, and he did not want to give Crook, whom he respected as a warrior, any excuse to come into Mexico after him. He was deeply disturbed, too, by Juh's recent vision. The Nednhi chief had been riding through the Cañon del Cobre one day when suddenly, out of a mist of pale blue, he saw thousands of phantom American soldiers marching off in the distance. "Ussen is warning us," said Juh. "The soldiers will come to the *Cima Silkq* and defeat us." *Cima Silkq* was the Apache name for the Sierra Madre.

In the aftermath of Chatto's brutal raid, Crook received permission from Washington to invoke the Hot Trails Treaty and take his troops into Mexico. Much to everyone's surprise—and the chagrin of many officers eager for glory in what would no doubt be the last Indian campaign in the West—Crook took only fifty soldiers and eleven officers with him.

"I have concluded that it would be practically impossible for white soldiers to defeat the Chiricahua, especially in the Sierra Madre. In operating against them, the only hope for success lies in using their own methods. That means employing Apache scouts."

Crook had recruited nearly two hundred Apaches for his purposes, the majority of them Coyotero and White Mountain. These Indians respected *Nantan Lupan* and were eager to ride with him, especially since it seemed likely that further depredations would result in the mass relocation of their people. They wanted to stop Geronimo and his *bronchos* every bit as much as George Crook did.

Among the white men handpicked by Crook to accompany him were Captain Emmett Crawford and Lieutenant Charles Gatewood, both gallant and intelligent soldiers. The latter was placed in charge of the Apache scouts. Al Sieber would be chief of scouts. Crook's fiercely loyal aide, John Bourke, came along, so that he could faithfully maintain a diary of his experiences as the trusted sidekick of the United States' most renowned Indian fighter. Crook also permitted Frank Randall, correspondent for the *New York Herald*, to accompany the expedition. Randall was packing photographic equipment as well as his writing materials.

Lieutenant Hudson Lane of the Ninth Cavalry was also chosen as one of Crook's officers.

When he heard that he had been seconded to Crook, Lane went immediately to Hatch and asked the Ninth's commander if there was any way out of the assignment. Hatch was shocked.

"Why, I thought you would fairly jump at the chance, Lieutenant," said Hatch. "When Crook asked me if I could recommend an officer to represent the Ninth, I immediately thought of you."

"I am honored that you think so highly of me, sir, but I would rather not go. Furthermore, I must request two weeks leave."

Hatch scowled. "Leave? In the middle of an Apache breakout? Have you lost your mind, Lieutenant?"

Impaled on the general's flinty gaze, Lane squirmed in anguish but stubbornly stood his ground. "Sir, I have . . . I have urgent personal affairs which require my immediate attention."

"You will have to tell me more about them before I will even consider your leave."

"Sir, I am engaged to Faith St. John."

"The scout's daughter? I wasn't aware."

"No, sir. I've told no one, sir."

"For a soldier, Lieutenant, duty takes precedence over romance."

"I realize that, sir. But just this morning I received a letter from Miss St. John, informing me that her father had been murdered."

"Good Lord." Hatch took a moment to absorb this news. "I confess, from everything I have heard of Clancy St. John, I assumed he was indestructible. Or at least that no mere mortal could get the best of him."

Lane nodded. "I felt the same way, sir." Clancy's death had hit him hard. He hadn't realized how much he admired and respected the Irishman. They had disagreed on some things, but that couldn't change the fact that Clancy had been a hell of a man. One of a kind.

The death of her stepfather had hit Faith harder still. And, Lane was sure, Laura and Charity, as well, although in her letter Faith had failed to mention them. Faith had admitted that Clancy's death came as a worse blow to her than the demise of her natural father. Knowing that his beloved was grieving so had prompted Lane to request the furlough at this, the worst possible time. Faith was hurting, and the last thing Lane wanted to do was disappear for God only knew how long into the Mexican malpais in pursuit of elusive Apache renegades who would surrender sooner or later anyway.

"Who did the deed?" asked Hatch.

"No witnesses, sir. But apparently Buckshot Reilly had threatened Clancy's life."

"The leader of that pack of scoundrels who attacked your detachment?"

"The same, sir."

"Are you contemplating a little revenge of your own, Lieutenant?"

"Absolutely not, sir. I will leave Reilly to the law. But I do feel that my place is with my fiancée in her time of distress."

Hatch frowned, shook his head. "I'm very sorry,

Lieutenant. I cannot agree. Miss St. John will have to find another shoulder to cry on, if she must have one. Your place is with General Crook in Mexico, doing your duty to make your country safe. If you wish to compose a letter to your betrothed, do so tonight and give it to me. I will guarantee its prompt delivery into her hands. Beyond that, I can do nothing more for you, Lieutenant Lane."

Lane rashly considered arguing the point, though he realized that further discussion would at best be futile and at worst detrimental to his career. Still, he would have made the attempt, in his desperation, had he not remembered how important it was to Faith for him to get ahead in the army. She would probably be pleased to know that he had been one of the chosen few selected by Crook to track down Geronimo. That in itself was a conspicuous honor, and if the campaign proved successful, every officer involved would find his career much enhanced.

With this in mind, Lane went to his quarters and wrote the letter, explaining to Faith why he could not be with her. He hoped she would understand. And yet one thing General Hatch had said nagged him mercilessly, keeping him awake much of the night. *Miss St. John will have to find another shoulder to cry on.* Lane fervently wished the general hadn't said that. Surely a young woman as winsome as Faith had many other admirers. What if one of them stole her heart away with those little attentions that meant so much to a woman? Faith would be very vulnerable now . . .

At reveille the next morning Lane and the other officers pegged to accompany Crook met the general in front of his tent. As usual, Crook was garbed in civilian clothes. His mule, Apache, stood saddled and waiting near at hand. Crook scanned the officers arrayed before him and smiled wearily.

"Gentlemen, we are about to embark on an historic undertaking. I will expect all of you to do your duty to the best of your ability. If you do, we shall, with luck, bring to a close at long last the final chapter of these bloody Apache Wars. But it will not be easy. In fact, it will be a damned difficult enterprise. If we all come back alive, I shall be very surprised. For we are going to do what has never been done. Many have tried, and failed. They usually paid for failure with their lives.

"Gentlemen, we are going to invade the Apache stronghold of the Sierra Madre."

Lane scarcely heard a word. He was brooding miserably over Faith.

35

For two months not a word was received from General Crook and his handpicked group of stalwarts. The American press and populace speculated that disaster had befallen the expedition in the Sierra Madre. But in the summer of 1883, Crook suddenly reappeared in the Arizona Territory. With him marched almost four hundred Chiricahua Apaches. Nana and Loco were among them. Geronimo, however, was not. Crook announced that Geronimo had promised to gather up the rest of his followers and come to San Carlos before the end of the summer.

Immediately upon his return to Fort Stanton and the Ninth Cavalry, Hudson Lane again requested, and this time received, his furlough. Mounting the fastest horse he could find, he rode like hell for Tucson.

He was relieved to find Clancy's family still residing at the Howell boardinghouse. In the downstairs parlor, he offered all three women his heartfelt condolences and apologized to Faith for being unable to come sooner.

"You must have been very proud to have been chosen by General Crook," said Faith, her eyes agleam with admiration. "Please, Hudson, you must tell us all about it."

"Yes, do," said Laura. Clad in mourning black, she looked very pale and tired. The passage of three months had not been sufficient time to heal her emotional wounds. "We've had so little reliable information."

Lane nodded, resigned. What he really wanted to do was steal a few minutes alone with Faith, to profess his all-consuming affection for her, and perhaps, if he were lucky, to taste the sweetness of her lips.

"What I will always remember about the entire affair," he said, "were the villages we passed through on our way to the mountains. I have never seen people so afraid. They are starving, because the men are too terrified of the Apaches to venture out into their fields. Utter the name Geronimo, and they will scream in terror and run away. Some of them are convinced that Geronimo is actually the devil, who has assumed human form and come to punish them for their sins. The renegades had struck countless villages in Chihuahua and Sonora. As you may know, Geronimo has declared war without mercy on the Mexicans. Apparently his family was massacred by Mexicans many years ago, and he has never forgiven them.

"We reached the Sierra Madre without seeing any sign of the renegades—unless you count all the new graves in the village churchyards. As soon as we got to the mountains we began to march at night and hide in the daytime. Frankly, I expected an attack at any moment, but, as remarkable as it must seem, we had probed deep into the mountains before the *bronchos* became aware of our presence.

"The going was very rough. Some of the mountain trails were so narrow and treacherous that we lost several mules. They slipped and fell to their deaths in the deep chasms below. Cactus and sharp stones cut through our clothes and boots and sliced into our flesh. I got a thorn more than an inch long in the heel of my foot, so deep I could not extract it. The wound became febrile, and the doctor, Captain Grogan, said I might lose the whole foot to infection if they did not operate. They cut the heel open and removed the thorn."

Faith gasped, a dainty hand covering her mouth. "Oh, you poor dear. That must have hurt terribly. But I'll wager you were very brave."

Lane smiled sheepishly. "Actually, I howled like a coyote in a trap. Eventually we came to a deserted village on a high ridge. Thirty or forty huts, all abandoned in a hurry. There were cowhides, meat drying on racks, blankets, and pots left behind. The scouts picked up the trail of the renegades then. It was only a day or two old. A few days later the scouts found a camp that was still inhabited. They attacked, killed a few, captured a half dozen children. The rest of the renegades escaped. We realized then that most of the *bronchos* weren't in the mountains. They were out raiding Mexican villages. We learned from our captives that the Mexicans were holding some of the Chiricahuas at a place called Casa Grande. Geronimo was trying to take Mexican hostages, to exchange them for the prisoners held by the Mexicans.

"We heard later that on the day our scouts attacked the Chiricahua village, Geronimo was a hundred miles away, sitting beside a campfire with his *bronchos*. Suddenly he jumped to his feet and exclaimed to his men that some of their people had been captured by American troops in the Sierra Madre."

"What nonsense," scoffed Faith.

"I thought so too—at first. Until I met Geronimo face-to-face. His followers believe he has this special power. The *bronchos* ran to their horses and began to ride for the Sierra Madre. They never doubted for a moment that Geronimo was telling them the truth.

"Anyway, General Crook hoped he could get most of the Chiricahuas to surrender before Geronimo got back. He released the captives and told them to go to Loco and tell him that we had only come to take them back to San Carlos. Then we made camp by a stream in a canyon and waited. We didn't know what to expect. Would the Chiricahuas give up, or attack us?

"The next day I was down by the creek filling my canteen when I looked up and saw a *broncho* watching me from the other bank. He had two pistols and a rifle, and his face was painted with a broad red stripe across the eyes. Tied to his pony's mane and tail were strips of red cloth. I confess, he gave me quite a start. I almost panicked. Thought about drawing my pistol and shooting him. Then some of the others saw him and ran down to the creek, and I felt better about my chances with them around. The *broncho* rode across the creek and right through us like he owned the place and we were of no consequence to him. He rode right up to General Crook's tent and told the general that Loco had sent him to say that his people had never wanted war. Geronimo had forced them to leave San Carlos, and they were ready to go home.

"By the following morning we had several hundred Apaches in our camp, mostly women and children. That same day Geronimo arrived. He and his men sat up on the canyon rimrock. Sometimes they would yell insults down at our scouts. I was convinced we were going to have a fight, and I wondered if our scouts would turn against us, as those who had served with Colonel Carr did at Cibecue Creek.

"And then a most astonishing thing happened. General Crook went bird hunting and got himself captured—by Geronimo himself."

"What?" Laura was sure she hadn't heard right. "Crook, captured?"

Lane nodded, grinning. "I know it sounds incredible, but that's exactly what happened."

"I would not have thought a man like George Crook capable of such foolish behavior."

"Well, the general won't say one way or the other, but I'll tell you what I think, and I'm not alone in this, ma'am. I think he deliberately set out to be captured."

"That would make him the bravest man I've ever heard of," said Laura.

"The most amazing part of it is that Geronimo did not kill him outright. Instead, he and Crook sat down and had a long talk. A few hours later they'd struck a bargain. We would leave the Sierra Madre, taking Loco's people with us. Geronimo would come to San Carlos with the rest as soon as he had exchanged his Mexican prisoners for the Apaches held captive in Chihuahua."

"The local newspaper has been berating General Crook for giving the Chiricahua complete amnesty," said Laura, "as well as for taking Geronimo's word that he will surrender. They claim the whole campaign was a colossal failure."

Lane shrugged. "Crook says it is unfair to punish the Apaches for violating a code of war they don't understand. He believes peace is more important than vengeance. I hope it works. I hope Geronimo comes in." He glanced at Faith. "I want these wars to be over, once and for all."

"Amen," said Laura. "I only wish Clancy had lived to see it. He wanted peace more than anything."

For a moment gloomy silence reigned, as each of them thought about Clancy St. John.

"You say you actually saw Geronimo?" asked Faith, deliberately changing the subject.

"Yes, and he looks mean as the devil, I can tell you. Has a scar from a bullet across his forehead."

Faith turned to Laura. "I think Hudson is a hero, don't you, Mother?"

"Faith, please!" exclaimed Lane, mortified. "I was just a soldier doing his duty. To be perfectly honest with you, I didn't want to go. I begged to be given leave so I could come to Tucson and be with you." He blushed furiously, glanced at Laura. "My apologies, Mrs. St. John, for being so forward. But I . . . I happen to be madly in love with your daughter."

"I see." Laura rose from the horsehair sofa. "Come along, Charity. Let's give your sister and the lieutenant a few moments of privacy."

Charity paused on the way out. "Hudson, have you seen or heard about Soldado?"

"No, Charity. I'm sorry. There's been no word of him for months."

Crestfallen, Charity followed her mother out of the room.

No sooner was the parlor door closed than Faith literally pounced on Lane. Arms locked around his neck, she sat on his lap and giggled.

"Did you miss me, Lieutenant?"

"Why, yes. Of course I did. But Faith—what if your mother returns and finds us like this?"

"Oh, fiddlesticks. What if she does?"

"Well, I . . . it's just not . . . "

"Proper?" Faith put on a pout. "Aren't you going to marry me, Hudson?"

Lane's cheeks were burning hot. "I certainly hope so. But your mother would probably forbid me to even see you again if she saw this."

"You're such a prude." Faith got up and flounced to the parlor window where she could frown at Tucson's dusty street. "I'm not sure I will marry you, after all, Hudson."

Lane was at her side in a flash. "Don't tease me like that, Faith. You know how much I love you. I would do anything to please you."

"You could please me most by taking me away from this dreary place."

"Where would you like to go?"

"Well, since you've asked, I'd like to see Paris, and Vienna. I'd like to take a European tour."

Lane's heart sank as he did some quick mental calculations of the cost of such an overseas excursion and then compared that sum to his paltry savings.

"But," she continued airily, "I would content myself with a city back east. St. Louis or New Orleans, or even New York. Some place civilized."

"I could request a transfer," said Lane dubiously.

She turned to face him, and her arms snaked around his neck again, and her body pressed against his. Lane very nearly broke into a cold sweat.

"You won't be sorry," she cooed, and kissed him.

The next morning Lane walked down to the boardinghouse from the hotel where he was staying. Any other time would have found him in a foul mood; he'd had to share his room with a singularly obnoxious whiskey peddler who not only snored all night but smelled bad into the bargain. But Lane could not in all good conscience lay all the blame for his lack of sleep on the peddler. He had been kept awake most of the night trying to figure out what he was going to do. If he wanted Faith for his wife, he would have to wangle a transfer east. This he was willing to do, but he knew it was much easier said than done. At least the Apache Wars were finally over. That improved his chances. He was an experienced cavalry officer now, and if the *bronchos* were still on the rampage, the army would never let him leave the district.

Then, too, his sleeplessness could in part be blamed on apprehensions about this morning's meeting with Laura St. John. He planned to illuminate her regarding his intentions towards her daughter. Would she give them her blessing?

Ensconced again in Mrs. Howell's well-appointed parlor, Lane informed Laura that he and Faith wanted to be married. It was the most difficult task he had ever performed, and he did not give his performance very high marks, thanks to utterly jangled nerves and a sudden affliction which rendered him nearly incapable of articulating the King's English.

Laura took the news calmly. "You are a fine young man, Lieutenant," she said.

And that was the sum total of what she said.

Lane was almost speechless with abruptly rising terror. "Faith wants to go east," he mumbled lamely. "I'm willing to put in for a transfer, ma'am. Of course, we would want you and Charity to come, too."

Faith stared at him, thunderstruck. This was news to her. He avoided meeting her gaze.

"I mean, there is nothing to keep you here, is there, Mrs. St. John?" asked Lane, with the unpleasant feeling that with every word he was digging a bigger hole for himself.

"You want to take care of the three of us?" asked Laura. "I am grateful, but—and I do hope you won't take this the wrong way—I'm not sure a lieutenant's pay would stretch far enough to accomplish that noble sentiment."

"Well, it's just that I don't think it's right to . . ." Lane came to a stumbling, witless halt.

"To leave me to my own devices?" Laura smiled sweetly, trying to put him at ease. "Clancy did not leave me destitute, Lieutenant. The sheriff has seen to the sale of the land and the cattle bearing the shamrock brand."

"I see," muttered Lane, feeling humiliated. He felt he had made a complete fool of himself.

"Besides," said Charity, "I won't go until I know Buckshot Reilly is dead and I see Soldado again."

"Soldado!" hissed Faith, exasperated. "Soldado, Soldado, Soldado. That's all I hear from you."

"Faith," said Laura, her tone firm and scolding.

"Well, it's shameful, Mother. Charity is in love with a filthy savage."

"That filthy savage, as you call him, saved your life, young lady. He is one of the most decent people I've ever known. I'm sure Hudson will agree."

Perfectly miserable, Lane kept his mouth shut.

"But he is an Apache!" protested Faith.

Charity was on her feet, features cloudy with rage and hands clenched into fists. "If you weren't my sister I would punch you in the nose!" she declared.

"You two may leave," snapped Laura sternly. "I would like to have a private word with the lieutenant."

Lane sighed, trying to brace himself, as Faith and Charity stormed out of the parlor.

When they were gone Laura said, "I will not stand in the way if you and Faith really want to be married, Hudson. But I agree with Charity. We cannot leave until Buckshot Reilly is brought to justice. I want to see him hang for what he did. I know how terrible that must sound, but it is the way I feel and I cannot deny it. And we must know what has become of Soldado. He was like a son to Clancy, and I will not leave the territory until I have some word of him. Will you try to find something out, Lieutenant?"

Lane said he would.

Back at the hotel Lane was accosted by the proprietor, who handed him a note.

"This just come over from the telegraph office, Lieutenant. It's them red devils again, ain't it?"

Lane read the terse message requesting his prompt return to Fort Stanton. No reasons were given. But then, none were really necessary.

"Yes," he said wearily. "I'm sure you are right."

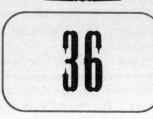

36

Geronimo had been one of the last of the Wild Ones to surrender, but finally he did come in, and Crook was there to greet him. The Bedonkohe leader was a man of few words. "Once I moved about like the wind," he told *Nantan Lupan*. "Now I surrender to you, and that is all."

He went to Turkey Creek, where the other Chiricahuas had been located, apart from the other Apache bands, an arrangement that suited all concerned. There were five hundred of them, and the officer chosen to supervise them, Britton Davis, did his level best to make their lives comfortable. Most of the Chiricahua were well pleased with Davis; he was a fair and honest man who admired his Indian wards. But Geronimo immediately began to sow the seeds of discord. He openly scorned Davis and refused to try his hand at farming. He made friends with a disreputable character named Tribolet, who smuggled whiskey onto the reservation.

Shortly after Geronimo's arrival at Turkey Creek, Britton Davis was made aware of a new breakout. Eighteen warriors led by Geronimo, Naiche, and Lozen had bolted after a night of drinking. They were accompanied by thirteen women and six children. Davis had high hopes of catching the renegades, as they had only a few horses and mules between them. But Geronimo was a master at eluding pursuit, and soon Davis had to report that the Apaches had vanished into Mexico.

At Fort Bowie, Crook received disturbing news from Washington even before he was made aware of Geronimo's successful escape. The new Commanding General of the United States Army was Phil Sheridan, and the new President was Grover Cleveland, and neither gentleman was willing to abide by the terms of the surrender which Crook had hammered out with the Chiricahua renegades in the Sierra Madre. Only "unconditional surrender" was acceptable, which meant Crook's promise of full amnesty for past crimes simply would not do. Sheridan ordered Crook to do the impossible—renegotiate with the Apaches while preventing their escape from the reservation.

On the heels of these unsavory orders, Crook received word from Britton Davis about Geronimo. The news devastated Crook. A few hardcase renegades like Geronimo and those brass-tailed idiots in Washington had unwittingly conspired together to ruin everything. Crook fired a brief telegram to Washington, asking that he be relieved of command. He had given his word to the Apaches and he would not break it. Sheridan was quick to accommodate him.

Crook lingered only long enough to formally transfer command of the district to General Nelson A. Miles. He offered to share all the knowledge of the Apaches he had acquired in eight years of campaigning against them. Miles wasn't interested, and in turn shared with Crook the news that, because of Geronimo's escape, President Cleveland and General Sheridan considered the surrender which Crook had negotiated to be null and void. All Apaches would be transported to a reservation somewhere in the east. In addition, the disbanding of the Apache scouts, which Crook had delayed in spite of unrelenting pressure, would be carried out forthwith.

And so George Crook bitterly took his leave. He

knew Nelson Miles all too well and concluded that the
Apaches were doomed.

The two men had served in many of the same Indian
campaigns. They had fought the Sioux and the Cheyenne
and the Nez Percé. Miles was not a West Point man; he
had served in the Civil War as a volunteer and risen in the
ranks more swiftly than any other officer. Crook and Miles
were as different as night from day. Miles was vain, arrogant, and an exceedingly ambitious man. He believed in
doing things strictly by the book. Where Crook scorned
the trappings of command, Miles had a fondness for gold
braid and the special privileges that came with those trappings. Worst of all, Miles was not one to concern himself
overmuch with the right and wrong of a situation when his
fame and fortune were at stake.

Geronimo and his *bronchos* were a desperate crew. They
believed they were dead men. As such they had nothing to
lose. They expected no quarter, and would show no mercy.
They would go out in a blaze of glory, so that the *Pinda
Lickoyi* and the *Nakai-Ye* would never forget the price they
had to pay for stealing Apache land, and would forever
tremble at their memory.

Before Nelson Miles could orchestrate a campaign
against the renegades, Geronimo struck, crossing the border with a handful of men to undertake what would be the
last Apache raid on American soil. They hit a ranch in
southern Arizona first, killing a few cowboys and forcing
the rancher to watch the rape and torture of his wife. The
man went insane, which saved his life, for to kill someone
who was "touched" was, to the Apache, strictly taboo.

There were more victims. Geronimo left a trail of
dead whites behind him—Happy Valley, Pantano Wash,
the Whetstone Mountains, Greaterville, the valley of the
San Pedro.

The population of the Arizona and New Mexico
Territories were in a panic. They screamed for army protection. They inundated the White House with angry let-

ters. There were hundreds of bloodthirsty Apaches prowling the malpais, they claimed. The Apache menace had to be dealt with, once and for all.

By early summer General Miles had five thousand men under his command. South of the border, Mexico had put three thousand troops in the field. Adding in the various groups of *vaqueros*, volunteers, and vigilantes scouring the desert for the Apache raiders, Miles figured there were nine thousand men pitted against eighteen *bronchos*. Good odds, if you could get them.

Miles sent detachments hither and yon to cover every mountain pass and water hole. Then he ordered Captain Henry Lawson to pick one hundred officers and men and pursue Geronimo, pursue him relentlessly—if necessary, to the ends of the earth.

Lieutenant Hudson Lane was relieved when he learned that he was not to be one of Lawson's chosen few. He knew Lawson, a hero of the Civil War, a big, brawny soldier much admired by his fellow officers and greatly respected by the men he had commanded. But privately Lane didn't think that even Harry Lawson, a natural-born warrior with the guts of a grizzly and the tenacity of a bulldog, could catch Geronimo.

Instead, Lane was given command of a twenty-five-man detail assigned to watch Skeleton Canyon and the nearby springs. Figuring that Geronimo would make a dash for the sanctuary of the Sierra Madre, Lane decided that his assignment, though not exactly pleasant, would not be particularly hazardous, either. The most recent sightings of the *bronchos* were far removed from Skeleton Canyon. At worst, he would have to spend long, uneventful weeks in a miserable hellhole of an encampment, out of touch with his beloved Faith, and unable to pursue his inquiries regarding Soldado.

The day prior to his departure from Fort Stanton, Lane dropped by the sutler's store to enjoy what he feared would be his last warm beer for who knew how long. The sutler, old Wiley James, could not help but notice the sour expression on the lieutenant's face.

"What happened to you, Lieutenant?" asked the irrepressibly good-humored James. "Did your dog die? Or are you down in the mouth 'cause you ain't ridin' to glory with the gallant Harry Lawson and his pack of heroes?"

"It's a long story."

The sutler planted his elbows on the counter. "I got all the time in the world."

Lane poured out his woes to the sutler.

"So, the long and short of it," said James, when Lane was finished, "is that you cain't win your sweetheart till you find out what happened to that scalp hunter and the Apache called Soldado."

Lane nodded. "So, as you can see, Geronimo is the least of my worries. He will run Lawson ragged for a few weeks and then he'll give himself up, as always, and that will be the end of that. Our soldiers probably won't have fired a single shot at a wild Chiricahua when it's all said and done."

"Hmm. Maybe, maybe not. Well, I cain't help you as far as Buckshot Reilly is concerned. But you should've come to me a long time ago if you wanted some information on Soldado."

Lane gaped at the sutler. "You know him?"

" 'Course I know him. Clancy St. John was a real good friend of mine, and Soldado was like a son to Clancy. I've been here for nigh on twenty-five summers, Lieutenant, and in this line of work I hear a whole lot of interesting things. Guess you could say I know just about everything there is to know about what's going on in this bailiwick."

"You're sure Soldado is alive?"

"I ain't sure of anything except that when I die and go to heaven, there'll be ol' Clancy in a foul mood wanting to know what the flamin' hell took me so long, and did I bring a bottle of who-hit-john with me."

Lane grimaced, suspecting Wiley James of being an old windbag who was just pulling his leg.

"More than a year back," continued James, on a more serious note, "Soldado headed down into Mexico. That was after Geronimo come up here and took Loco and his

Cherry Cows out of San Carlos, made 'em go with him whether they wanted to or not. Now, from what I hear, Soldado had in mind bringing Loco and his people back. He prowled around in the Sierra Madre, and before long he'd spirited more than a dozen away from Geronimo. He had a tough time of it, though, 'cause not only did he have to avoid the Wild Ones but he had to watch out for Mexicans, too. They say he even killed a couple of Geronimo's *bronchos*. After a spell, you see, Geronimo figured out what was going on, and sent some of his boys out to find Soldado and the *reducidos* he was hiding and taking care of. Never found them, though. That Soldado is one wily cuss. Count your lucky stars, Lieutenant, that he didn't turn out to be a *Netdahe* like Geronimo and them others.

"Anyhow, when Crook made his deal with the renegades, Soldado sent his group up here—there were about twenty of them by that time. But he didn't come himself. Seems some of the Apaches, mostly women and children, got themselves captured by the Mexicans."

Lane nodded. "Geronimo was trying to take Mexican prisoners so he could exchange them for those people."

"Yeah, but it didn't work. The Mexicans wouldn't deal with Geronimo. Far as they were concerned, he's the devil himself in human form, and they won't strike a bargain with such. But Soldado's still down in Mexico, trying to free those Chiricahuas."

"But how do you know all this?"

"From a half-breed by the name of Santiago, that's how. His mother's Mexican. She got took captive by the Apaches when she was just a kid. Santiago was born into the Chihenne band, and he was one of Loco's people. Soldado got him and his mother away from the *bronchos*. His mother came back to San Carlos, but Santiago stayed behind to help Soldado. Every now and then Santiago shows up here. Passes himself off as a *vaquero*, and he's good at it, though at heart he's an Apache through and through. He buys ammunition and a few other sundries for him and Soldado. Reckon Soldado deals with me 'cause he knows he can trust me, me being Clancy's friend and all."

"Can you get a message to Soldado for me, Mr. James?"

"What kind of message would that be?"

"Tell him Clancy's dead, and that Laura and Charity want to see him again. It's very important to them—and to me."

Wiley James rubbed his stubbled jaw. "I'll try. I never know when Santiago will pop up. And there's no guarantee Soldado will do anything about it even if he gets your message. He's a loner, that one. Guess you can't blame him."

"No," said Lane. "I guess you can't."

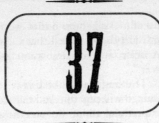

37

"Suh?"

"Yes, Sergeant." Lane did not look up from the evening fire, which he prodded with a stick. He continued to stare moodily into the dancing flames.

"Suh, you reckon this canyon is haunted?"

That snapped Lane out of his brooding. "What? Haunted?"

"Yessuh." The grizzled sergeant looked sheepish, but he plunged ahead, just the same. "Aint there been killin' done here?"

"Well, as a matter of fact, there has been some killing here. About twenty-five years ago, Mangas Colorado and a hundred Chiricahua Apaches ambushed an army detachment on its way to Tucson with a herd of cattle. Cochise was on a rampage, and the town was cut off and starving. A good many men were killed that day, as I recall."

And if memory serves me, thought Lane, *Clancy St. John was in that fight.*

"Well, suh, reason I ask, the pickets, they been tellin' me about hearin' some mighty funny sounds."

"What kind of funny sounds, exactly?"

"Voices. Real distant like. Shoutin' and moanin' and such."

Lane grimaced. "Tell them not to worry about all of that. Ghosts can't kill them. Apaches can. And they won't hear or see an Apache until it's almost too late for anything but a quick prayer."

"Yes, suh." The sergeant walked away.

Lane scanned the steep canyon walls looming up on either side. A strip of violet-blue sky was darkening as night came on, filling the defile with murky, indigo shadows. This was, he supposed, a pretty spooky place. His buffalo soldiers weren't afraid of a living thing, but a few did have a strong superstitious bent. They were edgy too, after more than three weeks of sitting here waiting for something to happen.

Not that Lane himself expected any action. He doubted if there was an Apache within a hundred miles of Skeleton Canyon. Geronimo and his renegades were probably hiding out somewhere in the Sierra Madre by now—assuming they were tired of running Harry Lawson and his command around in circles. Lane shook his head. This wasn't at all what he had expected when he had first come west, fresh out of the military academy. It occurred to him that after years of hard campaigning he had not even fired a shot at an Apache. The only action he had seen was against Buckshot Reilly and his crew of scalp hunters.

With a sigh, Lane got to his feet and kicked dust into the fire to extinguish the blaze. Going to his tent, he lighted a lantern and sat down on his cot and balanced a small writing table on his lap. Paper, ink, and other paraphernalia were inside the desk, beneath the hinged top. He began to write a letter to Faith. Tomorrow he would send a rider to Fort Bowie with his report—a report, he thought wryly, that would be notable for its brevity, since he had nothing to report. He would send this letter along, as well. General Hatch would no doubt frown on his using a trooper to carry his personal mail, but Lane was willing to take that chance. He had to let Faith know how much he missed her. How much he loved her. She mustn't have any doubts on that score.

Dearest Faith,

That was as far as he got in twenty minutes. Setting the lap table aside, he stretched out on his cot with a deep sigh. Hands behind his head, he frowned at the peak of the canvas tent. Increasingly, where Faith St. John was concerned, he was feeling like a fool. Why was he so persistently uncertain of her love that he feared she might meet someone else who struck her fancy? Why wasn't she the kind of girl about whom he could feel secure? And why was it that she put such pressure on him to earn a promotion? It seemed to Lane that, if she truly loved him, she would be proud of him for what he was, what he had already accomplished. Graduating from West Point was no mean feat. Being a lieutenant in the army was nothing to scoff at. But Faith wanted more.

To have so much expected of you was a very exhausting business. Might be that the only reason she had eyes for him now was because there was no one more attractive in her present range of vision. If he took her east, might she not see someone more to her liking? New York had many more eligible bachelors than Tucson. Lane shook his head. He was sure he loved Faith, but how could a man in love be so perfectly miserable? It didn't seem fair.

A shot rang out. Lane was on his feet in an instant. But there was no more gunfire, and the tension slowly drained out of him. Someone was shooting at shadows. He stepped out of the tent with a scowl already in place. Chewing on some trigger-happy trooper might make him feel a little better.

The sergeant was jogging towards him. "Lieutenant! We got us an Apache!"

"What?" Lane was skeptical.

"Yessuh. Look there." The sergeant pointed.

Two troopers were approaching, their carbines trained on the Indian who walked in front of them. The Indian led a wiry desert mustang by the reins.

As they drew closer Lane recognized Soldado.

"Thank God, you're alive!" exclaimed Lane.

The sergeant and the troopers stared at him, incredulous.

"He just come right in like he owned the place, suh," said the sergeant. "He had these." He held out a Winchester 73 and a Colt Army revolver.

Lane took the weapons and returned them to Soldado.

"Who's the idiot who fired that shot?" he snapped.

"That was me, sir," confessed one of the troopers. "When I seen he was Apach' I pulled the trigger."

"Lucky for you you're a poor shot, mister."

"Yes, sir."

Lane turned to enter his tent. "Soldado, come with me. Sergeant, get these men back to their posts."

"Yes, suh."

Inside the tent, Lane said, "So you got the message, after all."

Soldado nodded.

"I'm glad to see you again," continued Lane. "Laura and Charity will be relieved to know that you are still alive. I'm very sorry about Clancy. He was a good man."

"Reilly will die," said Soldado.

"I hate to be the one to tell you this, but the army is making arrangements to move all your people to a reservation in the east, probably Florida."

"I know. This Geronimo's fault."

Lane nodded. "In large measure. But perhaps it was inevitable. The people in these parts won't tolerate the Apache reservations here any longer."

"Apaches are not people?"

Lane blushed. "I mean the white people. They see the reservations as army-sponsored safe havens for Apaches when the bronchos get tired of raiding. Thing is, they'll want to ship you east, as well, Soldado. Somehow we've got to get you to Tucson to see Laura and Charity. That Charity, I think she's very fond of you. They want to see you and won't take no for an answer. Maybe if I escort you there, you won't have any trouble. You could even masquerade as a Mexican, like your friend Santiago does. I can go with you as soon as this campaign against Geronimo is over."

The ghost of a smile briefly haunted Soldado's gaunt, bronze features.

"Geronimo comes here."

Lane was sure he had misunderstood. "You don't mean to Skeleton Canyon . . . "

"*Anh.*" Soldado pointed to the ground. "Here."

"Good God. How close is he?"

"He attack at dawn."

"But why? What could he hope to gain?"

"He cut off from Pahgotzinkay. Now he must fight."

"He should surrender. He must know he can't win this war."

"All Apaches know they cannot win war. Know this for long time. No matter to Geronimo."

"So Lawson got between him and the Sierra Madre." Lane smiled grimly. "Well, Geronimo has less than twenty men. I've got twenty-five."

"No," said Soldado gravely. "You must leave this place. Tonight."

"But I have him outnumbered."

"It is not enough."

"I won't turn tail and run," said Lane. "The war between our peoples has been going on for twenty-five years, Soldado. It's got to stop. I won't have Geronimo killing ten or twenty more innocent people because I let him cross back into the United States through this canyon. Do you understand? You care what happens to your people, so you should want Geronimo stopped as much as I do."

"Yes," said Soldado. "He must be stopped."

"I will attempt to hold him here, and send a rider to Fort Bowie to get help. With any luck, this will be the end of Geronimo."

"I go to fort," said Soldado.

"You?"

"Geronimo will try to stop your rider. I go. Give me three good horses."

Lane thought, *Based on everything I've learned about Apaches, I should not trust this man under any circumstances* . . .

But for some reason he did trust Soldado.

"Okay," he said.

From the rim of Skeleton Canyon, Geronimo could peer down and see the cherry flickers of the soldiers' campfires far below. The stars in the night sky told him that in a few hours the new day would dawn. He could scarcely wait. His days were numbered, and he wanted to make each one count. It would be good to kill some of the *Pinda Lickoyi* here in this canyon which figured so prominently in Apache lore.

He had sent eight *bronchos* around to the other side—it would take them until nearly daybreak to get into position. Then he would have the yellowlegs in a crossfire. His palms itched from the anticipation that ran like acid through his veins. The *Pinda Lickoyi* were such fools!

Still, something was wrong . . .

Geronimo squatted on his heels and shut his eyes, concentrating, trying to summon his special powers. The eight warriors who stood nearby glanced at one another. Was Goyahkla having another vision? They waited and watched in breathless silence. Minutes passed. Finally, Geronimo's eyes snapped open. He rose abruptly and turned to face them.

"The soldiers know we are here," he said grimly. "They have been warned. They will stand and fight, and try to keep us here until more soldiers come from the fort. They will send one man to bring those soldiers. That man must be stopped."

A *broncho* stepped forward. "*Jefe*, I will go."

Geronimo nodded. "I cannot see this man in my mind. But somehow I know I would recognize him if I saw him in the flesh. He will not be easy to kill. Who else will ride with Yanozha?"

A second *broncho* stepped forward to stand at Yanozha's side.

"I will."

Geronimo blinked. This was Chapo, his own son. Chapo was not yet out of his teens, and this was his first raid. Before, when he and Juh had left San Carlos and sought refuge in the Stronghold, Geronimo had always forced Chapo to stay behind with the women and children, even though the youth had begged to accompany his father on one of the many raids against the villages of the *Nakai-Ye*.

With a sigh, Geronimo nodded again. Like all fathers, his first instinct was to protect his own flesh and blood. But it would be better, decided the Bedonkohe leader, that Chapo die a free man than as a slave of the White Eyes. Better to perish in combat than to rot in some faraway hellhole.

"*Enjuh*," murmured Geronimo. "Good. Kill this man who rides for the soldiers, or die trying."

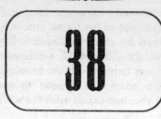

38

Before the sun had fully risen, Soldado saw the signs of pursuit. At this distance the dust could not tell him how many *bronchos* were after him. But it could mean only one thing: Geronimo had moved more swiftly than he had anticipated. The Bedonkohe and his "Wild Ones" were already at Skeleton Canyon. They had seen him leave the camp of the soldiers—or else Geronimo had used his power to "see" what was going on beyond the realm of his normal vision.

Two men. Possibly three. That was Soldado's best guess. Geronimo would be hard-pressed to spare more men than that, considering the size of his whole band. But he would want to make absolutely sure that Lane's messenger did not reach Fort Bowie, so he would send more than one.

Soldado rode his own horse, a wiry desert mustang, and led two more, the latter stripped of saddles and pads. To be on the safe side, Soldado assumed the *bronchos* who were after him also had extra mounts.

Every third mile or so, Soldado checked his pony and held it to a walk for another mile or more before urging it back into a ground-eating canter. The pursuers slowly gained on him; they were pushing their horses very hard.

When he judged that the distance had closed sufficiently that he could see something of the men who pursued him, Soldado curbed his horse, pausing at the top of a low hogback ridge, and took a pair of Vollmer field glasses from a leather case. He had acquired the Vollmers in Mexico during his long search for Najita. Now he used them to confirm that there were two *bronchos* on his trail. They were not close enough for him to identify. Each of them had two extra ponies on a long rope, tied neck-to-neck.

Soldado's features were impassive as he watched the *bronchos* come on. They would, he decided, ride their first mounts into the ground, in hopes of gaining on him. Soldado realized he would have to do likewise. A part of him wanted to stand where he was and fight it out with the Wild Ones. He had tangled with *Netdahe* before, most recently in the Sierra Madre, while he was endeavoring to spirit the peaceful Chihennes of Loco's band out of Geronimo's clutches. He respected them but did not fear them. He knew they could be killed, like any other man. But he also knew that many lives depended on his getting through to Fort Bowie. Not just Lane's and the buffalo soldiers', but all the innocent people, white and red, who would die if Geronimo wasn't stopped. So he would have to try to outrun them, and turn to fight only as a last resort, for in the latter case his odds of survival were two-to-one against him.

Switching to one of the cavalry mounts, Soldado continued on his way, pushing the big bay horse into a gallop. He was at a disadvantage now, because the cavalry mounts did not possess the stamina of the wiry mustangs that the *bronchos* were riding. For that reason Soldado decided to save his own horse for last. The decision had nothing to do with sentiment. Soldado knew that his mustang could run like the wind all day.

At midday he paused for a few minutes to let the horse blow. Wetting his bandanna with water from one of the two canteens he carried, he let each horse nibble for a moment on the moist cloth. He took no water for himself, saving it all for the horses. Again he used the Vollmers to scan his backtrail. The *bronchos* had managed to gain more ground. They were not much more than three miles behind him.

Soldado grimly swung aboard the big bay and rode on. The Colt Army was holstered on his hip, the Winchester 73 on a sling draped over his shoulder. He was fully prepared to use the weapons if he had to.

When the *bronchos* attacked, Hudson Lane had his men positioned in the rocks at the foot of the canyon slopes. Each man had plenty of ammunition and water, as well as a little hardtack, because Lane figured they would all be pretty well pinned down, at least until dark.

The horses were held in a steep, narrow draw, with a five-man detail assigned to guard them.

Lane thought his men were pretty well concealed, but when the first shots rang out, in an almost desultory fashion, two of the buffalo soldiers were hit. Spencer carbines began to speak, and in moments the crashing din of a full-fledged gun battle and the whine of hot lead filled Skeleton Canyon. Lane fired his revolver, aiming at puffs of smoke materializing in the rocks above him, but even after expending a dozen cartridges, he was fairly certain he hadn't done any damage to the enemy.

The shooting went on for about an hour and then, suddenly, deteriorated into occasional sniping. Lane nodded to himself with grim satisfaction. *Broncho* raiders usually suffered from a chronic shortage of ammunition. He hadn't expected the initial assault to be of long duration. His men had proved to the Apaches that they weren't going to bolt. He yelled to the buffalo soldiers, reminding them to keep their heads down. Every now and then an Apache would take a potshot.

A flurry of gunshots from the vicinity of the draw where their mounts were held was followed by the drumbeat of horses on the run. Lane's chest muscles seemed to contract, and he drew a long deep breath, trying to relax. A few minutes later, the sergeant ran to his position, dodging a few Apache bullets that kicked up spurts of dust at his heels. But he made it unscathed.

"Damn it, Sergeant," growled Lane. "Didn't I tell you and every other man in this outfit to keep his fool head down?"

"Yes, suh. But Lieutenant, the horses . . . "

"Yes, yes. I know. The Apaches have driven them off."

"How did . . . ? Beggin' the Lieutenant's pardon for stating the obvious, but we appear to be trapped here."

Lane nodded. "Quite right, Sergeant. We didn't need those mounts anyway. Because, you see, we weren't going anywhere. Now Geronimo thinks he has us boxed in good and tight. So he'll take his time trying to kill us. With luck, he'll stick around long enough for our reinforcements to arrive. Then he'll be the one in the trap."

The sergeant dubiously rubbed his jaw. "So we're the bait. Is that it, suh?"

"That's it in a nutshell, Sergeant."

An Apache bullet whanged off a rock a few feet away and both men ducked instinctively.

"I sure hope those reinforcements come," said the sergeant, prayerfully.

"They will. You'll see. Tomorrow noon at the latest."

Assuming Soldado gets through. Lane didn't have to say it out loud. The sergeant knew as well as he that their lives depended on Soldado.

Soldado knew an instant before it happened that the big bay was going down. The animal was wind-broken, making an awful wheezing sound as foamy slobber drooled from its mouth. Soldado showed no mercy, urging the horse to a final burst of speed that finished it quickly. Suddenly the bay's front legs buckled. Soldado was already leaping astride the second cavalry mount, which he had brought up alongside. It was no mean feat switching from one galloping horse to another, but he made it look easy. The bay went down, plowing a furrow into the ground, and Soldado rode on, leading his mustang. The bay lay still, its heart burst.

It was early in the afternoon. The two *bronchos* pursuing him had gained perhaps a mile since midmorning. Soldado could not be certain of this, but he assumed that they, too, had lost their first mounts. Soon they would be in rifle range. At issue was whether Soldado could keep beyond that range until darkness, his ally, came.

He rode hard for another hour. Then misfortune struck. The cavalry mount stepped into a hole, breaking a foreleg. Soldado heard the bone snap. The horse screamed, a sound almost human in its anguish, and went down. Soldado could not react quickly enough to avoid going down with it. Pitched over the animal's head, he hit the ground hard, jarring the wind out of him. Somehow he held on to the mustang's lead rope. Stunned, he lay there a moment, fighting to remain conscious. Then, getting unsteadily to his feet, he drew his Army Colt and shot the suffering cavalry mount dead. Vaulting aboard the mustang, he paused to check his backtrail.

He had lost valuable time, for in this life-or-death race every second counted. The relentless *bronchos* were not much more than a mile away now. He kicked the mustang into a gallop.

The *bronchos* began shooting, but they had no luck while mounted, as only luck could have guided their bullets to the mark, especially at this range. Finally, Yanohza shouted to Chapo, only a little behind him, that he was going to attempt a desperate measure. He urged his horse to even greater effort. After covering a mile he sensed that the animal was about to falter. But he had gained some ground. Curbing the horse sharply, he leaped down; on one knee he raised rifle to shoulder and took careful aim, making adjustments for windage and distance. Yanohza was one of the best shots among the Apaches, and he proved it when he squeezed the trigger.

Soldado knew as his horse stumbled that the mustang had been hit. He jumped clear as the animal went down.

Yanohza uttered a yelping cry of triumph as he saw this. In that instant Chapo thundered past him. Yanohza saw that his own horse had strayed, and he did not waste time trying to catch him, suspecting that the last burst of speed forced from the animal had left it completely spent. Besides, the day-long chase was over. Time to close in for the kill. Yanohza rushed forward, fleet as an antelope, in Chapo's dust.

Soldado waited until Chapo was two hundred yards away before firing. The Winchester 73 jumped against his shoulder. Chapo somersaulted off the back of his horse. As Soldado worked the Winchester's lever action to eject the empty brass and inject another cartridge into the breech, Yanohza fired again. The impact of the bullet spun Soldado around and knocked him off his feet.

"*Ya te da!*" yelled Yanohza, exultant. "I have hit you!" He raced forward.

On one knee, Soldado twisted around with the Army Colt in his grasp and fired all six rounds as Yanohza closed on him. Yanohza did not go down until Soldado's revolver was empty. But he was dead before he hit the ground.

Fighting off the nausea and dizziness of wound sickness, a white-hot core of pain growing in the numbness of his shoulder where Yanohza's bullet was lodged, Soldado reloaded the Colt, holstered it, and retrieved the Winchester. He checked both bodies, and recognized both men. He felt a twinge of remorse as he gazed upon the youthful face of Chapo, Geronimo's son. Chapo was scarcely more than an *ish-ke-ne*—a boy. Soldado murmured an entreaty to Ussen.

"Prepare a place of honor in the House of the Dead for this brave Apache."

He turned away. Vengeance had been wrought upon Geronimo for what he had done to the Chihenne.

Murmuring the soothing gutturals of "horse talk," Soldado enticed Chapo's mustang into letting him close enough to take up the dragging reins. He ignored the pain in his shoulder as he mounted. Pain was a fact of life. Warm blood soaked his cotton himper. He felt light-headed, his vision slightly blurred. But he rode on towards Fort Bowie, unerring in his sense of direction, true as an arrow in flight, knowing he had many more hours of travel ahead of him, and hoping he could reach his destination before he bled to death.

39

Before Geronimo closed his eyes, he appeared to Hudson Lane like the fierce warrior he had proven himself to be. But after a few moments, when he opened them again, he had changed. The Bedonkohe looked like a tired old man.

"I no longer have the power," he said, speaking in Spanish for the sake of the interpreter. His words were heavy with the dead weight of despair. Grief, as well, because although no one had confirmed it, he knew his son had to be dead. "I surrender for the fourth time, and it will be the last time."

Lane knew at that moment that the Apache Wars were truly over.

It had been a close-run thing. After a day and a half of being pinned down in Skeleton Canyon, his men being picked off one after another, Lane had begun to wonder if help would arrive in time. Maybe Soldado had failed him. Maybe they were all going to die, in just one more in a long list of army disasters in the Southwest.

Then help had come, troops from Fort Bowie. And still Geronimo had nearly escaped, fleeing south for the border only twenty miles away. But a force of two hundred

Mexicans blocked his way. Capture by the *Nakai-Ye* meant certain death. Geronimo had shown no quarter in his war against the Mexicans, and they would show him none. Not that he feared death. He just did not want to give the hated *Nakai-Ye* the satisfaction.

And so he had turned around and capitulated to the United States Army.

Lieutenant Charles Gatewood had conducted the initial negotiations, but the formal surrender had to await the arrival of General Nelson Miles. Miles knew perfectly well what Geronimo's surrender would mean to his career. He brought along a couple of reporters and a photographer, intent on milking the event for all it was worth. The ceremony took place in Skeleton Canyon and seemed to Lane to be something of an anticlimax. Geronimo and his people were resigned to their fate and did not protest when Miles informed them that all Apaches were to be transported to Florida.

"This will be a temporary relocation," said Miles. "Only until tempers cool and time heals old wounds. Then you will be permitted to return to the land of your ancestors."

Perhaps Miles honestly believed what he said, and the Apaches seemed to take his words at face value, but Lane knew it wasn't so. The Apaches would never return. He wished Clancy St. John had lived to see this day. Peace had come at last to the Arizona and New Mexico Territories. The last of the Indian Wars had been won. The Irishman would have been happy about that, but sad about the final fate of the Apaches.

Lane had learned one thing about war—there was no glory in it. As a cadet at West Point he had fretted constantly that he might not graduate in time to participate in a war. Now he realized how foolish he had been.

He wished, too, that George Crook had been the one to accept Geronimo's surrender, for he, much more so than Nelson Miles, deserved the honor. But another thing Lane had learned was that life could be eminently unfair.

His opinion of Miles rose a notch or two when, a little

later, and well out of Apache earshot, the general informed his subordinates that he had recently received a wire from President Cleveland, who wanted Geronimo and the *bronchos* turned over to the civil authorities.

"They will be hanged for sure!" exclaimed Gatewood in horror.

Miles nodded. "I have no intention of complying with the President's wishes. Further, I am confident I will be able to change his mind in this regard. Deportation will solve the Apache problem. But gentlemen, we must be sure, absolutely certain, that every last Apache is shipped off to Florida."

Lane's innate sense of fairness was offended. "That doesn't include men like Soldado, surely, sir. Apaches who have helped us in the past."

"Indeed it does, Lieutenant. Of course, in Soldado's case, he may not survive to see Florida. When I left Fort Bowie the post surgeon informed me that he had lost too much blood to have any real hope of recovery."

But Soldado did survive.

By the time he had regained sufficient strength to stand on his own two feet without help, Geronimo and most of the other Apaches had been transported east by rail. Fearing that Soldado might try to escape in order to avoid the same fate, Miles ordered him confined in the Fort Bowie guardhouse.

With the permission—one might even say the blessings—of General Hatch, Lane went before Miles to protest the treatment of Soldado in the strongest terms. Miles felt obliged to listen. Lane was the real hero of the final capture of the legendary Geronimo. Story of the lieutenant's valiant stand at Skeleton Canyon, at the cost of more than half his command killed in action, had spread like wildfire through the nation. Miles was secretly jealous. He did not like sharing fame. Yet he astutely realized that Lane was now a force to be reckoned with, a voice to be heard—realized this better than did Lane himself.

"I fully sympathize," said Miles, when Lane was finished. "But you must see that my hands are tied, Lieutenant. The orders are clear. *All* Apaches are bound for Florida. No exceptions."

Lane stared at the general for a moment. Further protest was useless. Considering his opinion of Apaches in general, which had not changed appreciably, his spirited defense of Soldado surprised even himself. Yet he could not in all good conscience stand by and witness such injustice being perpetrated.

"With all due respect, General," he said coldly, "this is wrong, and history will condemn all those involved."

Miles, a man acutely interested in his own posterity, frowned.

"I have not the power to change it," he replied, at length, testing for the first time the excuse he would give history. Rising from his desk, he moved to the door of the office in the fort's headquarters building. "However, before Soldado is taken to the railhead, I wish to interview him. Perhaps he will tell me whether there are any wild Apaches left in the Sierra Madre. I have heard rumors to that effect." He opened the door and called to his aide.

"General," said Lane, "give me permission to bring Soldado to you."

Miles looked narrowly at him.

"I would like the opportunity for a few last words with him, sir."

Miles nodded. "I see. Very well, then."

Lane promptly left the headquarters building. He did not go directly to the guardhouse, but when he did arrive there, the sentry gave him some free advice.

"Begging your pardon, Lieutenant, but it might be wise to let me tag along. You just can't trust these red devils, and I got a gut feeling that this one's the worst of the lot."

Lane almost laughed out loud at the strong, bitter irony of it. The sentry was merely expressing the sentiment he had held for years regarding Apaches. Had he not decided that even the so-called friendly Apache could not be relied upon? That they, endowed with the nature of the wolf, could turn against you without warning? And yet Soldado—and many Apaches like him—had never broken his trust. *And who are we*, mused Lane, *to be so judgmental? We who repay Soldado with treachery?*

But he concealed his true feelings and nodded gravely as though in full accord with the sentry. "I appreciate the offer, soldier, but no Apache holds terror for me, after tangling with Geronimo for two days."

"No, sir," said the sentry in haste, fearing he had offended the hero of Skeleton Canyon. "I reckon you can handle him, sir."

The sentry keyed the padlock and pulled open the heavy, iron-plated door. It was now a few minutes past sundown. The indigo shadows of night spread across the land, while overhead, strips of clouds captured the last golden remnants of the sunlight. The interior of the guardhouse was as black as the heart of hell. Lane drew his revolver. The sentry was partially right about one thing. Soldado *could* have been one of the worst of the "Wild Ones," had he been so inclined. He was an intelligent and dangerous man, quick and cunning, and it struck Lane that Soldado might not take kindly to the way he was being treated.

"Come out of there," said Lane.

Soldado emerged from the guardhouse. He was gaunt. His shoulder was cocooned in a tight dressing. His hands were shackled in front of him. He had a hollow-eyed look, the look of an animal in a steel trap, an animal in exquisite anguish. Lane figured Soldado's anguish was more than physical.

"General Miles wants to see you," said Lane. He motioned with the revolver, indicating that he wanted Soldado to precede him. "Carry on, soldier."

When Lane knew they were out of the sentry's sight, he told Soldado to stop and turn around. The Apache complied.

"Listen close," said Lane, looking about him. "We don't have much time. I don't approve of what they're doing, Soldado. You came through for me, and I intend to repay the favor."

Soldado said nothing. He watched Lane impassively. Lane was relieved there would be no display of sentiment here.

"My guess is you don't want to go to Florida. We both know you have some unfinished business here."

Soldado nodded.

"There's a horse waiting for you just down there." Lane gestured to a dark passageway between two nearby buildings. "I guess you must be wondering if this is a trick, if you can trust any white man." Lane smiled bitterly. "I don't blame you. You will just have to trust me."

"I trust you," said Soldado, and to prove it he turned away, loping into the shadows.

Lane counted to ten, then aimed his revolver at the darkening sky and squeezed the trigger.

"Stop!" he yelled, hearing the drumbeat of a horse's hooves.

He crossed Fort Bowie's dusty parade ground as soldiers boiled out of the barracks with shouts and curses flying. General Miles was on the porch of the headquarters building, scowling ferociously as Lane approached.

"What the blazes is going on, Lieutenant?"

"I regret to report that the prisoner has escaped, sir."

Miles glowered at him with more than a trace of suspicion stamped on his face. "If you are fond of your commission, Lieutenant Lane, I suggest you damn well better get him back."

Lane saluted briskly, spun on his heel, and jogged briskly for the stables, hoping to impart a sense of urgency he did not feel.

Trying, too, with less success, to suppress a smile.

40

Buckshot Reilly was in a rare good mood. He had spent most of the day and, now, several hours into the night, in the cantina of some nameless border town, drinking mescal and spending the pesos he had just received as a bounty for five scalps. Spending and drinking like there was no tomorrow.

The future didn't concern Reilly. A few weeks ago, Geronimo had surrendered to the Americans and been shipped east, and they were saying the Apache Wars were finally over. But Reilly didn't expect the government of Mexico to stop paying the bounty any time soon. The Apache scourge had left a deep, suppurating scar on the collective soul of Mexico, and as long as there was rumored to be even one wild Apache roaming the malpais, the bounty offer would remain in place. Which meant Reilly could make enough *dinero* to keep himself in whiskey and whores for a good while yet.

Of the five scalps he had turned in, only one was genuine Apache, and that one from a harmless old White Mountain man who had worked for an American sheepherder just north of the border. One of the other scalps belonged to a Mexican woman, and the other three to a Yaqui family he had bushwhacked down on the Rio Diablo. But the authorities didn't ask any questions. As long as he was careful and didn't get too greedy, Reilly figured he could keep playing this game.

That night Reilly had his eye on a little senorita who worked the cantina's clientele. She was getting prettier with every mouthful of mescal he swallowed. When she was pretty enough to suit him, he whispered in her ear and she laughed at his lewd suggestion, braying like a mule. In no time at all they were gone from the cantina, walking a short distance through dark, narrow streets to a little *choza* where she brought her paying customers. Reilly stayed conscious just long enough to cover her, and then passed out.

The woman wasn't finished working for that night, so she got dressed and returned to the cantina, leaving Reilly sprawled and snoring on the narrow bed. If she brought back another customer, she would roll Reilly off onto the floor, and if he was still there in the morning she would try to make some more money off him. Failing that, she would send him on his way.

The pickings were poor, though, and she failed to entice another man to the *choza*, returning alone in the early hours of the morning.

Her hysterical screams roused the entire village.

Buckshot Reilly was dead. He was sprawled on the bed, just as she had left him. Except for one thing. His head was missing. His blood thoroughly soaked the cornhusk mattress. Flies wallowed in big black puddles of blood on the hardpack floor.

Arriving in Tucson with his ten-man detail, Lieutenant Hudson Lane went straight to Mrs. Howell's boardinghouse. While the buffalo soldiers waited outside, he met Laura St. John in the parlor. He was glad to see that she no longer wore mourning black.

"I'm afraid Faith isn't here," she said. "Hudson, I don't know any other way to tell you this, except straight out. She has married another."

Lane was silent for a moment, absorbing this information, and quite surprised himself. The news came, not as a terrible blow, but rather as a vast relief to him, and he experienced only a twinge of something he put down as the irrational protest of a fragile ego being bruised by rejection. Irrational because he had already pretty much made up his mind about Faith. Or, more precisely, about his future with her.

"I can tell you had already had a change of heart about marrying her," said Laura, studying his sun-dark features.

"Yes, ma'am," said Lane, feeling a little ashamed of himself. "I guess I could have written to her, explained things as best I could in a letter. But I thought it might be better to speak to her about it. I apologize."

"No need, Hudson." Laura's smile was warm and friendly and a great comfort to him. "I never honestly thought you and Faith were cut out for each other."

"No, ma'am. I came to the same conclusion. It's not that I don't love her, but . . . "

"But she doesn't love you. It was . . . infatuation, I think. Frankly, I don't approve of her marriage to this other fellow. Oh, he's nice enough, I suppose. He's a mining engineer. Some years older than yourself. But he makes a very decent living, so I suppose he will be able to keep her happy."

Lane gave her a funny look, and Laura laughed self-consciously.

"By implication that isn't a very flattering thing to say about one's own daughter, is it? I love Faith. But I also know her."

"What will you and Charity do now, ma'am."

"Remain here in Tucson. I've found work as a schoolteacher. There is a house here in town, recently vacated, which I think I shall purchase."

Lane nodded. "Soldado is still alive."

"Yes, we know."

"You know? But how?"

Laura rose from the black horsehair settee. "Wait here for just a moment, Hudson. I'll be right back."

She returned a few minutes later carrying a Winchester 73.

"Do you recognize this rifle?" she asked.

"Yes."

"We found it one morning about a fortnight ago, at Clancy's grave. I'm so glad they didn't ship him off to Florida with the other Apaches. But I worry about him, too. He'll be a hunted man for the rest of his life. Alone, friendless."

"Not friendless," said Lane.

Laura smiled. "No, I suppose not that."

"And maybe not alone." Lane thought about Santiago, the half-breed, who, according to Wiley, was devoted to Soldado. "There may still be a few Chiricahua hiding out in the Sierra Madre. If they leave the Mexicans alone, a few Apaches could live in those mountains undetected for the rest of their lives."

Laura sighed. "But will he ever find happiness? He is a good man, with a kind heart, and he deserves to be happy."

"I don't know about that. Where is Charity?"

"Out riding. She's gone a great deal these days. I think she is hoping that one day Soldado will appear and whisk her away. Though I doubt that we will ever see or hear from him again. He left the rifle to let us know he was alive, of course."

Lane agreed with her. "I'm sorry I missed her. But it's been good to see you again, ma'am."

She kissed him on the cheek. "Come and visit us again. Our door will always be open to you, Hudson."

Rejoining his detail in the street, Lane led them out of Tucson. The grizzled old sergeant brought his horse alongside Lane's as they put the town behind them.

"Lieutenant, you reckon we'll ever catch this Soldado?"

"I doubt it, Sergeant," was Lane's cheerful reply.

"But you'll have hell to pay, sir, if we don't."

"I'll pay it."

As they passed the cemetery, Lane looked for Clancy's grave. What he saw there almost made him curb his horse. A gunnysack hung from the wooden cross that marked Clancy St. John's final resting place. Flies buzzed furiously around the sack. Lane had a pretty good idea what was in it.

Soldado had finally squared accounts with Buckshot Reilly, and paid his last respects to his white father.

Satisfied, Lane nodded and rode on.